CHARMED BY THE BILLIONAIRE

BLUE COLLAR BILLIONAIRES, BOOK 2

JESSICA LEMMON

CHARMED BY THE BILLIONAIRE

CHAPTER ONE

Cris

Working for Benjamin Owen is agony. Pure agony.

Not in the my-boss-is-an-A-hole way, which would be easier, but in the my-boss-is-my-best-friend way, which is much worse. Especially when said boss doesn't acknowledge me beyond my role as his friend and life assistant.

Pardon me, life assistant *coach*.

He's been vocal about the title adjustment, most notably to his brothers, who likely have observed me shadowing Benji's every footfall like a devoted Labradoodle.

He strolls into his kitchen where I'm waiting on the one-cup coffee maker to finish sputtering java into my travel mug. "Can I treat you to lunch, coach?"

I wrinkle my nose. I don't like that nickname.

There's nothing alluring or feminine or even personal about it. Not that I expect him to address me as "honey" or

1

"gorgeous." That would be unprofessional. But it would be alluring and feminine and personal. If he would bother to notice that I am, in fact, a woman.

Sigh.

"You're looking at my lunch." I elevate my mug of coffee, and his mouth pulls down at the corners.

I've yet to give you a full picture of Benjamin "Benji" Owen. I'll do that now.

The basic stats: he's thirty-three years old, having turned thirty-three on October thirteenth. He's six-feet, one-inch tall if you don't count his hair, which is fantastic. It's thick, ink-black, and tousled into a want-to-run-your-fingers-through-it style on top but short in the back with groomed, neat side-burns that aren't too long or too short. Eyebrows: dark, arched, and expressive. Eyes: brown but not dull cardboard brown. Caramel brown, golden when the sun hits them right, and almost always smiling even when his mouth isn't. Lashes: enviably long with a bit of curl at the tips. Nose: straight, narrow but not pointy. Mouth... Cue full-body shivers.

Give me a second to pull myself together.

Mouth: straight white teeth thanks to braces when he was a teenager, full lips almost always parked in an apprecia-tive, happy grin or a smirk hinting that an appreciative, happy grin is about to emerge.

Clothes: *divine.* I've never known a man who dresses as impeccably as Benji, and I've been around several well-dressed men in my line of work, mostly the Owens. Sure, his brothers dress well, but Archer and Nate do it in a rote way. Benji's outfits are carefully selected. His shoes are Salvatore Ferragamos, which cost between one and two grand per pair.

His shirts are usually button-down, most often a checked pattern, and his trousers encase long, strong legs.

He's slim but not "skinny," boasting a body I've admired when he wears a lot less. Like when he's swimming in his pool, his powerful arms slicing through the water, his torso leaving ripples in his wake. When he's in shorts it's hard not to notice the sharp definition of his calf muscles. They could whittle a chunk of wood into a replica of Aphrodite. An army of ab muscles marches down to a *V* marked by delineating lines at his hipbones. And—brace yourself—there's a tattoo on his flank between his ribs. The words "carpe diem" are etched there in careful cursive—his own handwriting.

Hey, I tried to warn you. He's damn near perfect from head to toe with but one glaring flaw.

"You can't have coffee for lunch, coach." His grin is mischievous and friendly. Sexy as hell. He doesn't mean for it to be. He oozes sex appeal from every pore as if he was crafted in a test tube to fulfill a woman's desires. Billionaire? Check. Well-dressed, well-spoken? Check, check. Painfully attractive and potent? Check *aaand* check. Clueless? Big fat checkity-check.

Other than being able to give a general description of my person (in case of my kidnapping, for example), he doesn't see me. At least not the way I see him.

"Oh, but I can," I argue, my smile a plastic version of itself. I've learned how to manage my attraction to my boss-slash-best friend over the years I've known him (ten of them), and over the year-plus I've worked for him. My tactic is simple, and judging by Benji's non-reaction to me each time we interact, it's working. Our friendship is solid, our working relationship steady. We are nailing it.

3

Even though I'd rather be nailing him. Ha.

"Anyway," I say, trying to sound breezy while my hormones crowd into a panting mass that would give boy-band fangirls a run for their money. "I have errands, so I'm on my way out the door."

"Okay, but we're still on for our jog at five today." His finger-point is as depressing as his wink. He may as well slug me in the shoulder and call me "sport." It's official. I am a nonsexual entity to him. Like a bagger at the grocery store. Or a turnip.

He sets his mug in the sink and slaps his flat middle. "I don't call you coach for nothing. You keep me in my prime."

"That's my job." I hope sarcasm didn't creep through. His eyes spark but the glint fades fast. I'm safe for another day. "I'll see you in a few hours."

Purse on my shoulder, I grab my travel mug and head out the door. Twenty minutes later I'm walking around Grand Marin, the open-air shopping center Benji's brother, Nate, recently built and opened here in Clear Ridge, Ohio. It's an absolutely gorgeous April day with plenty of sun, no rain, and mild temps. The shopping behemoth is a live-work facility housing and employing young entrepreneurs who run businesses and restaurants, and rent the offices atop those businesses and restaurants. Just being here makes me feel more successful.

I palm the door handle leading up to the property manager's office and then climb the stairs. The office sits at a corner overlooking Grand Marin like a castle in a kingdom. Or should I say queendom? Nate's fiancée oversees this place like the queen she is. She was a government employee with a secret history when she crashed into Nathaniel

Owen's life. He never saw her coming but shifted his entire world to be with her. A trait that evidently *doesn't* run in the family.

Inside the posh office loaded with live and fake greenery, a receptionist greets me. He's young, twentysomething, and knows me on sight.

"Ms. Cristin Gilbert." Sandy—a name he inherited from his father and refuses to be embarrassed by—stands and smooths his tie. "Vivian just finished with a conference call. Is she expecting you?"

"She is."

"Business or pleasure?" His forehead crinkles adorably, but I feel no zings of attraction to him the way I do to my boss and best friend. Sandy is a cute guy. From his high cheek-bones to a nice build suggesting he hits the gym at Grand Marin on the regular, there's plenty to admire. But at five years younger than me, he reminds me too much of my younger brother Manuel for me to find him truly hot. Though Manuel is more like my kid than my kid brother, given I've been raising him and my other two brothers since I was eighteen.

Long story.

"Pleasure," I answer. "I have a date tonight. I'm in need of duds." I gesture to my basic black dress and flats.

"Say no more. Please." He makes a face and the two days' worth of scruff shifts on his jaw. "I'll listen to you talk business with me all day," he says, already en route to Viv's office door, "but I can't talk about clothes."

He fakes falling asleep as his knuckles rap on the door, and I chuckle under my breath. Viv looks up from her desk through the glass—there's virtually no privacy in this office, save for the tinted windows in the conference room—and waves us in.

"Your date is here," Sandy announces. "She's cherubic, cute, and too good for the likes of me. I trust you two will be very happy together."

"Thanks, Sandy," Viv says with a laugh. He rushes back to his post to pick up the ringing phone. "I really like him."

"Told you." I buff my nails on my dress. I was the one who suggested Sandy work for Vivian instead of Owen Construction proper. His resume had hit Benji's inbox as Vivian was saddling up for her new position and was worried she'd never find good help.

"You ready to do this?" She stands and rubs her hands together. Her slimming plum skirt is fitted, her silk blouse a paler shade of purple bedazzled with winking rhinestone buttons. She's both professional and beautiful. I glance down at my plain dress and feel a stab of envy. I stepped it up today —I typically wear jeans to work—and I still can't touch Viv's fabulous style. Don't get me wrong, my clothes match, but I'm not winning any awards for costume design. Which is exactly why I called her.

"I'm as ready as I can be," I tell her as we exit the office. I wave goodbye to Sandy upon my retreat.

"I've chosen three boutiques to check out." We take the stairs, her incredibly tall high-heeled shoes ticking each step. I'd break my neck if I attempted stairs in shoes like hers. "Two of them are here, the other right up the road."

"I'm in your capable hands."

"It's not going to hurt to go on a date. A few dates," she says as if I'd argued instead. She flips her dark brown hair over her shoulders and slips a pair of sunglasses onto her nose, hiding chocolate brown eyes a few shades darker than Benji's. "If anything, maybe Benji will voice an opinion about who his life assistant coach is dating. And wouldn't that be fun to hear?"

He'd have to notice me as a being with two X chromosomes to comment. Which would be different, but I don't know if it'd be *fun*.

She spares me a grin as sunlight hits her hair and highlights the delicate freckles on her cheeks. You'd never know it now, but she was cagey and nervous after being outed as Walter Steele's daughter last year. Yes, *that* Walter Steele. She's not a criminal like her deceased father, but I could understand why she was worried about what others would think. Who among us isn't?

"Benji wouldn't notice what I was doing if I was doing it on his desk while he was typing up an email." I snort. The truth is always funny.

"We'll see," she promises. "We'll find you the perfect date ensemble and then grab lunch and martinis. I can have you back to your office by, oh, say six o'clock?"

"No can do." I turn her down with regret in my heart. Martinis and lunch sound *amazing*. "I promised Benji we'd jog at five. As his coach, part of my job is to keep him fit for his myriad girlfriends."

She hums, no longer looking pleased. "Who is she this time? Blonde? Redhead? Brunette?"

"Honestly, I don't know." I frown as that fact hits me square in the solar plexus. Since I've worked for him, Benji has had a revolving door of dates on call. Last year he was in a semi-serious relationship with a tall, leggy blonde named Trish. She was smart and nice, which sucked because I really

7

wanted to hate her. Vivian met her and agreed we couldn't hate her. She also agreed that not being able to hate Trish was a bummer.

"Well, who cares." Viv waves a hand. "Time to move on. Or at least sideways. Take it from me, Cris, life has a way of working out the way it's supposed to. Especially when you least expect it."

Easy for her to say, I think without animosity. Vivian and Nathaniel are in love, and it's adorable and beautiful and enviable. As a closet romantic (though I came out to Vivian), I watch them together and internally swoon. I want that someday. Not with Nate, obviously, but with someone.

Time to go into the big, bad world and find him.

CHAPTER TWO

Benji

Each pounding footfall thumps in my ears, my heart keeping time like an orchestra conductor. I hear my own steady, rhythmic breathing over the sounds of my steps and heart.

Thump, beat, puff. Thump, beat, puff.

The day is mild, warmish, but a cooler breeze keeps me from sweating too much. The park is moderately occupied, but it's also large, so there's plenty of room on the path for us to run. Cris is ahead of me wearing a pair of hot pink shorts and a white T-shirt with the words "my favorite brother gave me this shirt." The first time I saw it I had to smile, not because of its outwardly snarky message but because there is zero chance she could pick a favorite brother out of the three her mom stuck her with.

Stuck is a harsh word. I didn't mean it that way. Let me explain.

Cris's mom, Selina, bailed on her daughter and co., aka

9

her three bros, when Cris was eighteen years old. Selina, who I'm told goes by Lina, moved to Vegas to marry a guy she's since divorced three husbands ago. I think she's on marriage number seven, but it's been four or five months since Cris mentioned her, so who knows if Lina has moved on to number eight by now.

So, Lina went to Vegas and Cris stayed here in Clear Ridge with her brothers, who at the time ranged from ages seven to twelve. This was while she was grinding out a college education *and* working part-time. Talk about a full schedule. Cris said her mom promised to send money regularly when she left, but only ended up sending it semi-regularly. Like sending cash was going to make up for not being there. I know firsthand how nice it is to have money, but it's no substitute for a parent.

When Cris turned twenty, she started working as an intern for William Owen, better known as "Dad," but he's not my birth father. Sadly, my birth father (and birth mother) are no longer alive. It's not a circumstance I like to think about, but there's no escaping it. They're gone and have been since I was ten years old. I've missed them every day since.

Anyway. We're talking about Cris.

I remember the first time I saw her. Spunky, adorable, blond. I thought she'd come and go as most interns did at Owen Construction, but she stayed on full-time, working for my dad before I hired her myself. I had taken to working at my home office more often than not. Traveling to headquarters is a drive to the tune of ninety minutes on a light traffic day which allows me to get almost nothing done, so I limit my visits to the big HQ. Plus, I like my home office. And my home gym. The in-ground pool in my backyard is heated. I'm not trying to sound like a dick, just illustrating how everything I need is at my fingertips. Including my life assistant coach.

It's a title I made up. I needed an assistant, but I also needed a life coach. Her position is bespoke. I'm thrilled she was willing to mash together two seemingly random job titles into a Franken-position we could stitch up or bolt together as I saw fit. We were acquaintances at best when she worked for William. Our friendship grew once we started spending a lot of time together. Now I don't think I could do anything without her. At least not well.

When we moved her from HQ into my house, I noticed tenfold how spunky, adorable, and blond she was. How she hums when she takes her first sip of coffee. How much she enjoys going to the post office to buy stamps. She always buys the LOVE ones with puppies or cartoons on them, but I don't complain. Whenever she uses one, her gray eyes light up and a sweet smile spreads her mouth. Unfortunately, she's not the kind of assistant you hire and then seduce. She's practically family, though "family" takes on a broader meaning in the Owen family.

William and Lainey Owen have one child of their own. Archer Owen is three years older than me but not the eldest of the Owen sons. He's the middle by a technicality. After they adopted me, they went and adopted a rough Chicago teen straight out of juvie. Nate is one year Archer's senior. Ours is a patchwork family. I've heard Archer refer to Cris as our honorary sister, but I can't agree with him there. She's a lot of things to me, but sister? *Yikes*. I've admired far too many of her body parts for that not to be creepy.

And man, is she hard not to admire when she's running

ahead of me, her round ass jiggling enticingly every time her shoes hit the pavement. Dappled sunlight streams through the leaves on the trees and lights her curly blond hair. Her fair skin is what most would consider "tan" but given my bronze hue, I only see "fair."

So there she is, a blond-haired, gray-eyed, petite, strong, smart woman with an ass that won't quit...who works for me. As her boss I overlook her questionable professionalism—the aforementioned cutesy stamp fetish and her typical ensemble of Chuck Taylors and ripped jeans at the office. As her best friend I overlook her glaringly obvious hotness and wish I'd developed a fascination with her before hiring her. I could have asked her out in some neutral capacity back then. Now I have to settle for stolen glimpses and pretend not to notice her admirable attributes. Whenever we stretch side by side after a run, I glance at her bare legs, pale next to mine, and entertain what they might feel like wrapped around my waist while I roll my hips and give both of us the ride of a lifetime.

"Race you to the parking lot." She interrupts the vision beginning to form, which is probably for the best considering it's hard to run with a boner. She spins around and runs backwards, her curly hair bouncing with her every step. Now I have a view of another jiggling part of her, those incredible breasts I try to ignore every single day.

"Try and keep up." I take off.

I reach the parking lot before she does, no surprise since I was half-killing myself to do it. I hate losing. Not as much as Archer, but still. I wait for her to catch up, bent in half, sucking air through my open mouth and balancing my palms on my knees. She's not far behind.

She slows to a walk, arms heavy at her sides, cheeks pink

and eyes dancing. "When will you learn"—she pauses to take a breath—"that I'm baiting you"—another pause, another breath—"when I say that?"

"Never." I straighten, grinning. She grins back. My winning made her feel like she won and that is good for everyone.

"You clocked your steps for the day, I bet." She nods at the watch on my wrist. It tracks a million things, the number of steps I take in a day included. Look at that. I just rolled over my goal. "Nice."

"You're welcome." She winks.

I *am* welcome. She takes care of me, which I need. I have a tendency to lose myself in the numbers the way some might get lost in the woods after dark. I go into a deep, trancelike state when I'm thinking around, over, and through financials, rendering me unable to tend to my most basic needs. Like eating, drinking. Blinking, on occasion.

Cris happily refills my water, buzzes up the occasional smoothie in the high-powered blender, or delivers a takeout container filled with chicken and spring mix salad to my desk, lid off, fork stuck in it like a flag. Hell, she brought me vitamin C the other day because she heard me coughing and worried I might be coming down with a cold.

She does all of this while also managing my calendars (personal and business), preparing reports, interviewing candidates, spellchecking my letters, and traveling with me to a variety of affairs. She's made reservations for dinner with the woman I happen to be seeing (whichever woman it is at the time) and has set up lunch dates so I can end the "seeing" part, which always happens no matter how great the woman I'm dating is.

13

She is Super Cris! More powerful than the Calendar app on your iPhone, able to leap tall deadlines in a single bound. I have no idea how I did my job before I hired her. I shudder to think what would happen if she left. Which is why I pay her an exorbitant amount of money to do what she does.

Her attentiveness to my needs escalated noticeably last fall when her youngest brother Timothy went away to college. It's like she has empty-nest syndrome at only thirty years of age. Damn her mother. And damn Cris's father and each of her brothers' fathers for that matter. They stuck my chipper blond best friend with their adult responsibilities at a time when she should have had the luxury to learn more about herself. My parents would have never left me by choice. Not ever.

Without picking up her feet, Cris shuffles to the car and grabs our water bottles, insulated so the water stays ice cold. (She thinks of everything.) As we rehydrate I make my way to a bench and sit, watching people in the park run along the path in between admiring the sway of the trees against a blue sky.

Spring in Ohio. It's my favorite season. There's a whiff of newness in the air. I love the scent. It reminds me of a Monday, truly the best day of the week. Well, if you love what you do. I adore my lot in life. After all, I structured it.

She settles in next to me, her knee bumping mine, the innocent touch sending a blaze of heat up my thigh. Hers are not long legs, but they are toned and sexy—if I allowed myself to consider Cris "sexy" which I, of course, don't.

"What are you looking at?" She examines her leg.

Unable to share that my thoughts have devolved into a visual of her back against the wall while I'm driving hard and deep into the heart of her, I shake my head. When she frowns, I think fast and poke a purplish splotch on the outside of her thigh.

"Ouch! Is that a bruise?"

"Appears to be," I say. "How'd you do that? Are you a violent sleeper?"

"It's my new WWE boyfriend." She rolls her eyes. Wide, big, expressive. Innocent. There is a sweet, generous nature under the naiveté, but the naiveté is there all the same.

"If you have a boyfriend, WWE or otherwise, this better not be how I find out." I suck down more water as a pleat forms between her pale eyebrows. It's followed by a lip bite, and her eyes skitter away before landing on my face again. My Spidey senses tingle. She's not the only superhero in this park.

"What was *that* about?" I can't help asking. She shakes her head a little guiltily. I'm suddenly queasy and I don't think I can blame it on exercising. "Tell me."

"It's just..." She seesaws her head back and forth twice before continuing. "I have a date tomorrow night."

"A date." I tried not to let that sound like an accusation. I'm not sure I was successful.

"I didn't tell you because, well..." Her eyes are on her water bottle as she runs a thumbnail along the lid.

"Because well what?" Cris doesn't date. Or she hasn't dated since she started working for me, anyway. Now I'm frowning.

"I worried you'd lecture me. I don't want a lecture. I want to go on a date without anyone offering their opinion. Except for Vivian. She helped me pick out a dress for tomorrow."

That was the errand she ran today?

"You took her opinion," I say, stung.

Further avoiding my eyes, she rests one heel on the bench and reties her shoelace. I'm still wrapping my head around her not mentioning—even in passing—having a date tomorrow night. It wasn't as if I wasn't standing right next to her in the kitchen this morning. She had ample opportunity.

"You go on lots of dates. I reserve comment all the time." She holds up both hands in her own defense.

"You don't have to comment since I can read your expressions. I know when you don't like who I'm seeing."

What might be panic briefly crosses her pretty face. "Like who?"

"Trish."

"I liked Trish!"

"Your voice goes high and squeaky when you lie, by the way."

"I'm not lying."

"You laughed during the word 'lying' which further indicates you're lying." I stand and offer my hand. She slaps her palm into it and I admire the way we look together. Her small, pale, pink-hued skin against my large, long-fingered golden brown. A fierce protectiveness rears up inside of me before I can question it. Whoever she goes on a date with better be a gentleman or I will dropkick him into the stratosphere.

"Tell me about this dude—your date." I let go of her hand and walk with her to the car, irked and not entirely sure why.

"I don't know. I've only messaged him a few times on the app."

"You used an app?" I regard the sky. "A little help?"

"Who are you talking to?"

I look at her. "The Universe. Have you recently consulted your spirit guides?"

"In case you haven't noticed, I do almost nothing but work and hang out with *you*."

"Yowch." I rub my chest like she just shot me.

"You know what I mean." She rolls her eyes, not indulging me. "Timothy's gone. The house is empty. It was easier when he was at home waiting for me to help him with something. It's like he doesn't need me anymore, and I—" Her voice cracks the slightest bit, revealing the tender emotions she tries to hide from me.

"You're lonely." I wrap my hand around the back of her neck. Her skin is damp with sweat but not in a gross way.

"A little." She glances to the side like she had a hard time admitting the truth.

And like that, I can't fault her for going on a date. I know what it's like to be lonely. I've felt lonely since I was ten years old and heard my parents were in a car accident and wouldn't be coming home for Christmas.

Ever.

I was lonely even surrounded by my giving, loving, adoring adoptive family during the very next Christmas. Sometimes I still am. Loneliness, I understand. And dating, I *really* understand.

Which is why I tell my best friend, "You're lucky you have me." Her gaze snaps to mine over the roof of my car. I give her an unflappable, trademarked Benji smile. "I can give you some pointers."

CHAPTER THREE

Cris

I'm halfway through a glass of wine with my date, and all I've managed to do so far is obsess about the "advice" Benji gave me. It wasn't so much helpful as a hindrance. What he told me burrowed into my brain, which is now an echo chamber of distraction.

Beware small hands.

I've been staring at my date's hands on and off while he's been talking. I haven't been able to stop myself. I'm sure he thinks I have some strange fetish.

Do not let him choose the restaurant.

I was too late on that one. My date—Clark—chose an Indian restaurant and I agreed. I love curry, but this place isn't as good as the restaurant at Grand Marin. I should know since Vivian and I ate there last week. I'm already obsessing over what to order from the menu, and praying I don't hate it.

And whatever you do, don't mention you haven't dated in a while.

After dispensing that piece of advice, Benji narrowed his eyes, gave me an accidentally sexy head-tilt, and asked, "You haven't dated in a while, have you?"

I flubbed over my answer which was something like, "No, of course not!" followed by a dismissive, "Who has the time?" Now I'm here with Clark, undecided on my dinner, after having blurted the very phrase I was tasked with keeping to myself. *"It's been a while since I've dated."*

I actually said that.

My smile is frozen in place as I simultaneously wait for him to react, and consider running out of the restaurant before he can.

His eyebrows are sitting atop his forehead, which is a little too large for his face. He's pleasant enough to look at, but he's no Benji.

Not that I'm comparing them.

"How long's it been?" He casually lifts his draft beer to his mouth. His chin is sort of small. I've heard the phrase "weak chin" before, but never understood it. I think Clark is suffering from the condition. I stop staring at his chin, rerouting my attention to his mouth when he licks his lips. His lips are nothing like Benji's. They lack the fullness I'm so fond of. Clark swipes his mouth with his fingers, and I can't help noticing his hand is a little small. Also unlike Benji, there is no smile lurking behind that hand. Rather than slanting me a warm smirk that lights his eyes, Clark merely gives me a bland blink.

Anyway. I'm not comparing them.

"Long enough I can't recall the exact date." Well, that's a lie. I'm not even sure why I lied. Maybe nerves? I remember the *exact* date of my last date. It was the day of my mother's wedding. One of her weddings. I didn't go to her last *three* weddings. Including the most recent, which was not in Vegas like the last two, but in California at a vineyard. She didn't invite me, and I didn't offer to show up.

So, I went on a date two and a half years ago. July 2nd. His name was Phillip, and we went to a pottery class. It sounded romantic and sweet but ended up being uncomfortable and inescapable. Either because the class was three hours long, or because Phillip was sculpting the naked torso of his ex-wife and crying about how much he missed her.

Clark blows out a breath, looking bored. "I'm so tired of dating. Tonight is already tedious."

I blanch.

He catches my expression and smiles. It's not a warm smirk, but a creepy curl of his thin lips. "No offense."

"Would you excuse me a moment?" I'm on my feet before I think about it. He waves me off, lifting his beer and draining the mug.

I thank the good Lord the bathroom is by the front door and also behind Clark's head. He can't see me when I duck out the exit instead of powdering my nose. Outside, I suck in a gulp of air as relief swamps me.

Freedom.

I walk briskly to my car, looking over my shoulder before enclosing myself inside and taking a deep breath. As I reverse from my parking spot, I send another furtive glance to the door to see if Clark is chasing after me, shaking his fist and demanding I pay for my drink. He's not there. I drive away feeling as guilty as if I robbed the place.

Nerves and fear give way to anger. Soon, I'm fuming over several things. I'm upset with myself for being a coward and running away. I'm angry at Clark for being so good on text and so abysmal in person. And I have a bone to pick with Benji for planting a dozen poisoned seeds into my head before my first date in two and a half years.

I can't do much about the other two, but Benji I can confront, which is probably why I drive to his house instead of my own. I slam my car door and stomp up his driveway to the front door, growing angrier along the way. I knock, wait for him to answer, and then knock again. The door swings aside. Instead of being momentarily stunned by his beauty the way I normally am, I throw my hands into the air and roar, "Everything is terrible and it's all your fault!"

He blinks, does a once-over of me and my dress and heels, and says, "It's still daylight. What are you doing here? Shouldn't you be on a date?"

I glare and he steps aside, sweeping his arm to invite me in. I tromp past him and into the kitchen where I plunk my purse onto an empty barstool. I hear the front door shut, and then Benji is on the opposite side of the counter regarding me with raised eyebrows.

So, I continue.

"Your pointers were *not* helpful." I briefly recap the dinner leading up to what brought me here. "It's irresponsible to give advice that can cause this much destruction."

"Sounds like I saved you from destruction, coach."

I glare some more.

He slides a glass of wine across the counter. "Just poured. I haven't taken a drink yet."

I quirk my lips, dissatisfied with his response, but I take the wine anyway.

He pours another glass for himself, returns to the

21

counter, and opens a large paper bag. The scent wafting out is heaven. He ordered takeout from the Indian restaurant in Grand Marin. The one I love. He notices me salivating and offers, "I'm happy to share if you're hungry. I ordered extra. You sound like you might qualify for *hangry*."

"Entirely possible considering I've had nothing to eat since lunchtime." And that was a few crackers slathered with peanut butter.

He gestures for me to go on as he begins dishing food from plastic containers onto plates.

"How can you tell if someone's hands are small?" I ask. "Is it in reference to their head? The rest of them? What if they just have really big arms?" I was being serious but he laughs.

"He had small hands?"

"And he chose the restaurant." I prop my chin up on my fists, elbows resting on the countertop. The scent of curry curls into my nostrils, and my stomach growls.

"Which one?"

"The one on Berkley."

He cringes. I'm oddly satisfied it's not just me.

"I was willing to rough it for the sake of being agreeable."

He shakes his head. "No good, coach. You choose. Letting you choose is the right thing to do. If he doesn't know that, he's a clown." Benji sets a piece of naan bread on the edge of a plate piled high with rice, curry, and tender grilled chicken. Rather than offering up a plastic fork from the carry-out, he digs a real one out of the silverware drawer and hands it to me.

"I didn't want to be rude," I explain, taking the fork.

He settles in next to me with his own plate of food and his own real fork. He drinks his wine before asking, "And how did that work out for you?"

I sip my wine. It's fifty times better than the half of a glass I sipped on my disastrous date. "This is delicious."

"Archer ordered it for Club Nine. He bought an extra case and divvied it out between us. *Us* meaning Nate and me. Mom's wine cellar is stocked."

He can say that again. Lainey Owen has a robust wine selection. She often lets me pick the bottle I want when I'm over there for dinner. I've always loved that about her.

I take a bite of my food and moan in ecstasy. "This is exactly what I wanted tonight."

Around the bite of his own food, Benji says, "Like I said, you should always pick. Did he break any of my other rules?"

"No, but I did. I mentioned I hadn't dated in a while. He said dating was tedious, and included me in that generalization."

Instead of laughing, Benji frowns, the corners of his mouth pulling down as his thick eyebrows slam together. "What a dick."

Proud of myself for not seeing through to the end what would have only gotten worse, I straighten my spine and pull my shoulders back. "I excused myself to the bathroom and then I ran out the front door."

My best friend laughs, proving his jovial self wasn't buried too deep beneath his previous reaction. "That's my girl."

There's an awkward pause where we lock eyes for a truncated beat. I can't remember a single time he referred to me as "his girl." Or maybe it's the intimacy of this moment—me being here, dressed nicely, sipping wine and eating Indian food like we're on a real date.

As if he senses the awkward pause, he clears his throat. "You are a lot of things, Cristin. Tedious isn't one of them."

That was nice to hear. "Thanks."

"So, when's the next date?"

"With Clark?" I ask, mildly alarmed. His answer pleases me.

"Hell no." He gestures with his empty fork. "I mean the next date from your app."

The *his girl* comment was clearly a throwaway if he's so eager to share me with someone else. I try not to let the idea irk me. "Oh I don't know, maybe in another two years or so." I offer a demure smile before eating another bite of my delicious dinner.

"You can't let this stop you. Also, did you say his name was Clark? No wonder he was a dud."

"Clark Kent wasn't a dud. He was secretly Superman."

"Wrong. Superman was secretly Clark Kent."

"I don't know how you can pick on anyone's name, *Benji*. You are named after a dog."

He lets out a big, appreciative laugh. The lightness I'm feeling makes tonight's debacle worth the trouble.

"What I'm saying," he goes on, "is you can't give up because some moron says dating is tedious. Plus, you have me. I can give you a few more pointers for your next one—"

"Don't you dare. I don't need any more of your input beforehand. It made me a nervous wreck."

"After, then. We'll do a postmortem on your next few

Friday nights. You can come here after your date and give me the play-by-play."

"And then what?"

"I'll tell you if or when you can improve, though most likely I'll point out why the guys you're choosing aren't worth your time. Other than me picking your dates for you, that's the best way for me to help."

"You are *not* picking my dates for me," I tell him sternly.

Hands up, he declares his innocence. "Understood."

Benji

Well. That was quite the suggestion.

And not one I planned on making. I hate the idea of her believing she's not worthy of choosing where to eat, or worthy of having dinner with someone decent—a complete dinner. Including dessert. Instead she had to settle for half of my carryout.

A dating app, though? Could there be a worse way to meet someone? I bet I could find five better candidates with my eyes closed. Not that I would dare set her up. I would be too picky. Nobody is good enough for Cris.

"You're serious?" she asks, sounding both curious and interested. "About the postmortem thing?"

"Absolutely," I answer, as far from absolute as can be. "I'm your best friend. That's my job." Technically, it's true. My job as her best friend is to be there for her. She didn't ask me to be her wingman, but I refuse to let her fly solo. She hasn't dated in years. I date like it's a sport and I'm preparing for the championship. Reason being, I'm not the marrying type. Companionship must be found in spurts.

I understand why it's been a long time since she's gone on a date. Between work and home, she doesn't have a lot of free time. Hell, I take up a lot of it by asking her to attend various functions with me after-hours. Awards dinners, company hobnobbing, etcetera. For years, her excess free time was spent taking care of her brothers. Whether they lived with her or not, when one of them needed her, she answered the call. Always. Cris is reliable to a fault.

"As your life assistant coach, that's technically *my* job." She flutters her lashes. She looks cute when she does that. I mean, she looks cute when she does anything, but especially cute when she's trying to look cute.

"Fine. You can charge me." Before she can argue, which she is poised to do, I add, "If you make it through dinner with your date we'll have a nightcap. If you don't, I'll have carryout at the ready."

She blows out a sigh that sounds more like capitulation than refusal. "Why?"

"Why?"

"Yeah. Why not let me do this myself?"

Because she's tender and vulnerable. Because the idea of one of the guys she dates insulting her or manhandling her makes me want to howl. Because I want her to have a safe refuge in case she's angry or sad, or if she's happy. All of that sounds too mushy so I answer, "Because I'm a pro."

"You know what? I don't have the strength to argue with you." She lifts her glass. "I have just enough strength to finish this delicious dinner and wine. And then we'll talk strategy."

She lifts her glass and I clink mine against hers, but my "cheers" doesn't feel celebratory. I tell myself I'm doing what any good friend would do, but I'm not sure a "good friend" would root against her.

Like I said, no one is good enough for Cris.

CHAPTER FOUR

Cris

Date *numero dos* happened the following Friday, aka tonight, at Benji's urging for me to "get back out there." He insisted a delay would make me more skittish. I figured since I was as skittish as a rabbit who'd encountered a cat in the carrot bed on my date last week—and ran away like one—he had a valid point.

"I can't even call it a date," I comment, half humiliated and half relieved. I'm at Benji's, bellied up to the kitchen counter, my shoes tossed onto the floor, and a margarita glass in my hand. I lick the salted rim and take a tart, cold drink as he portions out shredded-chicken enchiladas, smothered with the amazing white cheese sauce the local Mexican place is known for, onto our plates. He sets foil containers filled with Spanish rice and refried beans between us so we can serve ourselves. Before he takes his seat next to me, he tops off our margaritas and tears open the paper bag of tortilla chips for easy access.

"Maybe I'm cursed," I say as I scoop rice onto my plate.

"You're not cursed." He takes the rice and trades me for the beans.

"He texted me twice to say he was on his way. Twice!" I point to him with the spoon and then set the container aside. "Did you order guacamole?"

"What am I, an animal?" he asks rhetorically before handing me a small Styrofoam container loaded with rich, yummy green guacamole. "Extra spicy."

I almost blurt "I love you" to express my appreciation for the guac, but I bite my tongue, suddenly feeling awkward.

I cut a corner off a steaming enchilada. "I don't know why he texted me twice and didn't bother showing up. Unless he was in an accident." A scenario flits through my head but I promptly dismiss it. I have that bad habit with my brothers too, but they've earned my worry. This jerkwad is not going to raise my cortisol levels.

Benji halts my fork's incline. "What are you doing?"

"Eating?"

"If you put that into your mouth without salsa, I'll have to report you."

Properly corrected, I lower my fork and wait while he dollops fresh tomatillo salsa on top. "I was remiss," I say after I swallow the bite. I wash it down with my drink. "This is a good margarita."

"I can't cook but Archer taught me how to mix a cocktail. Or was it Nate?" He regards the ceiling for a second before giving up. "I don't know. One of them."

At the mention of the Owen brothers, I smile. The Owens have been good to me. I'm lucky to have piggybacked onto a family with healthy parental units. I didn't have great

29

examples growing up, what with my mom gallivanting off with a revolving door of deadbeat husbands.

To be fair, Dennis's dad was a great guy. When Mom moved to Vegas, Dennis was nine years old. His dad had died at work the year prior. Heart attack. I always thought, had he lived, Larry Brunswick would have supported his son when Mom didn't. He was very involved in Dennis's life.

Manuel, my oldest brother, has a father who isn't a deadbeat but definitely isn't involved in a personal sense. Jake L. Rivera is a criminal defense lawyer. An incredibly successful one. He's sent money over the years, and he paid for Manuel's college, but beyond that he doesn't believe he has parental duties. Now that Manuel has graduated with a bachelor's degree in business and has opted to pursue his master's, attorney Jake L. Rivera can't be bothered with paying for more school.

Timothy is my youngest brother and might be the most brilliant. His father, Clay, lived with us until Timothy was born. One day he went out for cigarettes and never came back. Timothy doesn't remember his father, which is probably for the best. Almost one hundred percent of his four-year college plan has been paid for by scholarships. He's taken two quarters so far. He's always been easygoing and rarely caused problems, which might explain why I didn't lose my mind trying to raise him alongside my other two (more headstrong) brothers.

My own father's identity is a mystery. Mom described him as the "most attractive man on the planet." After he knocked her up, he left and she never saw him again. Sometimes I wonder if he was the one who drove my mom to marry and marry and marry again, as if searching for that kind of elusive first love.

Initially, when I was an intern at Owen Construction and working directly under Benji's dad, William, I tried to manage both school and work. Something had to give. And since my quest was to raise three strong men to be good fathers and decent humans, I dropped out of school and kept what became a well-paying job.

I don't think William or Lainey or the other Owens knew how much child-rearing I was doing back then. I didn't share a lot of details. I worried if they found out how distracted I was at home, they'd never hire me on. I was desperate to stay at Owen Construction. I couldn't think of any echelons higher than working for the Owen family. They're well-known, their reputations and good works preceding them.

I didn't expect sympathy back then—didn't want it either. I was grateful to have a job (my internship quickly turned into a paid position), and when Benji hired me I was thrilled to have a pay raise and move to a more casual work environment—Benji's awesome house.

Which is probably why lounging at his breakfast bar and chatting over enchiladas feels like a natural part of my day.

"Well, it's very good," I comment about the margarita.

"I'm sorry, Cris." Benji, suddenly sincere, places his hand on my knee. It isn't a sexual touch or an inappropriate one. It should be bland at worst, friendly at best. So why do I feel electricity shoot from his fingertips, up my thighs, and straight to my—

I fake a cough, moving my leg out from under his hand. He hops up to pour me a glass of water. I wave him off and take a gulp of my margarita instead. "I'm fine. Honest. And why are you sorry?"

He takes his seat and regards me like I'm daft, or suffering from short-term memory loss. "Because you were stood up."

"Oh, that." I momentarily forgot why I was here. I'd rather be here than out with that A-hole anyway.

"His loss."

I offer my best friend a warm smile. He's sweet.

"Give me your phone." He holds out a palm.

"No." I'm already suspicious of his motives. "Why?"

"I'll set up your next date. I can't bear to watch you go through this again. Maybe I can offer some insight. I am a guy, you know."

"You are a guy," I agree, mentally adding a few adjectives. Hot. Gorgeous. Funny. Intelligent. Good with his hands... I mean because he woodworks as a hobby, not that he—never mind.

"Show me the candidates." He claps once. "Let's do this."

"Hard pass, boss. I'm not letting you choose." I'm embarrassed about not being able to make it through a dinner. Tonight I didn't even make it *to* a dinner. The last thing I need is Benji going through the candidates on the app and pointing out how small their hands are.

His turn to give me a bland blink. "Cris, it's eight thirty at night. I am not your boss right now."

"Don't play the best-friend card. I wouldn't let *any* of my friends choose my date." I fold my arms over my chest in challenge.

"Is your phone in your purse?" He's already off the stool and rounding the couch where my purse is sitting. Unattended. Rather than dig through my personal items, he plunks the bag onto my lap. "Do you need a shot of tequila to bolster your courage?"

"If I have a shot of tequila, I'll have to sleep on your couch." I swear I see a flash of heat...or something...in his eyes. It banks instantly when he smiles, making me wonder if I imagined it.

"No tequila. Got it." He holds out his hand. "Phone."

I fish my phone from my purse. I do not hand it to him. "Here's the deal. You see only the screens I want you to see. And you can have a vote, but not the final say."

"Deal." He holds up a finger. "But you have to set the date for this weekend, and you have to insist on picking the restaurant. Also, if there's a picture of his hands I want to see it."

I burst out laughing. I knew it.

Half an hour and more laughter later, both plates of enchiladas have been annihilated and we've combed through the database on the app. We've narrowed my options down to two men. Benji approves of neither but admitted they were as good as we were going to find on the "stupid app." He maintains this is a compliment to me rather than an insult. I remind him I know whose side he's on.

Mine. Always. That's how he became my best friend, after all.

"Should we flip a coin?" he asks.

"No. I choose Dennis. Except he shares a name with my brother, which is a little disturbing."

"Agreed. What about the other guy? What's-his-name."

"Rick."

He makes a face. "If you must. Make sure he's available this weekend. Do you need help drafting your message?"

I whip my head around. "I'm insulted. Do you know how many emails I draft on any given day? I am capable of texting coherently."

He holds up his hands in surrender. I type in a message to Rick, telling him I'm available on Saturday. I look up to ask Benji if I should suggest Italian food, but he's staring forlornly at his margarita glass, so I don't.

"Done," I say after I hit send.

"Which restaurant did you pick?" His smile appears a touch disingenuous, but it is going on eleven o'clock, so maybe he's just tired.

"Piccoly's."

"Italian. Nice choice."

"Hey, if I'm lucky I'll get to eat there."

His laugh is forced. I assume I've overstayed my welcome.

"I'm going to go. Thank you for the recap dinner."

"Sure you don't want to practice not blurting out how green you are at this whole dating thing before you go?"

"Absolutely not." I shoulder my purse. "If I practice I'll sound like I practiced. I want to be genuine and see what happens."

"Well, we have all week." Again with the dark, contemplative look. It's so foreign parked on his face I don't know how to react. He's typically a happy person. I've always found it remarkable how a kid could lose both his parents and come out the other side as optimistic and pleasant as he did.

Dennis lost his parents too—though our mother is very much alive, "lost" seems an apt descriptor—and we had him in and out of school psychologists for years. Thank God I had power of attorney and no one looked too deeply into our home life. I wonder if Benji went through a dark period when he was a teenager. I never asked. It seems like I should have asked sooner since I've known him for ten years. We only became close recently, so now it's like I *can't* ask. We talk about current events and physical fitness. We talk about work. Talking about my dating status and how to proceed is new. And weird.

He opens the front door and I step over the threshold, turning to say goodnight. He leans one hand on the door over his head and props his other hand on his hip. His hair is stylish and messy. His eyes are tired in a good way—the way that makes me imagine snuggling against him on the couch and listening to jazz while sipping a glass of wine. Then retiring to bed for a little fun...

I stop short of imagining more, lest I have to go home and have fun without him. It's never as satisfying as I hope, and I usually feel guilty for objectifying him afterward.

"Night, Cris," he says, looking tall and strong and delicious and perfect.

"Night." I turn and walk to my car, waving one last time. He waves too, and then shuts the door.

CHAPTER FIVE

Benji

I'm carrying a bag filled with sushi rolls, hand rolls, fried rice, garlicky green beans, and various other foodstuffs from a sushi restaurant in Grand Marin. I could've ordered pizza, but in the event Cris's date doesn't work out—a high probability at this point—I want to be ready with a meal that will knock her socks off.

On my way out, I cut over to the corner where the management office is located, when I see a beautiful brunette in expensive shoes step outside. She slides her sunglasses onto her nose and rests one manicured hand on the arm of a good-looking son of a bitch with a crooked nose.

She sees me approach before he does and waves.

"How's my favorite almost-sister-in-law?" I call to Vivian as I cross the street.

Nate dips his chin in greeting before admiring his fiancée unabashedly.

"Charmer." She grins. She's not wrong.

Since my brother met her, he's been over the moon and not the least bit shy about admitting it. The cliché that the bigger they are, the harder they fall is true in his case.

"Eating for two?" He nods at the bulging bag of takeout in my right hand.

"I have extra in case Cris shows up hungry tonight. We've, ah, been working late nights."

"Uh-huh." His eyelids are at half-mast, his mouth a knowing tilt. "Vivian said she's dating and it's not going well."

"Nate!" she admonishes. "That's proprietary!"

"I don't count," he informs her.

"I'm helping her out," I explain, sweat prickling the back of my neck.

"You are?" Vivian asks. I'm surprised she didn't know. I thought she and Cris talked more often than Cris and me.

"Yeah. We're doing postmortems after her dates. Sometimes she comes over hungry and I have to be ready."

"So, she leaves her date and then comes to your place for dinner and drinks?" Viv's eyebrows leap over her dark sunglasses, her slight smile almost accusatory.

"What are friends for?" I say with a shoulder shrug. Cris is at my house a lot. Now, a little more than usual. I'm not seeing the big deal.

"Be good to your life assistant," Nate warns, his mouth screwed into an amused tilt.

"Life assistant coach," I correct automatically.

He laughs. I wish them well and turn to leave. Nate has been giving me shit about Cris for a while now. He maintains she has an incurable obsession with me, but I can't let the idea take root. She's my best friend. Did that sound defensive? Anyway, he's my oldest brother and ribbing me is part of his job.

At home, I stash the sushi in the fridge and glance at the clock. If things go bust with Rick tonight, Cris will have the finest sushi to ever touch her tongue. Nate doesn't fuck around when he puts businesses in his live-work facilities. They are top-notch or bust. Probably because the big bastard likes to eat. I'm grateful to any restaurant making amazing food because I also like to eat. And I *really* don't like to cook.

At my countertop, I drum my fingers on the surface and consider the clock on the microwave. Six thirty. I wonder how her date is going. If he picked her up or she met him there. If they are laughing over a glass of wine, or she's fretting about how long she should stay to be polite before leaving and coming to me.

My mouth shifts into a sly smile. Before I know it, I'm hoping she has a reason to run to me from her (likely shitty) date. Not that I want Cris to fail, but honestly, like one of these chuckleheads could be good enough for her? Highly doubtful.

Then another thought hits. What if the date's going *well*?

What if she's touching his arm and telling him how much she enjoys talking to him? I saw a photo of the guy and even I can admit he's not unattractive. Unbidden, a vision of them at a candlelit dinner pops into my head. What if they finish off a bottle of wine and then order a second, lingering over crème brûlée? What if they leave the restaurant hand in hand, her rosy-cheeked and doing that cute eyelash-batting thing she does, while he slides an expectant, feral gaze down her body...

Wow. That got dark.

I stop drumming my fingers and stand. I'll reroute my nervous energy and grab a workout and a shower. Or maybe a swim and then a shower. I debate for a few moments before deciding a swim would feel better. It's cool-ish outside but the pool is heated. And concentrating on laps will quiet my lizard brain.

Anything to keep from imagining what might happen if the next few hours pass and I end up eating sushi for two alone in my kitchen.

TWO AND A HALF HOURS LATER, I've swum, showered, and returned to eyeing the clock. I poured myself a glass of wine a few minutes ago, having given up on Cris showing. I'm guessing her date went well. I resisted texting her for a status update.

Barely.

But then her telltale knock comes—three in quick succession. I race to the door trying not to look like I'm racing for the door.

"Hey." I sound a little out of breath. I check her person for signs she's been kissed within an inch of her life—or closer —but her curls are un-mussed, her lipstick on, and her black dress pants and flowy red shirt are in pristine condition. There are no wrinkles suggesting the outfit was recently plucked off the floor, which is a big fucking relief. I'm not ready for that discussion. (If ever.)

"Hey," she says, her tone muted. I love that her tone is muted, and hope it's because she's disappointed. I realize this makes me sound a dick. Trust me, I don't want Cris to have a horrible life. I want her to have an incredible life, complete with her knight in pressed khakis. I just don't think she's going to find him on a freaking dating app.

"How'd it go?" I shut the door behind her and rub my hands together, realizing I might've assumed too much. She could be disappointed because she had sex with the bastard and it was bad. That...I really don't like thinking about.

"Well, we made it to dinner." She lets out a gusty sigh and drops her purse on the sofa. "And then he drove me home."

I tense.

"He was such a pretentious asshole. I should have run out before dessert, but like an idiot, I let him pick me up so he was my ride."

"You could have called me," I growl, my tone harsher than I intend. "You can always call me. Tell me you know that. You're not at the mercy of some douche-nozzle because he shelled out money for dinner."

Her cupid's-bow lips curve into a soft smile at my creative insult. She pats my chest, the warmth of her palm leaving an unexpected imprint on my shirt. "You think he paid for dinner. That's cute."

I clench my jaw.

"There's one thing I didn't have my fill of tonight. Wine. Rick was a self-professed teetotaler. I followed suit to be polite."

"I have a lot of opinions," I let her know. "I won't start my lecture until after I've poured." I point to my glass. "Red?"

"Is white too much trouble?"

"Not even a little." Nothing is too much trouble for her.

Her phone rings from her purse and she pulls it out to check the screen. "Vivian," she informs me. "I'll be fast."

"Take your time. I'll pick out the perfect vintage."

She heads out to the pool, sliding the patio door shut behind her. I jog downstairs, whistling as I go to the large wine cooler and study the contents. I feel a hell of a lot better knowing she didn't sleep with the guy, but he better not have done anything untoward or I'll have him killed.

I'm kidding.

I'll kill him myself.

Upstairs I uncork the wine and pour a glass. I stick the bottle in the fridge, palming her glass and mine to take them outside. The night is cool and pleasant, and the pool sparkles, lit from below with soft violet bulbs. She's still on the phone, arm crossed over her middle, eyes on the water. I slide the door aside and open my mouth to ask if she wants me to leave her glass for her when I hear:

"It wasn't the worst date ever, but close. He expected a kiss good night. Ha!"

I freeze, my interest piqued. I listen in for a second. Just long enough to feel relief that her derelict date didn't get a kiss good night. *Idiot.* I pull in a breath to announce myself, but what comes out of her mouth next causes my tongue to stick to the roof of my mouth.

"At this point I'd pay a thousand dollars for an orgasm from someone other than myself."

Swear to God that's what she said. I nearly face-plant onto the patio and give myself away. Her sweet, musical laughter draws me in as my mind spirals to the gutter. I don't know what's more appealing. The visual of her giving herself an orgasm, her legs spread wide on her bedsheets, her mouth open in a moan or...

Yeah, that's the best visual. I can't come up with a single better one.

"Vivian!" she admonishes with another laugh. This one is playful, open, and a touch naughty. Cris is not naughty. At least *I* haven't heard her say anything naughty. I lean out the door further, too rapt to turn back now.

"Oh great idea, Viv," she says, the words heavy with sarcasm. "Should I mosey down to the wine cellar? And then what? Slink up to him—" Her hand goes to her hip and she shimmies, making her black dress pants look a lot sexier than they should.

My eyes move over her pert ass and up to where her curly hair brushes her shoulders. I make no move to go inside or announce my presence. I have to hear what comes next or I'll explode like a confetti cannon.

"And then I'll soften my voice like this—" Her voice slips into a seductive husk I've never heard before. Her red shirt is cut in a V, revealing her bare back—no bra strap. All I can think about is how silky her skin would feel under my fingertips and how good her blond curls would smell if I buried my nose in them.

My brain goes offline when she purrs, "Excuse me, Benji..." But her eyes are still on the pool, her purring only for Vivian. I'm riveted, mouth agape, frozen with one foot on the patio outside, my palms strangling a pair of wineglasses. I take a shallow breath and another, anticipating what might come after hearing her say my name so sensually.

She doesn't disappoint.

"How about you slide one of those talented hands into my pants..."

Beads of sweat form on my forehead while I hang on to the word "pants" with both hands. I find myself wishing this was a choose-your-own-adventure story. I lapse into a fantasy about sliding my hands into her pants, which is probably why I didn't notice she turned around.

Her voice trailed off some time ago. Now she's staring at me, phone to her ear, her mouth gently agape—ironically *not* unlike the Cris in my debauched fantasy. And here I am, in limbo at the open patio door, statue still. It's painfully obvious I'm eavesdropping.

Well. Painful for her. I'm so intrigued I can hardly think straight.

"I have to go," she says to Vivian. Then in a harsh whisper adds, "Call you later."

She ends the call and slides the phone into the pocket of her pants. The same pants she suggested I slide one of my "talented hands" into.

Her smile brightens as if by force. "Hey! Change of plans. I'm going to head home after all. I am beat. Sorry to make you go through the hoops for the wine." She laughs, but it's not the sinful, playful trill from before. No, no. This laugh is bordering maniacal.

"What a night!" she says. Loudly. She steps around me, careful not to bump the wineglasses or brush against so much as my arm.

Surely she's not going to pretend she didn't say what we both know she said—what she *has* to know I overheard.

I follow her brisk steps into the kitchen.

"Sorry again about the wine," she calls, moving away

43

from me as I set down our glasses on the bar. She shoulders her purse and walks away. I jog to catch up.

"Oh, hell no." I press my hand against the front door as she attempts to pull it open. "You're not going anywhere. Not until you explain what just happened."

CHAPTER SIX

Cris

Crap. I knew that wouldn't work.

I turn slowly to face him. He's close. Too close. Regret surfs on the crashing waves in my stomach. "I should go."

He shakes his head. "You're not leaving until we talk about your date."

The date. He wants to talk about my date? Maybe he didn't hear what I told Vivian. Maybe there was a blip in the universe, and the words I thought were overheard instead frittered off and vanished into the atmosphere.

Then he tacks on, "And whatever you said about your pants."

Double crap.

This is Viv's fault. She called to say she felt betrayed because I've been giving Benji the lowdown on my dating life rather than talking to her. In my defense there wasn't much to tell. She then accused me of using the postmortems following my dates as an excuse to date Benji. I laughed and explained those were his idea, and then possibly protested a wee bit too much.

To throw her off my trail, I recapped my date with Rick Backer, who might be the penny-*pinchingest* man I've ever been in the presence of, and I'm including my maternal grandfather who died a millionaire and left his money to my uncle—my mom's brother—but lived eighty-eight years as a miser.

Vivian then mentioned I'd better step up my frequency of dates since I needed to cash in my V-card (the V is for virginity), and that's when I blurted out I'd love an orgasm. She suggested Benji. I laughed again and acted as if it was a ludicrous suggestion. She is engaged to Benji's brother. I don't want how I feel about Benji getting back to Nate.

"Have a seat." Benji tips his head toward the bar where our abandoned wineglasses sit. I shake my head. "*Cris.*"

"*Benji.*" I guess I can be thankful I didn't mention the V-card thing or else I'd have a lot more explaining to do. Although judging by the look on his face, I already have plenty of explaining to do as it is.

Viv loves to tease me about him. I've done a good job pretending I don't find my boss attractive since I met her, but she doesn't believe me. I'm a horrible liar. On the phone, she suggested I solve my orgasm issue by approaching him, and I deflected. But my joking might've gone too far by the time I committed to the character of seductress, and wouldn't it figure that Benji was standing right behind me when I spun my R-rated fairy tale.

The key to problem-solving is to start from the square you're in, which means I can't deny what he heard. He's too smart for that. Even if he was as dumb as a brick, I'm transparent. Any claim he misheard me would be an obvious lie. My remaining option, which he is thwarting, is to flee.

"Can we do this later? The wine went to my head tonight." I pin a smile into place and try option C: reason.

"You didn't have a drink at dinner because Rick is a teeto-taler." Benji's eyelids lower into a deliberate blink. He points to the full glass of white wine sitting next to his red on the counter. "And you haven't touched your glass yet."

"Benji, please," I whine. Begging is all I have left. I put my hands in prayer pose. "Please can we forget this happened?"

His full, delicious mouth tips up at one corner. "How'm I supposed to do that?"

"Easy, you shake your head like this." I demonstrate, shaking my curls and closing my eyes for effect. I smile brightly. "Voila! All gone!"

He takes my hand and leads me past the sofa and to the counter, then spins to face me. He's not as close as before, which is good. I really needed to take a breath not steeped in Benji. He drops my hand.

"You can't say..." He pauses, and I pray he's not going to recap. "What you said while looking like you do and expect me not to think about it."

I blink at him, stunned. "You...thought about it?"

"I'm still thinking about it." He adjusts his fly rather deliberately and my eyes follow the movement. I don't mean to look but here I am, looking. I'm not saying there's a flagpole down there, but there is a bit more, um, *lift* where there wasn't before.

"Oh my God." Did I do that? I don't know whether to cry or throw a party.

"You understand my dilemma," he rumbles. His voice is raw and sexy. My nipples tighten and press against the silky fabric of my bra.

Triple crap.

"Cris, I am capable of giving you an orgasm."

Whimper.

"Uh, that's okay. I'm okay. It's okay." Next tactic: denial.

His expression reads "bullshit" but what he says is, "I wouldn't charge you a thousand bucks for it either."

A laugh stutters from my lips. I put my hands over my face and literally hide. He pulls them away, which brings him closer to me. I'm so humiliated I might spontaneously combust. I open one eyelid a crack and admit, "This is so embarrassing."

"Wine. You're overdue."

I'll say. He takes my purse and drops it on the couch, and then hands over the glass of wine he poured for me. Resigned to my fate, I accept. Clearly, he's not going to let me exit his house before he's given a reasonable explanation. Drunk was a convenient excuse but with that off the table, I find myself reaching for another. Insanity? Would insanity work?

I take an unladylike gulp of my wine. He notices.

"There's plenty more where that came from."

"What a relief," I say, deadpan.

His laugh is rumbly and gentle. I wish I could vanish into thin air, but alas...

He pulls out a stool for me. I don't want to sit, but arguing is futile. He settles onto the stool next to mine. "So this Rick guy left you sexually frustrated?"

"What? No!" I can't help laughing at this entire absurd situation. Me, busted after Vivian suggested I seduce my boss-slash-best-friend who's determined to continue the date's postmortem in order to deduce the reasons behind my mentioning his hand in my pants.

Groan.

"Cheapskates who do nothing but talk about how smart they are, and brag about the awards they won at work don't do it for me."

"And I do?" He smirks. Before I can have a panic attack, he frowns. "Was he inappropriate with you?" He's angry at the idea of Rick being improper with me, which makes my tummy grow as warm as my cheeks.

"No. He tried to kiss me, but when I refused he didn't press." What he did was shrug and say "whatever" before walking off my front porch. Then he loped back to his car and gunned the engine, his tires squealing as he sped down the street. I don't mention that.

"And then you drove here."

"Yeah. I thought it'd be nice to finish the night on a positive note." My voice is small. The truth ekes out next. "It's depressing to think I can't meet anyone halfway decent."

He consoles me, his voice gentle, but it takes me a second to unpack the sentences he says because they are not the ones I expect.

"You're a woman with needs, Cris. It's nothing to be ashamed of. All you have to do is ask. If that's what you really want. Is what you said out there what you really want?" He tips his head toward the patio door, the pool's cool violet lights glowing beyond.

I try to laugh, but a thin wheeze exits my throat.

"This doesn't have to be weird."

"Too late!" I try to sound offended. I'm not offended. I'm so turned on I'm in danger of setting off the smoke alarms.

"Sex is a basic need. If you meant what you said..." His non-question is more of a challenge.

"I was just..." Nothing comes after those words because I wasn't *just* anything. I wasn't kidding, even though I tried to convince Vivian that I was. I have been sexually frustrated for a number of years. I haven't done much of anything with anyone to know what it would feel like to have relief from that frustration. Which is, well, frustrating. The prospect of a stranger's hands on my body below the waist is terrifying. The thought of Benji's hands down there...

Oh, this is such a bad idea.

"Drink your wine. I'll give you an orgasm and then you can go home." He shrugs. "You'll feel better."

Why, *why* does that sound so damn good?

"Wh-what about you?" I croak.

"What about me what?"

"Won't you feel frustrated? More frustrated?" I ask on a strangled whisper as I glance at his lap. Not that I'm considering this, but I am curious.

His lips pull into a full-fledged Benji smile that never fails to weaken my knees. "Honey, giving you an orgasm would make my day."

Before I can wrap my mind around those words, especially the "honey," he continues. "Who would you rather stroke you to orgasm? Some loser you found on a dating app or your best friend?"

It's so close to what I imagined I worry briefly that I said it out loud.

"You can trust me. I won't pressure you into doing anything else. You'll enjoy yourself, guaranteed. I'm very, very good."

Before my stomach can sour at the idea of the plethora of practice he's had in the past, I laugh again. "Now you're giving me your resume for the job?"

"It won't be a job for either one of us. You'll sleep better too."

His offer isn't a profession of love or even lust. I'm trying to decide if I care that he doesn't want me but is offering the very thing I've been dreaming of since I started working for him.

"It's just sex," he states plainly, murdering any remaining hope that he might be overcome with passion during. "And it's not even real sex. It's fingering, which barely counts. I can go down on you if you want."

I make a little "meep" sound in the back of my throat. He chuckles.

"Okay, too much. That's fair." He holds my hand. "We can start with kissing, see how that goes. Do you like nipple play?" he asks casually as he helps me to my feet. He watches me expectantly.

I nod my head. "I think so."

His eyes flare, burnishing the browns to vivid gold. Not so impersonal for him after all. "I'm your best friend," he repeats. "Completely safe."

Oh, but he isn't safe. No, he wouldn't hurt me, and yes, he'd likely give me the orgasm of my life, but he is not safe. I have to set my mind on not allowing this to mean anything. Or worse, not allowing this to mean *everything*.

He grips my hips and tugs me so close our chests almost

touch. "It won't be weird if we don't let it. Your body is in need and my body is happy to give yours what it needs. It's simple."

"It is?" I have my doubts. When it comes to relationships, it's never simple.

"Yep. We'll start with a kiss and if it's weird, we'll stop and pretend it never happened."

"You swear?" I ask hopefully. I wish he'd forget the phone call instead, but if he won't, maybe one kiss will lead to us calling it off, and then we can embrace our agreed-upon amnesia.

It's as close to a time machine as I'm going to get.

Not that I could forget kissing Benjamin Owen. No way, no how. My gaze strays to his full lips, his rounded shoulders. He fills out his pale blue dress shirt better than any man I've seen. His torso is slim and fit, giving him a V formation thanks to his religious gym habit. Home gym, with a trainer. God bless Vlad. He's an artist. I make out the outline of Benji's pectorals through the shirt and imagine his abs—which I'd love to set my mouth to. *Oh my God.*

"I can't do this." I shove his chest. "I—"

"Cris." Both his hands rest on top of mine. "Do you trust me?"

"Yes, but—"

"It's me. The guy who's known you since you were a college dropout working for my dad and I was a horny, annoying twenty-three-year-old." His lips quirk. "Now I'm a horny, annoying thirty-three-year-old."

I blow out a short laugh. Remarkably, he's setting me at ease.

"You can trust me," he insists.

I trust him more than anyone. He's been there for me even when I didn't work for him. I fold easier than I would have thought.

I nod. He leans in. I don't stop him this time.

Gently, his mouth presses mine. The touch of his lips melts me like warm chocolate. The hand I put on his chest fists, and I grab a handful of material and pull him to me, slanting my mouth and deepening our kiss. It's every fantasy I've had about him come to life. And proof my imagination is blurry black-and-white compared to the crisp, bright technicolor of this moment.

He returns my kiss with vigor, opening wide and touching my tongue with his. A bolt of lightning streaks through my body and ignites between my legs. He wraps both arms around my back and smashes my breasts against his torso. Then he's diving in with renewed vigor, the scrape of his five o'clock shadow rasping my jaw.

It's incredible. It's amazing. It's...

I whimper and my hips roll forward, my belly bumping into a telltale hard ridge. He grunts and then pulls his amazing mouth away.

I'm dazed. Uncertain.

He draws his chin back and smiles down at me. "Damn. You're a firecracker."

Then his smile blooms into one of his infectious grins.

CHAPTER SEVEN

Cris

"I've never had a panic attack before but I'm fairly certain if I did it would feel like this." I tap my breastbone with my fingers and nod to back up my own theory.

Vivian is grinning like crazy. Maybe she *is* crazy. She'd have to be considering what I'd shared with her was not good news. Meanwhile, she looks like she's ready to burst with excitement. I decide she is definitely crazy when the words, "You kissed Benji!" fly out of her mouth.

It's Sunday afternoon and I should be at home, cleaning and doing laundry and preparing a few meals for the week. Instead I called Vivian and told her I had to see her in person. So here I am. We're sitting on opposite sides of a beautiful sofa in Nate's—and well, now Viv's too—gorgeous home. The living room is posh yet comfortable. Take-charge, confident Vivian is sitting, legs crossed, her hands folded in her lap. I feel better about my predicament being next to her. If I'm lucky, maybe some of her confidence will spread to me. I have to go to work tomorrow, after all. After a sleepless night last night I realized I couldn't face Benji until I unpacked what happened.

"Technically *he* kissed me. But I kissed him back," I say. "And then he really kissed me. Like, with his whole body."

She giggles. I've never heard her giggle. I grouse at her. "You're losing your edge."

"I'm a woman in love. Sue me." She gives me a contemplative scowl that turns into a self-effacing smile. "Wait, don't. I've had enough legal issues for a lifetime."

I shake my head when she grins wider than before.

"I can't believe you didn't leap into his arms and have sex with him right there on the floor!" she shouts as Nate steps into the living room with our drinks.

I give him a wan smile. "Sorry you have to hear this."

"You're secret's safe with me." He hands me a glass garnished with a sprig of rosemary and a lime wedge.

"Nate's not a gossip." She beams up at him. He bends and gives her a soft kiss. God, they're sweet.

I take a drink of the clear liquid as Vivian does the same. "This is delicious."

"It's one of my favorites. He's been creative lately," she says.

"I'm a man in love." His smile is easy. He's the happiest I've seen him. He deserves it. He's such a great person. "I'll leave you to it. I'm going to do some work."

Viv blows him a kiss, and he walks his big body past the glass partition separating the living room from the staircase and walks up.

"So then what happened?" She folds her leg beneath her

on the couch and settles in for story time. "Tell me about your first Benji-assisted orgasm."

I send an uneasy glance over my shoulder even though I watched Nate walk upstairs with my own two eyes. Then I face my friend. "Why do you want to know?"

"Because! Since I first met you and Benji, I've sensed sparks. And what I want to know, in as much detail as you're comfortable with, of course, is what sort of sparks you threw. Was it sizzles and pops like oil in a pan, or a raging, unstoppable forest fire?"

"It was... It was..." I want to lie, but I'm awful at it, so I tell her the truth and save myself the trouble. "I left after the kiss. Nothing else happened."

It was not the answer she wanted to hear, but to be fair, it wasn't the one I wanted to give her. My shoulders sag. I'm both disappointed for her and in myself.

She sighs, her mouth screwing to one side. "Bummer." Then she takes a gulp of her drink and sets the glass aside. "I thought the whole reason you were dating was to celebrate your life—the one you finally have since your last baby bro left the house."

"I do. I *am*," I defend.

"Then why wouldn't you do the one thing you wanted to do most?" she asks gently.

"I panicked."

"The virgin thing," she guesses incorrectly.

"The best-friend thing. The *boss* thing. Benji is very intertwined in my life."

"He's also not seeing anyone at the moment, which is as rare as a snowman sighting in the desert." She takes a breath before offering a soft smile. "I'm not trying to pressure you,

Cris. I'm encouraging the outcome I thought you wanted."
She props her elbow on the back of the sofa and rests her
cheek on her fist. "It's obvious he's totally into you."

At this news, I blink. "Pardon?"

She reaches for her drink again. "Benji. He's into you."

"No, no. He's offering to help me out of a bind. Trust me,
if you heard his sterile explanation of how I was a woman in
need and he was capable of fulfilling that need, you would
not say he was into me."

"Oh yes, I would. No man offers to give a woman an
orgasm out of the goodness of his heart. Usually it's so they
can talk you into more sexy things." She shimmies her
shoulders.

"Really?"

"*Yes.*"

"But Benji is... I mean, he's probably not lying. He knows
what he's doing. He's had plenty of practice," I mumble
against the rim of my glass. "He did offer to go down on me
instead if I preferred." I pluck the neckline of my shirt and
use it to fan my face. I'm suddenly hot. Vivian has a way of
watching me like she's KGB and I'm under a very, very bright
lamp.

"He did *not*."

"He did. I think he was joking. Why are you
whispering?"

"Cristin—what's your middle name?"

"Joy."

"Aw, that's pretty." She smiles.

"Thanks."

Her smile erases and she explodes, "Cristin Joy Gilbert!
You and Benji circle each other like there's an impenetrable

57

forcefield between you. Now you've broken past the barrier and learned you have some serious untapped sexual chemistry." She softens her voice. "This is your chance to explore it. Sounds like he's willing to take your relationship to the next level."

"Not the next level," I correct. "He said after, we could go back to life like nothing happened. Tomorrow when I show up at his house for work, that's exactly what I'm going to do. Pretend he didn't offer to...you know. And I'll act as if he didn't kiss me."

"Mm-hm." Her mouth is a firm line of disagreement. "And how well do you think that will work after last night?"

"I am positive it will work," I fib. "As in one hundred percent positive," I further fib. "Benji will be as relieved as I am for not taking him up on his offer to put his hands in my—"

The clearing of a throat draws my attention over the back of the couch where Nate has reentered the room. He gives me a pleading, earnest expression. "I implore you, Cris. Do not finish that sentence. Refill?"

Vivian dissolves into laughter.

I smile up at him. I've always liked Nate, but now I like him even more. I drain my glass and hand him the empty.

OTHER THAN THE first time I met him, I can't remember being truly uncomfortable around Benji. Well, aside from Saturday night. This morning isn't looking so hot, either.

As usual, I arrive at seven thirty, park in his circle driveway, and grab the bag holding my laptop, planner, and other office necessities from my front seat. In my other hand are my keys and a travel mug of coffee. My keys, I always have. My travel mug, I always have but never fill at home. I make coffee at Benji's. Today, I filled it at home. I didn't want to risk lingering at the coffee pot until I was sure he was either downstairs working out, or entrenched in an important phone call.

Which means I'm already overthinking. Which means I probably should have called in sick. I thought about it. I did. But then I worried he might show up at my house and offer to nurse me back to health, and when he found I didn't need to be nursed back to health might offer to do other things to me —which, as previously discussed, we are *not* doing.

I'm still team Bad Idea on the Cris-Benji pairing while Vivian, up until and through drink number two on Sunday, remained team Just Do It Already. Nate remained neutral. Or as Viv said, *in denial*.

I clear my throat, linger by the car, roll my shoulders, and stare at the front door.

The door is outfitted with a code, but Benji rarely locks it as his neighborhood is gated and luxe. Just driving past the rows of manicured lawns feels like entering a different town altogether. Where the sidewalks in front of my house are cracked with grass growing between the splits, there isn't a weed that would dare grow outside of its sanctioned zone in this part of Clear Ridge.

I would be overwhelmed by his house if I hadn't been to the Owen house multiple times while I worked for William or visited Lainey whenever I was invited to family affairs. I've been around them often enough that their regal lifestyle seems almost commonplace.

Not that I had time to be intimidated. I had way too

much on my mind back then. Was Dennis passing algebra? Did the school nurse remember to give Timothy his antibiotic? Did Manuel forge my signature on his report card, or did he just not show it to me yet?

All of those issues were rattling around in my head in addition to appointment after appointment I had to keep track of. Work hours, conference calls, sports games, pickups, drop-offs... It wasn't any wonder I ended up leaving college. School is expensive, and there wasn't a lot of time left in the day to dedicate to studying in between grocery shopping, cooking, and helping Dennis with his algebra homework.

It also wasn't any wonder how I ended up a thirty-year-old virgin. I was busy. Too busy to date, and when I did date, there wasn't much room for intimacy. Once Manuel was off to college, I still had Dennis and Timothy to look after. And trust me, Dennis was a handful in his teen years. He's twenty-one now and still a handful, but he's not a big drinker, and enjoys the company of his girlfriend, Amara, who he's dated for six months. She's a good girl and has agreed to keep him out of trouble. God bless her.

I'm not completely inexperienced, though. I took matters into my own hands as needed. I'm not denying I'm a sexual creature with "needs," as Benji called them. But involving someone else was a layer I didn't have the luxury to explore back then. Basically, I put off my sexual needs until they morphed into a beast that grew bigger and scarier than it should've been.

As I consider Benji's front door, I wonder if fear is the reason I turned him down. I certainly felt something akin to fear the other night. It was a small miracle he let me leave.

Even though the kiss was a success, judging by the tent in

his pants and the dampness in my own, I insisted on going home. He didn't argue, and even stranger, changed his tune. I'm guessing one of the reasons he let me go was because he'd kissed his life assistant coach-slash-best friend and realized we were about to make a big mistake. I also think that sucks, which is at odds with the amount of relief I feel.

Do you think I need therapy?

One more shoulder roll, and I walk inside, steeling myself for seeing him. He's not in the living room/kitchen area, no surprise there. Occasionally he's refilling his coffee, but more often he's in his office.

The house's layout is absolutely perfect. If I had a billion dollars lying around—and didn't have three boys living with me up until fairly recently—it's one I would have chosen for myself. The living room is wide and open, outfitted with comfortable black leather furniture save for a deep red, tufted chair serving as a focal point. There are two paintings in the room, both abstract, with splashes of red and burnished gold crisscrossing the canvas. Painting was his birth mother's hobby. I'll never forget his fond smile when he told me they were amateur, but beautiful. The frames are handmade. By Benji. He sanded them until they were smooth, lovingly etched a design into the wood, and stained them.

My heart grew three sizes that day. I was twenty-two and not yet in love with him, or so I like to tell myself. The day I felt his sadness as he remembered his beautiful mother and admired her paintings, I'm pretty sure I toppled over Love Cliff like a heartsick lemming. But again, I had no time to react to it or entertain it. I was busy. And that was more than a convenient excuse. It was also the truth.

The attached kitchen runs the length of the living room.

A countertop with barstools offers space to address the person on the other side of it like a bartender, like I did last year when Nate screwed up with Vivian and was moping at Benji's house. I'm not sure Nate appreciated my help at the time, but he's since apologized for being a buffoon. His word. I laughed and he smiled. You've seen him. How do you not adore a lovable teddy bear like Nate? Anyway, where was I?

Oh, right. The kitchen. Lights strung from wires spotlight the bar. The fridge and cabinets are shining wood and very modern. Off the kitchen are the patio doors, a patio covering, the in-ground heated pool, and a huge yard. A huge yard I could have been pacing rather than standing *right next* to the dang patio door so as to be overheard talking about Benji putting his—well, you've heard this. The side yard wraps around the house and opens to a large backyard with plenty of trees and garden beds packed with flowers. Mostly roses, cultivated by Lainey Owen.

I walk past the kitchen and down a wide corridor to the left. There are several doors, one leading to the basement. The downstairs is cool and inviting. The perfect place for a wine cellar, outfitted with lots of tall wooden racks for bottles and a double-sided wine cooler. A table and stools sit in what he called "the tasting room" during the few times he invited me to belly up. There's also a gym down there, a pool table, and another room he rarely uses with two arcade games and a poker table. Other than the wine cellar, of which I am a semi-frequent regular, and the gym, of which I am a *regular*-regular, he doesn't spend his free time down there.

Probably because like me, he doesn't have much free time. Well, he doesn't allow himself to have much free time. He's a workaholic, and I suppose I'm guilty of that as well. As

Manuel went off to college, and then Dennis, and now finally Timothy, I should have an increased amount of free time on my hands. I seem to have filled it with Things To Do. Usually those things are Benji-related. I like to be near him, and he always has things to do.

Now, I have no boys at home, tons of time on my hands, and plan to avoid Benji, which will leave even more time on my hands. I'm sort of scared of what that will look like. My house used to be a bustling throughway of activity and noise, but is now a cavernous, empty vessel. I considered talking to Lainey about being an empty nester. She went from three boys at home to zero. If anyone can give me sound advice, it's her.

I wasn't relieved when Timothy went off to college or when Dennis stopped needing me. Then there was Manuel, who took the role of oldest male in the house seriously. Like me, he grew up too fast. He's independent and strong and appreciates how hard I worked to keep our family together.

As I pass various rooms in Benji's too-big-but-freaking-beautiful house, I call myself on my bullshit of "not having enough time." I have time to have a life. I made time to go on three terrible dates and shop for clothes over the last month. I found time to lounge around with Benji after, regaling him with tales from the dark side of my dating life.

Had I been lying to myself for years? Saying I didn't have time because of housework or yard work? Doctor's visits, college applications, workouts, repainting, changing the batteries in the smoke detectors... All those tasks were necessary, but did I turn life into a series of chores without allowing for the flexibility I so desperately needed?

Here I am, a third of the way (or less) into a life lived.

Have I lived it well? I will never regret raising my brothers. I'd do it over again. But I'm allowed to have romance too, aren't I?

And what is the real reason for my intact virginity? Did I truly "forget" about it? Did I slot it as unimportant? Or was there another, sneakier underlying reason for saving myself?

I walk through Benji's office on the way to my own. He looks up from his laptop and sends me an easy smile. In an instant, I realize what I've been doing for the last ten years. I wasn't "too busy." I've been waiting for the right man to come along. A man who sends heat to both my cheeks and my nether regions. A man whose smile lights up the room and my soul. Granted, he isn't the smartest choice—and makes no logical sense—but I know in my gut I'm looking right at him.

I've been saving myself for Benji.

CHAPTER EIGHT

Benji

I heard the front door open and close and readied myself for Cris. Meaning, I muted the video conference call I am on and listened for her approach rather than to the team meeting.

When she stops in front of my desk, I pop out one earbud and give her my attention. She looks different than she looked on Saturday. And I don't mean because she's wearing a pair of dark blue jeans and a yellow T-shirt that says, "Que sera sera" instead of black dress pants and a sexy red shirt with the back missing. I mean she looks *different*.

Her chin is higher, the set of her shoulders firmer. She's decided something, and she's come in here to tell me. I bet you a million dollars her speech is going to have to do with how she shouldn't have kissed me.

I let her have Sunday to herself. I didn't text or call, figuring she'd like a day to regroup. And possibly to rethink my offer. An offer as sincere as it was exciting. Cris plus an orgasm? Sign me up. *Twice.*

When my lips touched hers Saturday night, I wasn't expecting her to turn me on. Don't get me wrong, she's sexy as hell. I just didn't think of her that way. I couldn't afford to. She's the best assistant I've ever had. She's close friends with my family. She's...Cris. And yes, I admit, overhearing her talk dirty on the phone riled me up. How could it not? Since when did my angelic best friend start suggesting I put my hands in her pants?

I shift in my seat, aware of a certain part of me very much onboard with that plan. Thank God that part is hidden under my desk.

"Morning, coach." I paste on a (hopefully not lecherous) smile.

Some of the fire in her eyes dims, but she recovers quickly, shifting her body like she's preparing a speech. I glance at my screen where Josie is speaking about the effectiveness of a new software tool we're testing out while using a lot of hand gestures. I turn my attention back to Cris to tell her I can disconnect from the call in five minutes.

My life assistant coach starts talking before I can stop her.

"On Saturday I decided that allowing you to, um, *service me* was not the smartest, best design for our future. I was so sure that when I visited Vivian and Nate on Sunday, I was singing the same tune. She argued, saying I was crazy not to take you up on the offer, but I stayed firm." She makes a fist to illustrate. Damn, she's cute. Even while turning me down. I fight a smile.

"All the way up to the point I left their house, I was certain. Hell, all the way up until I walked into *this room*, I

66

was certain. My plan was to come here with my coffee already made"—she holds up her travel mug—"and walk directly to my office, not bother you, and then keep busy enough so you'd be discouraged to bother me. Not that you bother me." A pleat appears between her eyebrows. "What I mean is, I was planning to avoid you. In the hopes you would forget we kissed. And then we could pretend I never said I'd pay a thousand dollars for"—she motions with her hand—"you know."

I open my mouth again, but she holds up a hand to silence me. I press my lips together.

"The thing is, I'm tired of sex being this big taboo issue. I never meant for it to be! I never meant to preserve my virginity in a jar of formaldehyde. I told myself I was too busy to think about it, which was sort of the truth. But it was also sort of a lie because I've thought about it, Benji. Especially lately. My house is boy-free for the first time in twelve years. I'm practically an old maid at age thirty. And if that's the wrong word, then I am at least out of touch with reality. I was never waiting for marriage. I was never waiting for anyone." She mumbles the next part under her breath. "Or so I told myself."

My mind is stuck on one word in particular, like tires in the mud. Did she say she was a *virgin?* Cris Gilbert, adorable, petite, fit, cute, funny, smart Cris Gilbert has never had sex? Like *ever?* I can't wrap my head around it. The video call on my screen blurs into the background, Josie's voice in my ear nothing but white noise. The only thing I can focus on is that Cris is a virgin and I recently offered her a free-of-charge orgasm.

I swipe my forehead. I'm overly warm. More than a little

confused. A tad regretful I offered so callously. I should apologize, at the very least.

"I had no idea—"

"Save it." She stop-signs me again and continues. "I don't want to be treated like I'm precious or clueless. I want to be treated the way you promised. Like a woman who needs what you have to give. You did say you were very good."

I stare at her and imagine crickets sawing away inside my ears. Or a high-pitched hum when a loud sound renders you temporarily deaf.

"I did say that," I admit.

She walks toward me, cup of coffee and her bag in hand, the fiery determination in her eyes appearing hotter than when she first stopped at my desk. I thought she was going to tell me we were not going to do what I offered. I'm not sure that's the case anymore.

"You don't have to have sex with me, Benji." She says it so earnestly, I choke on a sound that might be a plea in the making. "But I would like to have some experience before I do it for the first time with someone. If—" She points at me, scarily serious before qualifying, "If you keep your word that things will not be weird between us. And if they do, promise you'll let me off the hook and we'll go back to being best friends and coworkers. I need to move on to the next stage of my life. I'm stuck. Maybe this will loosen me up."

"Oh, I guarantee it," I murmur, still in awe.

While she's been talking she's walked closer and closer. Now that she's next to my chair, her eyes snap to the screen where four of our company's team members are partitioned into squares. Josie notices Cris standing there and waves. In my ear I hear, "Hi, Cris!"

Cris doesn't wave back. She turns ghost-white, her gray eyes growing wider. I stand from my chair as she backs toward the door.

"Cris, wait—"

"Seriously?" she hisses before she runs from my office. By the sounds of the footsteps growing farther and farther away, and the answering slam of the front door, I assume she's not planning on coming back.

"Guys—" I start but realize the video conference is still muted. I click the button to unmute, say a prayer of thanks for the foresight I had to mute myself in the first place, and try again. "Guys, I had something come up. Go on without me. Josie, can you email me anything I miss?"

"Sure thing, Benji." Everyone looks as bored as before. I was definitely on mute. If I wasn't, I'm relatively certain not all of them could keep their expressions in check after hearing what Cris admitted. As bombs go, the one she dropped was Hiroshima in scale.

I make it out the front door as she throws her car in reverse. I move to her open driver's side window and put both hands on top of the car's roof as if I can physically prevent her from leaving. I bend down and lean on her open window. Tears shimmer in her eyes. She cries when she's angry. Not my favorite look on her, by far.

"You're an ass!" she shouts. "How could you let me say all that?"

"You were on a roll," I explain, backing up an inch when she taps the gas and almost runs over my foot. I move to the window again and shout, "It was on mute!"

She blinks at the steering wheel, then at me. "What?"

"The meeting. It was on mute. No one heard anything

you said. By the time I turned back to tell them I had to go, they couldn't hear me because I was still muted. I was going to tell you good morning and ask you to give me a few minutes, but you started talking before I could."

She blinks back the mist of tears beginning to form. Embarrassment takes over and her cheeks go ruddy. Then her eyebrows slam down. Her expression shifts back to anger so fast, I step away from the car just in case. "And you let me think they heard everything? You are an ass!"

I let out a light chuckle—carefully, as she's not yet put the car in park. "Like I said, you didn't give me a chance to inter-rupt. They didn't hear anything. I, on the other hand, heard every word of what you said. By the way, I have a few follow-up questions."

She licks her lips, and I feel a twitch in my pants again as I remember how she tasted Saturday night. How she kissed me back. She just propositioned me in my office. I'm not sure I can successfully go back to spreadsheets and email after her offer. I'm not sure any straight man could.

"Can we talk about it?" I approach her open window while she studies me warily.

"I don't know..."

"I'll make you coffee."

"I have coffee."

"I'll make you better coffee."

She sighs. I can tell a yes is forthcoming. She shakes her head and gives it to me. "Fine."

"Fine" isn't a "yes," but it's the best I can hope for. No way am I letting her leave my house before we have exhausted the topic at hand. Which, unless I hallucinated the last five minutes, was Cris asking me to give her an orgasm—

possibly more than one—before she bequeaths her virginity to some other dude.

And that, my friends, requires a lengthy discussion. With as many details as I can wring out of her.

Cris

He's taking this well.

Not that I tried to guess how he'd react. I decided on a fresh tactic while standing outside his office, which gave me about .02 seconds to react to the news myself.

Did I *really* proposition my best friend and boss?

"One oat milk cappuccino," he announces, sliding a foamed-to-perfection mug over to me.

"It's hard to believe you don't cook. You can be so fancy when it comes to drinks." We're not exactly in a comfort zone, but this feels normal. Sitting at Benji's bar in the kitchen and joking about his rad drink-making skills isn't new territory. Unlike the other territory we're tiptoeing around like un-sprung bear traps.

"You said a lot of things while I was on that call." He sits, resting his expensive shoes on the stool's rungs. "I was trying to tune out Josie and pay attention to you, then you said something that grabbed every last ounce of my attention."

I gulp. I know what that "something" was.

"You're a—a virgin?" His entire face screws into an expression I've never seen on him. It's one part confusion, two parts disbelief, and one part excitement. I'm not sure what to do about the excited part.

"It's not a big deal. Or it wasn't. Until recently." *Quite recently*, I think as I sip my cappuccino. Perfection. Of course. Like any orgasms Benji would gift me. If he accepts my offer I'll be doomed to wander the earth alone, scarred forever after having the perfect guy's hands on my body and never again finding his equal.

Or maybe I'm being dramatic.

"Where I come from, being a virgin is a big deal," he says.

"Virginity is a big deal in Idaho?"

"No idea. I was only in Idaho until the fifth grade. I was still wearing superhero pajamas."

"You could still totally pull off superhero pajamas," I tease. His expression shifts into one I've seen before but never had directed at me.

Sliding one elbow along the counter, he leans closer, his eyelids heavy. He tips his head to the side and in a seductive voice murmurs, "Role-play is an advanced level, coach. We should probably stick to the basics."

I was melting toward him, but now I bristle. "Can you not call me that?"

"What? Coach?"

"Yeah. It's...sexless."

"It's a nickname."

"It's not a sexy nickname." My voice is a whisper.

His gaze is cunning and knowing. "Would you like a sexy nickname?"

I exhale, breathless at the offer. "I don't know why I said that. Ignore me."

"Yeah, not gonna happen."

I'm overwhelmed. When I'm overwhelmed, there's one surefire way to combat it. Control.

"We should lay a few ground rules." Before he can argue, I go on. "I can call a halt at any time, and you have to agree to forget everything we did up until then. We go back to being best friends and coworkers and never speak of it again."

"I agree to everything but the middle part." He shakes his head. "No way I'll forget it."

Good point. I won't forget the offer, let alone the kiss a few days ago. I imagine anything more will be seared into my brain like grill marks on a Fourth of July hot dog.

"I say we do it now. The buildup is hard on everyone." He literally rolls up his shirtsleeves, revealing strong forearms with a dusting of dark hair. He wiggles his fingers and then winks. "I'll be gentle."

"You're insane." I make a defeated sound that might be a laugh. "Ugh, I don't think I can do this. *I* am insane."

"You can." He takes both my hands and gently squeezes my fingers. "And you're not insane. You're horny."

"Don't act like this is normal."

"Fuck normal. What's normal? Do you think it's normal for an orphaned kid to be shuttled from Idaho to Ohio and adopted by billionaires? To become one himself at a crazy young age? To be this good looking and exude so much charm that every female in a one-hundred-mile radius faints dead away at the sight of him?"

I shake my head. He's incorrigible and completely desirable. "You are too much."

"I am just right. As you're about to find out." He stands, tugging me up.

"Not at work. That's my other rule," I argue. "I can't do sex stuff during work hours."

"Why not?"

"My head is in work mode. I have to check my schedule and yours. I have to return the fifty emails I know are sitting in my inbox. I have a report to finalize. I have office supplies to order because I ran out of time to do it last week."

"We're not having no-holds-barred fun in your pants because we're out of Post-its?" he asks, droll.

"Pen refills, actually."

"Oh, well in that case." He wears sarcasm as well as his clothes, which he wears damn well. "Come on, Cris. You'll be glad you did."

"Nope. I mean it. I need to compartmentalize my day."

"Okay." He gives in with a full-body sigh. "When is the sex compartment?"

The questions stumps me. "I...I'm not sure. I've never had a sex compartment."

His grin is devious and beautiful. "I was right, Fire-cracker. This is going to be fun."

I return his grin, warmed by the idea we have something to look forward to. Warmed further by my new nickname. *Firecracker* is much sexier than coach.

CHAPTER NINE

Cris

My alarm pings, reminding me it's nearly five o'clock—the end of the workday. Some days it would also signify the beginning of a workout, but Benji lifted weights at lunch while I went for a quick walk around the neighborhood.

I love walking in his neighborhood. The gated community is called Three Palms. There are no palm trees in Ohio, but the name doesn't take away from the beauty of the immaculate houses and peaceful setting. While I walked I listened to a podcast rather than turning over what we talked about earlier. When I came back to my desk I was hyper-aware of the clock ticking the minutes away, eating up what was left of the hours of the day.

And here we are at day's end. That was fast.

I'm sending one last email when he appears in my doorway. My office is connected to his expansive one by a short hallway and outfitted with a white French door I never bother closing. He leans on the jamb, and I freeze, my fingers prone on the keyboard as I admire the long line of his body.

"Workday is over," he states.

My heart hits my throat.

"Looks that way," I say. Half of me is worried he's going to walk in and take care of me right here at my desk, and the other half of me is worried he's changed his mind and isn't interested after all. Neither halves are satisfied when he says something I didn't anticipate.

"I made dinner reservations for seven o'clock tonight."

"For...?"

"Are you serious?" When I don't answer his question he adds, "For us."

For us.

"You didn't think I was gonna come in here and take your pants off at your desk, did you?"

I laugh. A little too long and a little too loud. I pull myself together enough to say, "Someone very wise and experienced told me I should never let my date pick the restaurant."

He doesn't miss a beat. "Yeah, because you have been dating idiots. I know exactly what I'm doing. And I know how you like to be treated. Isn't that what you're counting on?"

There's something sweet about him knowing me. And how he's taking his knowledge and funneling it into treating me well. I haven't been the recipient of many selfless acts in my lifetime.

"I'm not counting on anything," I say. "I'm winging it. Totally and completely at your mercy." It was supposed to be a joke, but his brow darkens as he pushes off the doorframe. He stalks to my desk, all potent, masculine energy, and bends down in front of my chair. He sets his palms on my knees and turns my chair to face him. His face is chest-high to me, his golden eyes peering up beneath thick, dark eyelashes. I can't think of a single reason why we should go to dinner when we could do what I have wanted for as long as I can remember.

"You're not at anyone's mercy, Cris," he reminds me. "Always remember that. What you're asking for is not out of the ordinary. It's not ridiculous. It's nothing to be ashamed about. And it's definitely not something you should let happen without your express permission."

"I know. But you're...you."

"I am me. And you know you can trust me. I'm glad you know that. What I need you to remember is that with this physical stuff comes great responsibility on the part of the other person. He has to please you. He has to be good to you. He has to put you first. If he doesn't, move on. Every time."

I think of the experience Benji has had. He has treated quite a few women to his goodness, his way of pleasing. He's no doubt put them first. I have seen it time and again when I'm at professional functions and he brings a date. Especially when he was seeing Trish last year. Whenever she was around, it was like there was no one else in the room. His focus was on her. I figure he's always treated women well. In or out of bed.

"What if he does all of those things and leaves anyway?" I realize how transparent my question is the second I ask it. I'm not talking about a mysterious stranger from the dating app. I'm talking about Benji. He's the one who's going to leave. Yes, he'll still be my friend and we will work together afterward. But we're not going to be showing up hand in hand at family functions. We're not going to be holding each other on the dance floor at Archer's newest nightclub. That's not what this is about.

"If he leaves, he's a moron. You're a keeper."

I don't know what comes over me, whether it's his proximity, the open, kind way he's watching me, or the compliments he's laid at my feet, but next I surprise both of us.

Placing my palms on either side of his face, I bend and touch my lips to his.

Benji

Her lips. Her soft, soft lips.

I thought I exaggerated in my mind how soft those lips were, but as they move gently along mine, I realize I didn't exaggerate at all.

I've received plenty of kisses to know this experience is unique. It holds an entirely new facet than any in my past, given I know Cris better than I knew anyone in my past.

There is a deep trust between us, and I refuse to lose it. I know how tough it's been for her to relax and unwind with her responsibilities at home. I didn't realize it involved her intact virginity and the claim she'd "forgotten" about it—still not sure how that happens. But I refuse to let her feel like an outcast.

I'm going to show her how good it can be—how good it *should* be. Knowing I can deliver better than any bumbling moron she's dated before me strokes my already stroked ego. Speaking of strokes, her tongue comes out to play. I tip my head and allow her to deepen the kiss. Her hands slide from my cheeks to my neck and rake upward into my hair, sending chills down my spine. I scoop up the back of her hair with my hand and pull her seeking mouth to mine, tighter than before. The tiny whimper from her throat is like a gun signaling the start of a race.

And they're off.

I love physical affection. Touching, kissing. Delivering what the other person needs or wants. If I had any idea Cris was lacking in that department, I'd have leapt on this opportunity way before now. I wasn't trying to be cocky when I said I was good. I was sincere. There has always been a clear demarcation between my head and my heart. My body and my soul.

I pull away to take a much-needed breath, floored by the heat simmering in her eyes. I can't help smiling since I'm responsible for putting it there.

"Firecracker," I whisper. She smiles a demure, pure Cris smile that tugs the vicinity of my groin.

Not my heart. Never my heart.

"Can we skip dinner?" she breathes.

"But—"

"Benji." Her fingernails stroke my scalp. "I've waited years for this. Now that I've accepted, I'm pretty damn anxious."

Fuck, she's cute.

It'd take superhuman strength to turn her down knowing she wants what I want. To show her the time of her life and send some of the heat in her eyes skittering down her entire body.

"Still want me to slide my hands into your pants?" I murmur against her lips. She squirms and scoots to the edge of her chair, a nonverbal *yes*. "Do you want me to kiss you anywhere else? Like here?" I ask before I place a long, open-mouthed kiss on the underside of her jaw. She sighs.

"Or here?" I rake my teeth down the side of her throat before soothing it with another kiss. She moans. Her fingers go tight in my hair, and she pulls at the longish strands on top.

"Or lower?" I drag my tongue along her collarbone.

"J-just above the waist," she amends. I raise my head and find her looking adorably nervous. "But your hands can go below."

"That I can do." I stand and she stands with me. She's drop-dead gorgeous today. Even in the simple ensemble of jeans and a T-shirt. She's wearing a gold ring on her index finger and no other jewelry. Her beauty has always been understated. You have to look closer to see what's there. Simplicity. Honesty. Once I noticed, I couldn't unsee it, but seeing it is never a hardship.

I lead her to the loveseat on the other side of her office. It's dark brown, matching the earth tones of this room. Beige walls with green and beige and orange artwork on the walls— not my mother's work, but I made the frames.

I sit and she sits with me. Leaning in, I kiss her, this time untucking her shirt from the waist of her jeans as I do. She lets me lay her back, her big gray eyes looking so hopeful it hurts—in a good way.

"Trust me?" I ask, knowing she does.

"Of course." A shaky smile follows.

"We'll keep it light. This is supposed to be fun." I raise her shirt and kiss her stomach, her ribs and then up, up until I press a kiss between her breasts. They're the perfect size. B-cup, I'd guess. The bra she's wearing, a pale spring green lace, gives me enough of a peek of her pink nipples to spur me on. "This okay?" I kiss the swell of one breast over the demi-cup of her bra.

"Yes." It's more of a breathy sigh than a word, but it was a yes, so it totally counts.

"What about this?" I slip my tongue past the bra to taste her areola.

"Yes!" That was a borderline shout. Her eyes open, and her head jerks off the sofa. I lay my palm flat on her chest and push her down. "Don't even think of stopping me," I warn. "Not when you're enjoying yourself."

I wonder if this will take long at all. Let's find out.

Reaching behind her back, I unhook her bra. Then I sit back and bring her forward. "Shirt off okay?"

She nods, a little dazed, a lot beautiful. I try not to gloat as I take her shirt and bra off and set them on the low table next to the couch. She's in such good hands. She has no idea what she's in for, but I do. She crosses her arms over her chest and lies back, watching me with curiosity and something else I can't name. Anticipation, I think. But I have to ask. No way do I want her regretting anything. She's either all in or this is all over.

"What's wrong?" I touch the cleavage she's giving herself by pushing her breasts together, dragging my finger along the soft swells of each breast.

"What if—" She cuts herself off to smile, teeth and all. "What if I...can't? I've never let anyone other than myself touch me down there."

Rather than argue she most definitely *can*, I say, "Behind performance anxiety is usually worry you'll let the other person down. You can't possibly let me down. You have nothing to lose. I'll do my thing. You relax. If I don't hit the right buttons or ring the right bells, you can call it quits, or you can instruct me and I'll keep trying until I succeed."

She shakes her head, but it's not so much a "no" as it is expressing wonder and surprise. "Why are you doing this?"

"With great power comes great responsibility. Just so happens I have a lot of power in this realm. Are you going to let me prove it to you or not?" I reach for her crossed arms. She lets me pull them away from her body to reveal two of the most beautiful breasts I've ever laid eyes on.

"Oh, Cris. You're gorgeous, honey."

She blushes. It's amazing.

I lower my head, place her hands in my hair, then I stroke my tongue over one of her nipples. I go slow, licking, suckling, laving. She tastes incredible. She can't hold still, her hips wriggling beneath me. Her whimpers of ecstasy let me know I'm on the right track. I continue kissing her while moving one hand to the button of her jeans. By the time her zipper is down, her hips lift.

She's ready.

Sliding my hand past the barrier of her jeans, I find matching silky green panties. I stroke my finger over the fabric panel. She's wet. Ready. But to be sure, I ask. "Ready?"

"Yes."

It's the sincerest one I've heard yet. Slipping past the silken fabric, I touch her bare pussy and feel my cock grow heavy. The hardest part (no pun intended) is going to be remembering not to take this further. This isn't about me. She is looking for an orgasm. She didn't ask to lose her virginity to me. Although, I don't see why I couldn't help her out in that area as well. One thing at a time.

Focus, Benji.

Stroking her damp folds, I move up her body and kiss her mouth. Against those soft lips I instruct, "Spread."

Her legs fall open like I command, and damn, is that heady. I deepen my touch as her tongue explores my mouth with vigor. Her hips lift and drop in a rhythm she's setting. I'm just keeping time.

When she's close, she pulls her mouth from mine to suck in a few quickened breaths. Her brows dive inward, her eyes shut. She licks her lips. Her hands are clutching the couch cushion beneath her. I insert one finger incredibly gently, and for a moment she goes rigid before she relaxes into it. I press her clit with my thumb and, knowing she's close, dip my head to take a nipple on my tongue to send her over.

She comes on contact.

Her cry is hoarse, desperate, satiated. I continue stroking until I feel warmth on my fingers. Her entire body tenses and relaxes until finally, her hand grabs my wrist. I flatten my fingers against her sex and feel her pulse out the end of her orgasm. Her breasts lift. I take a moment to place one final kiss on the tip of each one.

She's so responsive. So bare. So open. So *ripe*. I was not wrong. This is damn fun. My cock disagrees, pounding against my fly with angry fists.

Down, boy. Greedy bastard.

"You're much better than I am at that," she mutters sleepily, her cheeks the perfect shade of rose. Her eyes flutter open. Her gray irises appear darker with blown-out pupils. "You weren't exaggerating. You are very good."

I kiss her again, unable to stop myself. I pull my hand from her panties, zip and button her up, and then I retrieve her shirt and bra and lay them over her chest. She clutches her clothing to her body and watches me from beneath heavy eyelids.

Seriously gorgeous.

"Any time you need my assistance," I tell her, trying to shift around a burgeoning erection without being noticeable about it, "you let me know."

She opens her mouth, maybe to laugh or maybe to tell me something. I don't find out because my phone buzzes and rings in my pocket. "Shit. Sorry about this."

I move to silence it as she sits up and snaps her bra. "Don't be sorry. Answer it if you need to."

Trish's name lights the screen. My phone rings again. I feel the weight of Cris's eyes, but she looks away as soon as I look at her. She redresses as I stand and silence the call.

"Not important," I tell her. She returns my smile with a tight-lipped one of her own.

"Well. Thank you." She fluffs her hair and tucks the front of her shirt into her jeans. I have a brief thought about how creamy she was, how good she might taste. But the timing is wrong to ask for more. I reroute my gaze to her face.

She's already snapped out of her post-orgasmic haze thanks to me not leaving my phone in my office or silencing the fucking thing. Now who's the idiot? She redresses quickly, and then shuts down both her laptop and her sated expression.

"Maybe we can have dinner another night," she says, all business once again.

I want to argue, but I sense she's not in the mood to discuss. She took what she needed and she's done. Not that I didn't have fun giving her what she needed, but I didn't expect to lose her company so soon.

"Anytime, Firecracker."

The nickname slows her hasty movements. She watches me, her purse in one hand and travel mug in the other. "I'm being weird, aren't I?"

Just like that, I have my Cris back.

"I'm sorry."

"No. No," I repeat emphatically. "Do not be sorry. See you tomorrow. Take all the time you need. I understand the need to recover." I wiggle my fingers for effect. "There's a lot of power in these babies."

She rolls her eyes and then surprises me by coming to her tiptoes to place a sweet kiss on the corner of my mouth. "See you tomorrow, boss."

With that, she's out of her office. A few minutes later I hear my front door open and close. I'm left with eight inches of hard-on I refuse to take care of with Cris on my mind.

That's not what this was about.

I'm not what this was about. This was for her.

Irked by her absence and several other things, including the call from Trish when I haven't heard from her in months, I stroll to my office and resume working.

CHAPTER TEN

Cris

Benji texts me the next morning to let me know he has a "thing" across town I didn't know about, and that he'll be back late morning. Fine by me. It's not like I was looking forward to bumping into him in the office and explaining my bizarro reaction yesterday.

Rather than drive straight to the office, I swing by Grand Marin, which is nowhere near on the way to Benji's, but the coffee and muffin joint there is calling to me. I plan on indulging in a triple chocolate with chocolate chunks muffin plus a matcha latte. And maybe I'll buy an extra muffin to indulge in later this afternoon. This is shaping up to be a week of indulgence and it's only Tuesday.

Bakery bag in hand, I'm sipping on my latte and wondering if I should drop in on Vivian. I decide that's not the best idea. Not that she wouldn't be supportive. She'd probably throw me a party. I'm not ready to tell her—to tell anyone. This secret is mine, all mine. Well, and Benji's. It's precious. Special. Now a memory, but a really friggin' good one.

He kissed me and then my breasts, and in the span of a few minutes—if that—I was shouting my release and riding his hand. I feel my face heat, my body responding as the memory of yesterday loops in my head. Truth? I've been reliving it since it happened. At home I zoned out during dinner, staring at the TV without seeing the screen, and then later I lay wide awake in bed. I replayed how his tongue felt on my nipples. The way his finger felt moving inside me.

It was a totally new experience with exactly the right person.

Aware I'm grinning like a moron, I lose the smile and shake the thoughts out of my mind. I'm determined to shore up today. To be professional and focused on work. The last thing I need is to complicate the one uncomplicated relationship in my life.

Benji is easy, and if I didn't think so before, I know so now. He had my shirt off and his hands in my pants and was A-okay letting me bolt from my office. He didn't chase me or insist on dinner. He didn't act like it was strange or awkward to give his best friend an orgasm on the guest couch in her office, so I'm not going to act that way either.

He gave me what I wanted. Little did I know when I was joking with Vivian on the phone I was placing an order he would happily fulfill.

That perfect, blissful moment was ruined when I spotted Trish's name on the screen of his ringing phone. I shouldn't have let her call ruin everything, but down deep, it hurt. I didn't know they were back in touch, which means he's kept that information from me. I also didn't miss the spark of apology in his brown eyes when he noticed I saw her name.

That said, he doesn't owe me anything, not even an explanation. He didn't promise me anything other than what he gave me. It was a gift he offered, one I accepted, and that should be enough. He didn't expect anything in return. All I have to do is convince my body we are moving on, because parts of me want more.

Throbbing, neglected parts.

I take a different street so as not to pass Vivian's office—no way am I laying this out for her while she's at work. I'll wait until a girls' night out when we both have cosmopolitans the size of our heads in front of us on the bar top. I turn the corner where a nail salon sits next to a posh boutique selling accessories. Maybe I'll pop in and buy myself something nice. I'm not much of an accessory person, but I do like the occasional ring or purse—

The thought freezes in my brain like I stepped into a subzero chamber. And like the cold sucked the oxygen from my lungs, for a second I can't breathe.

It's Benji, as in Benjamin Owen, standing on the sidewalk in a walkway between storefronts. In the shadows, he's talking closely with a tall, leggy blonde I know well. Patricia, better known as Trish, better known as his longest relationship. Not only did she call yesterday, they evidently arranged to meet. And here they are.

Meeting.

I back around the corner from whence I came and hide behind a small decorative tree. It isn't concealing me completely, but Benji isn't looking anywhere but at Trish. She looks sad. Her shoulders are hunched. While I watch, he pulls her into his arms, hugging her as he places a kiss on her temple. Her face screws into pleats as she wraps her arms around his waist.

My stomach sours. My heart aches. I look down at the bakery bag holding two fat chocolate muffins. I've lost my appetite. I come out from behind the tree and toss the bag into the nearest trashcan, throwing one final look over my shoulder. I don't know why I do it. Seeing him with Trish is sheer torture. If he kisses her, I might throw up.

As if he feels me watching, he turns his head. He scowls as a flash of blond hair vanishes behind a door bisecting the alley. She must work in that building. He dips his chin, giving me a stern look before checking for traffic and jogging over to me.

I can either run away or stand here and listen while he tries to make me feel better about what I just witnessed. Instead, I smile and pretend like the chill seeping into my bones doesn't exist.

"Hey! This is a surprise!" I say cheerily. He's still scowling when he comes to a stop in front of me. "I should have listened to my first instinct and bought two matchas. Here you are, and I only have the one." I elevate my cup. "I can go back and pick one up for you. I know you like coffee better than matcha, though. Would you prefer a cappuccino?"

"What are you doing here?" he interrupts my inane, and possibly insane, monologue.

"Matcha latte." I hold up my cup. "What about you?" My tone loses some of its chirp.

"I know you saw me with Trish."

Crap. This is the problem with lying to your best friend. They can tell you're doing it.

"Is that who that was?" What can I say, I'm committed to my path.

"You know it was. She—"

"You don't have to explain." The sad part is, I mean it. I don't want him to break up with me when we aren't dating. I don't want to see the pity in his eyes when he tries to let me down easy. "You and Trish were close. As close as I've ever seen you to anyone." It's miserable to admit but no less true. Worse, I remember vividly how she had his undivided attention when they dated. She's smart, savvy. Fun. "I imagine it'd be easy to fall in with her again given you broke up so recently."

"Six months ago." His expression is unreadable.

"Has it been six months already?" My high-pitched tone betrays me.

"You know it has been." He takes my hand in his. "Come on. We're going somewhere we can talk. I'll buy you breakfast."

"But—"

He leads me to the corner to a restaurant called Your Daily Brunch. He releases my hand to open the door for me, but I don't move.

"I'm sure they wouldn't like it if I took this inside." I hold up my matcha. "Why don't I finish drinking it while you grab a table?" I read somewhere that nodding while you speak tricks the other person into agreeing with you even if they don't. My tactic fails miserably on him.

"And let you drive off to parts unknown? Forget it. If the staff complains about your matcha, I'll deal with it." His hand wraps around mine again. Less than one minute later we're seated by a window in a cozy corner at the rear of the restaurant.

The waitress doesn't bat an eye at my matcha. She takes our orders and leaves us alone. Meanwhile, Benji is staring a hole through my head. I can feel it. I finally look at him, but I am not letting him speak before I get in at least one preemptive strike.

I lower my voice but speak loud enough so he can hear me over the din of diners. "Let's call yesterday a one-off. It's already weird, and you promised if it was weird we could forget it happened and go back to normal."

"Wrong. I told you I wouldn't forget."

"But you did agree to go back to normal." I point at him. "I won't stand in the way of you and Trish patching things up, especially when she—"

"Her mom's dying."

I blink. "Her—what?"

"Her mom. She's dying. Terminal cancer. They only gave her a month. Trish doesn't have any family in town. She found out yesterday and needed someone to talk to about it. When she called again this morning, I picked up and she was crying and asking for advice. I drove over to be here for her. I didn't want to do it over the phone. That's it. That's all."

My heart melts.

He's such an epically kind person.

"I'm so sorry to hear that." And I am. Truly. My mom and I may not be the most stellar example of mother-daughter camaraderie, but if she was sick and dying it would leave a scar. A deep one. "Poor Trish. Do you want me to send flowers? Or a fruit basket? Or if she's leaving town to visit her mom, we could send a Starbucks gift card for her travels."

When I tip my head to look up at him, he's smiling. Soft, easy. "You're always thinking of everyone else, aren't you? Even when I offer to give you something, you're worried about my pleasure more than your own."

"It's a habit."

"It's a bad one." He's no longer smiling. "Here's the deal, Cris. We're not done. We're not remotely done. We're not only going to do it again, we're going to push this to the edge of what you can take. To the pinnacle of what you really want. I'm not saying you have to sleep with me, but I am saying you have to allow yourself to take and take until you can't take any more. It's no less than you deserve."

I'm staring at him, my latte cooling in my hand. He's staring at me, unblinking. The waitress sets our plates in front of us. I blink first.

"Anything else?" the young girl asks, having no idea what she walked into.

"Do you want anything else, Cris?" Benji raises his thick eyebrows. "Are you brave enough to ask for it if you do?"

His challenge is about more than breakfast accoutrements and we both know it. The waitress doesn't, offering to bring hot sauce or their specialty house tomatillo salsa for our eggs.

"It's up to the lady," Benji says, his eyes glued to mine.

"You were the one laying down the law a second ago." I fiddle with the saltshaker.

He dips his chin into a barely-there nod, and then addresses the waitress. "We'll take both. And anything else to put this breakfast over the top. We've never been here before." Eyes back on mine, his voice dips low and seductive. "We don't want to miss a thing."

The waitress leaves. I wrestle my gaze from Benji and take in the crowded restaurant. Not exactly the most private place for a discussion of this magnitude.

A second later he stands and moves to my side of the booth. His hip bumps mine as he scoots me over. He folds his hands on the tabletop, tips his head, and watches me. Up close he's glorious. Perfect golden skin almost bronze in color. Dark hair I intimately know the feel of between my fingers. Eyes so expressive I'm held captive by them. Those half-open lids fringed with a million black lashes. I'll never forget him. Never. Even if we burn our friendship to ash and I never work in this town again.

I doubt either of those things will happen, but I justify he would be worth it. One orgasm at his hand was already worth it. Touching him once more would be worth it...

"Do you know what I saw when I was on my knees in front of you yesterday?" His voice is a low rumble. Seductive. Husky.

I shake my head. Paralyzed by his intensity.

"Numbers never lie. So I'll give you the numbers."

I'm not sure I follow, but I'm riveted.

"*Four.* That's how many seconds passed between your yes and the moment I slid my hand into your panties. *One.* How many fingers it took to take you there. *Six.* The number of times your eyelids fluttered when you came on my hand. *Three.* How many times you moaned while you were coming." He's leaning close, talking quiet. My breathing has escalated like I'm jogging instead of sitting still.

"*Two*," he murmurs next. "How many fast breaths you just took. Kiss me, Firecracker. No one's paying attention."

I can't resist so I do as he asks, my eyes closed, my lips parted. He's proven wrong a moment later when our waitress interrupts. She loudly settles a plate filled with ramekins onto the table. In those ramekins are sauces in an array of colors.

"Here you go," she announces, before asking if there is anything else. There's not, so she moves away from our table.

Benji dips a finger into a creamy aioli and sucks it clean. He's smiling when he asks, "What do you say, Cris? Should we try a bit of everything?"

I swallow thickly. And then smile as I nod.

Yes. *Hell yes.*

CHAPTER ELEVEN

Cris

By the end of the week I'm fairly certain the conversation at the restaurant was a vivid hallucination.

I could have sworn Benji's offer meant he'd be in hot pursuit, but he backed off. We left Grand Marin after breakfast, which was delicious once I committed to eating instead of melting into a puddle of hormonal goo at his feet, and then we returned to the office. Other than a few teasing winks, which I thought (and hoped) would lead to more, nothing physical happened between us. The only other time he touched me that day was when he gripped my hips to slide me to one side and open the refrigerator while I waited for my coffee to brew.

Then...nothing.

He wasn't being rude. He didn't seem upset. But this isn't the same "friend" who didn't touch me before either. We don't act like two people who recently spent intimate time together. Was it so impersonal for him?

Gone was the dirty-talking Benji reciting numbers to me in the most delightfully filthy way. Gone was the "let's try a bit of everything" talk.

Maybe he's distracted and the change has nothing to do with me. This could be Benji being Benji. He has a habit of hyperfocusing on whatever task is at hand. Unfortunately, life-coach Cris shares headspace with received-orgasm-from-Benji Cris. The waters are completely muddied.

So much for things not getting complicated.

But it doesn't *have* to be complicated, I find myself arguing. The benefit of him being my best friend and my boss is I know how him well. He's been rushing around here the last few days, eyes unfocused, phone in hand as he swipes the screen and refreshes his email. He's impatient. He's distracted. He zones out at his laptop when he's not rushing around.

I refilled his water several times this week. He paused to flash me a grateful smile each time. It wasn't a seductive one, though. It's his default smile, the amenable one he shares with everyone. I can tell the difference.

I stretch in my chair and check the clock. It's after six, and I should have gone home by now. My stomach rumbles, reminding me the granola bar I ate for lunch is long gone. I stand and look out my office window. The clouds hang low as a light spring rain sweeps over the yard. It's peaceful, and after a stressful week I could use some peace. Unfortunately, it's also making me tired. I yawn behind my hand.

After a quick bathroom trip, I pack up. I'm not sure what happened to Benji. I heard him on a conference call an hour ago, but then his voice faded as he moved from his office to pace through the house. He likes to walk around while he talks. Although I'm not sure if it's a preference as much as it's a compulsion. He's always had restless energy to burn.

Purse and laptop bag hooked on my shoulder, I stroll into the kitchen to grab my tumbler drying on the dish rack when I hear a quiet snore from the living room. I set my things down on the counter and round the couch. Found him.

He's lying on his back, eyes closed, mouth slightly ajar. He sucks in a heavy breath, and I squat down in front of him. I'm trying to decide whether to tell him I'm leaving, or if I should let him sleep.

I move to stand, but my eyes snag on the sight of his body sprawled the length of the couch. His button-down shirt, purple and white checked today, is rumpled but still partially tucked into charcoal gray slacks. The dark leather belt matches his shoes, Ferragamos of course. Him and his fancy footwear. He's beautiful. Just sinfully gorgeous. I sigh, my hands on my knees as I begin to stand. I purposely resist the urge to look at his face where his dark lashes are probably fluttering in sleep, and his thick hair is tossed rakishly over his forehead. There's only so much torture a girl can take.

A hand catches my wrist before I stand all the way up. When I jerk my attention down, I find those dark lashes shadowing open eyes. He blinks. Slowly. He doesn't say anything as he tugs my wrist. I sit on the cushion and twist to face him. Given the limited space, I have to lean one arm on the back of the sofa—the one he isn't holding.

He licks his full bottom lip. I stare at the dampness, wanting to lean in and have a taste.

"You were sleeping," I say to break the silence.

His grin is honey slow and his heavy-lidded eyes lower in another sexy blink. This man kills me. He's a god fallen to earth and I'm a mortal, weakened by his beauty.

So, I offer no excuse when I curve my body toward him and put my lips on his. The kiss is sweet, brief.

Too brief.

When I would've stopped, he lets go of my wrist and uses his hand to cup my jaw. He pulls my mouth to his and kisses me again. This kiss is sweet like the last one but unlike the last one, not brief. He lingers, his lips on mine for a deliciously long time. Long enough for my heart to shimmy around my chest untethered, knocking into my ribcage like a drunk at a rave.

"What's wrong, Firecracker?" he asks against my mouth. "Am I moving too slow for you?"

I have to process the question. I think of the past few days, my worry that he was no longer interested. My frustration at not knowing how to act or what to say.

I back away and frown. "Is that what you're doing?"

He props himself up on an elbow. "No."

I let out a disbelieving grunt.

"I didn't realize you were in a hurry."

"I'm not." Defensiveness is a bad look on anyone. On me especially. I'm unaccustomed to asking for what I want, to putting anyone out for what I want.

"That kiss suggested differently."

"I wasn't planning on kissing you, but you looked so..." I press my lips together, unwilling to finish.

His eyebrows climb his forehead. "So...?"

I dare myself to say it and then surprise myself when I do. "Hot," I blurt.

"You're the hot one, Firecracker. By the way, do you still like that nickname better than coach?"

"Much."

He grins, pleased.

"Are you on your way out?" he asks. Talk about an abrupt subject change.

"It's after six," I say, when what I should have said was yes. Or no. Hell, I don't know.

He hums in his throat. The noncommittal sound doesn't clue me in to what he's thinking.

"You've had a busy week," I say. "I can see how you would forget...things. Why don't I head out and plan on seeing you Monday." I stand. He stands with me. He's no longer smiling.

"You think I forgot?"

"Didn't you?" I whisper.

"You said no work hours. You've hustled me out of here every day to go jogging at five. You made the hastiest of escapes afterward."

"You stopped acting interested," I accuse. "I didn't want to be presumptuous." I hate arguing. I hate that I might have been wrong—might still be wrong.

He shakes his head. It's almost a sad shake, one that has me quaking down to my toes.

Crap. I was wrong. He was being nice, hoping I'd forget the promises he made over breakfast. The sincerity in his eyes is too much to take. I wonder if Trish called him this week and wormed her way back into his life. She's sad about her mom, and as a guy who's lost parents, he can sympathize. They've probably forged some unbreakable connection. I can't fault him for it. I might feel the same way in his position.

What's between us was only temporary anyway. It was a fantasy. I'll take my one Benji orgasm and tuck his dirty-talking brunch speech away in the back of my mind. I'll save them for future sexual encounters with myself. I'll—

"Cris. You're freaking out," he states.

He's right, so once again I go on the defensive.

"No, I'm not." Bright smile.

"Yes. You are." He's calm. Too calm.

"I'm fine. I need to go home...and— What are you doing?" I ask, even though I know what he's doing. I'm watching him do it.

My flimsy vinyl belt is open and he's unbuttoning my jeans. The zipper goes next. My mind on his recent reunion with Trish, I say, "You don't have to do this."

"Wrong. You don't have to let me do this. But knowing how good it's going to feel for me to do what I'm about to do to you, I *strongly* suggest you let me do this."

"I remember the loveseat."

He nods. "So do I. But I'm not going to do that. I'm going to do something better."

He shoves my jeans past my hips. The rain falls faster outside, giving way to a rumble of thunder as a storm rolls in. The one within me feels the same: volatile, overwhelming. I'm not going to argue. The heat in his eyes promises the same good things his mouth just promised.

"Like?" I whisper.

His eyebrows jump. "You want me to explain."

I give him a jerky nod. He grins to beat all. Not the for-everyone Benji smile. This one is just for me.

He tugs my jeans up and takes my hand. "First off, not on the couch. I need room to move. And you need to be naked."

"N-naked?"

His hand in mine, he leads me down the hallway. I scamper to keep up with his long-legged gait. We pass the door to the basement, his office, a bathroom, a guest bedroom, and finally wrap around to the master suite which takes up a goodly portion of the rear of his house.

His bedroom is like a fancy getaway to an island. A wicker ceiling fan turns lazily over the bed. The comforter is made neatly, black with a barely visible pattern of deep gray palm fronds. His pillows are fluffed, the requisite two, no decorative ones, in matching black pillowcases. The walls are a pale, pale green, and white-and-green vertical striped curtains hang from black iron rods. The floor is shining wood, the dresser a deeper tone of wood than the floor. A black wrought-iron mirror stands in one corner.

His fingers dance along my neckline, bringing my attention to him. "That okay with you?"

"What?" I've totally lost track of the conversation. Maybe I have some sort of protective mechanism to keep from anticipating what he's going to do to me. It will be amazing, I'm sure, but suddenly everything is moving at warp speed. "You're right." My voice is slightly strangled. "I'm freaking out."

He chuckles. "Tell me something I don't know. Here's the plan. You want to amend any of it, let me know."

He doesn't give me time to mentally brace before he outlines his plan.

"I'm going to take off your T-shirt and bra, kiss each of those nipples I've missed so much. Then I'm going to slip you out of those jeans and ask you to shimmy out of your panties. I can't wait to see what color they are today, by the way." He offers a devious wink.

I'm already warm and damp from what he's saying, and he hasn't said anything particularly dirty yet. Incredible.

"Then I'm going to ask you to lie on your back on the bed, and I'm going to kiss you here." He cups my sex. "Fuck, Cris. You're burning up down there."

"I might die if you do that," I whisper hoarsely. I'm not sure if I'm kidding or not.

"You won't die. You might have to take a nap after, which is fine by me. I have a big bed."

My mind is racing. No one has ever kissed me *down there*. I have always wanted to experience it. I've never pictured Benji doing that. I've pictured him—oh, trust me I have—but not *doing that*. I don't know why. Maybe as a safeguard to keep my best friend and boss where he belonged. Maybe I was protecting myself by managing my expectations.

"What about your clothes?" I finger a button on his shirt.

"My eating you out doesn't require clothing removal for me."

My finger stills at his raw description.

"It'll be sexier if I stay dressed. Think of it as being serviced by a concubine of sorts. I don't expect anything in return." His lips quirk. "At least not yet. You start feeling experimental, honey, sign me up."

"You're too much." I palm my heated cheek and avert my eyes. "When did you become a...a"—I gesture at his long, strong body—"Casanova?" But I know. I've seen him schmooze at functions. I've watched him set a client at ease with a drink in his hand and a sparkle in his eye. I've seen him with the women he's dated. He's as smooth as Skippy peanut butter. He's just never been that way with me.

"This is part of the deal," I conclude. "The sexy version of you comes with the sex."

"You wanted the package, Cris. This is it. Since you're a fan of dirty talk, I'm obliging. I customize. No extra charge."

His fingers go to the hem of my shirt and pull it off. My bra follows. As promised he bends and takes a nipple into his mouth, suckling it to a turgid peak while his hands dip into my pants. Over my panties his fingers gently move, and then my jeans are pushed past my hips and I lose his mouth. I kick off my shoes as he tugs my jeans and panties to the floor. He instructs, "Lie down on the bed."

"On top of the covers, or..." I'm stalling. I both can't wait and don't want to rush. I already know it'll be over too soon. I'm halfway to my second orgasm with Benjamin Owen, and he's barely touched me.

"Your choice."

He picks up my clothes and tosses them onto a dark green chair in the corner. He tucks my shoes under the chair. Once I'm settled on top of the comforter, he stalks over to me and puts a knee between mine on the bed.

"Spread."

I loved that the first time he said it. I love it as much now. My body jolts as a rush of pleasure slides through me, as thick as honey. Slowly, I spread my legs.

He looks unashamedly at what I'm showing him. With a quick headshake and smile, he starts to unbutton his shirt. "I take it back. I'm going to need to take this off. If that's okay with you."

I give him a jerky nod since I'm incapable of speech at the moment.

He unbuttons his shirt and tosses it over my clothes on the chair. I like that our clothes are all over each other the way we're about to be. It's so wrong. It's so right.

I've seen his chest before. At the pool. It's glorious. All that flexed, toned skin punctuated by flat brown nipples and a belly button above a trail of dark wiry hair that disappears into his shorts. Then there's the tattoo etched onto his ribs, as enticing as everything else about him. His chest is broad at the top, bookended by strong, rounded shoulders. Then his torso dives in, narrowing at his waist. I wish he'd take off his pants. He doesn't, but before I can complain he tosses my legs over his shoulders.

"Relax. If you can." That's the last warning he offers before lowering his face.

His mouth is soft, firm, hot, attentive. I can't tear my eyes off his jet black hair or the motions his head makes as his tongue strokes and strokes and strokes again. My legs quake even though I will them to stop. I fist the blankets while lecturing myself to loosen up. To go easy. To slow down. I don't want this to end.

But it does. Quickly.

An orgasm rages through me at the same time a low roll of thunder shakes the windows of his bedroom. My eyes shut of their own volition as a wave of warmth washes over me. My body buzzes. My mind blanks.

That was...

That was...

Amazing.

Beautiful.

Perfect.

Way too damn fast.

Devastation comes on as fast as the orgasm, the blissful rush receding like it was never there. I feel the wet in my eyes and blink them open. Benji is smiling, clueless to the direction of my thoughts.

It's over. My one chance to savor him and I blew it.

"Let's hear it," he says. Obviously, he's figured out I have something on my mind.

"I wanted that to last longer," I murmur, my throat constricted from thick emotion. "It went too fast."

"Sure, but that was only the first one. Haven't you had multiples before?" His eyebrows pinch like he's legitimately confused.

My mouth hangs open for a second. I, of course, have heard of multiple orgasms. I have also heard of unicorns and fairies. I have never had more than one at a time—orgasms, that is. I break it to him by saying, "I'm more of a one-and-done girl."

He's already shaking his head. "Not true. I bet you have four or five more in there. You ready?"

He's propped on his elbows, shoulders still positioned under my legs, his beautiful face framed by my knees, his dark hair perfectly ruffled, and offering me four or five more orgasms. That he will deliver with his tongue.

"Hell yeah," I say.

He bursts out laughing. I do the same. This time the tears springing forth are from relief. It's not over. Good news.

My second orgasm arrives with the same force but lasts longer than the first.

The third one is longer still, and the waves washing over me pummel me with pleasure.

The fourth is so intense, I kick Benji out from between my legs and writhe until I've wadded up his fancy comforter.

I don't make it to five.

When I finally open my eyes, I find him on his side watching me, his head propped on a fist, his elbow resting on the mattress.

I can't make myself regret it. Any of it.

CHAPTER TWELVE

Benji

Cris is sitting at her desk, Chuck Taylors off. One leg is folded, her bare foot hanging off the edge of the chair, the other is on the floor, toes pointed.

Her thumb is between her teeth as she concentrates, and her pale, curly hair is hiding half her face. Her shirt is loose and floral-patterned. Her jeans strategically ripped.

She's the sexiest woman to grace my bedsheets, and I haven't even slept with her. *Yet.* I can't wrap my head around how attracted I am to her. Before I delighted both of us with her four orgasms, she was my cute, sweet, irreplaceable best friend who, yes, I found attractive. Now she's all those things, but also makes me hard and distracts me in a way that's unhealthy for the bottom line.

I've dated a lot of different women. I don't gravitate to any certain type. Round women, stick-thin women, Black women, Caucasian women, Hispanic, Asian, or Israeli women. Each of those other women, while different, had one thing in common. They worked in proper office settings and dressed in outfits more expensive than mine, which is saying something as I have very, *very* expensive taste.

I don't go jogging with the women I date, mainly because the women I date either don't jog or prefer to run on a treadmill. I don't do treadmills. I run outside or not at all. Who wants to run on a moving belt? It's impersonal. And the scenery fucking sucks.

Even on a weekend, the women I've dated usually donned a full face of makeup. And while I have seen a lot of bare feet, they usually poke out of a slimming pencil skirt or a short dress. Jeans, yes, but I can't recall any of them wearing a pair as well as Cris does. She must feel me lingering at the doorway of her office. She looks up from her laptop.

"Hi." Her smile is cautious, anticipatory, reminding me of last week when I buried my face between her legs and feasted on her like a starving man. *Four times*, I remind myself with a proud roll of my shoulders. I counted.

Although number four should've counted as two, given how powerful it was. She literally shoved me away, then curled on her side and shouted the completion of her release into a pillow. Meanwhile, I went for the world's record on the most painful chubby of my life. Seriously. I could have carved my name in the wall with it.

I survived. I was doing it for her. I wanted to prove multiple orgasms were not an urban legend. She deserved her own "Bigfoot sighting," if you know what I mean.

And I nailed it.

We lay there a while after and she touched my chest, casually running her fingers over my pecs and down my abs and up again. She chatted about nothing while my skin caught fire. It took everything in me not to strip off my pants and sink into her wet pussy, and then fuck her until we were both screaming for the Almighty.

I swipe my forehead and shake the incredibly distracting fantasy from my head. "Did you read my email?"

"Oh. Not yet." She clicks a button and her eyes scan the laptop's screen. I walk into her office and lower my ass onto the corner of her desk. Her gray eyes track over to my leg and then up to my face. "We're going to Venice, Florida?"

"Evidently."

"I didn't realize they were hosting the fundraiser at their main office," she murmurs. "I'll have to clear our schedule. Book a flight, rooms..." She grabs a pen and jots down a few notes for the trip.

Typically, we (Owen Construction) attend the annual charity fundraiser for Heart-to-Teen here in Ohio. The charity helps home kids between the ages of ten to seventeen. They have branches throughout the country. The Ohio one is huge since the Owens support it biannually, and with a lot of money. My adoptive parents have always given generously, but they give more to Heart-to-Teen than anywhere else. Trust me, I see the reports.

This year is different since the charity is hosting a fundraiser specifically for their biggest donors. Archer, Nate, and me included.

"Room, *singular*," I correct. She blinks up at me, half lost in thought as she absorbs what I'm saying. "I already took care of reserving it. We're staying in a neighboring hotel rather than where they're holding the event. I booked a room with a view of the ocean."

"One room?"

"You're staying with me. We can take care of your lingering virginity issue while we're away. If that's all right with you," I tack on, since her expression has morphed into a bizarre mixture of anger and anticipation. She usually loves when I talk about sex. And she's loved everything I've done to her so far. A very large part of me—not that one—wonders why we didn't do this a long time ago.

She sets her top teeth to her bottom lip. "Benji—"

"Look," I interrupt before she can ruin my plans, "I know you haven't made a habit out of letting people do nice things for you, but you're going to start." She's taken care of a household, raised three boys, and put herself partly through college. She dropped out when said household was too much to juggle alongside her schoolwork. She started working for Dad, and then later started working with me. Short of recently when I've made her moan in ecstasy, I'm not sure anyone has done anything for her without considering what they might get in return. It's vexing.

"This is your opportunity to allow yourself to be treated the way a woman should be treated," I explain. "So far you've taken care of everyone else. It's time to let someone take care of you."

"That's not necessary." She shakes her head, her smile soft. Like she's suddenly uncomfortable with the idea of me doing things for her. And *to* her.

"Necessary has nothing to do with it." I stand from her desk. "The hotel room and travel are sorted. Got it?"

She sighs, a sound of capitulation. "Got it."

For years she has been a busy "mom" to her brothers and a busy worker bee for Dad and me. It's her turn to be served.

I'm going to gift her what she's been missing. Explosive, care-free sex with someone she can trust.

Just as soon as she grants me access.

"Are we still on for a run?" I ask.

She glances at the clock on the wall. "Wow, is it that late already? I was in a zone."

"It's okay if you want to postpone."

"Actually, I may cancel. I have to finish up something today. Why don't you go to the gym instead? We can run tomorrow."

I picture her running in front of me, her tight ass in short shorts, her smooth, strong legs... My general stands up and salutes. Shit. This is torture. I have to work with her another few days before we go to Florida. Before we "seal the deal." I'm not taking her virginity in my bed. We need neutral terri-tory for her first time.

"Gym. Got it." Hands hiding a certain swelling part of me, I dip my head to indicate I'll be in the basement.

Forty minutes later, I'm done with my HIIT workout but my erection rages on. I'm lying, back to the floor on the mat, all but one "muscle" complete mush. I manage to push myself up and limp into the cavernous open shower. I also have a sauna, but I don't need heat right now. I spin the knob to cold.

Stepping under the spray, I quickly determine that a cold shower, while effective, isn't the most pleasant way to handle my problem. I warm up the water, hissing through my teeth as my skin goes from chilled to warm, and then I grip my cock and begin to stroke.

Cris

I wasn't planning on a late night, but since we're going to spend the upcoming weekend in Florida at the event by Heart-to-Teen, I have extra tasks on my burgeoning to-do list.

Since Benji informed me we'll be sharing a room he booked, I've been unable to chase a single coherent thought to its end. I've mostly been imagining what it'll be like to have his undivided attention, to be the center of his world. To sleep in a bed next to his hot, naked flesh.

Shiver.

He's making every one of my fantasies come true. I know I should be cautious, but honestly, I would rather lean all the way into what he's offering. I can draw the necessary boundaries when we're back from the trip.

As much as I adore him, I am aware that "forever" and Benjamin Owen don't mix. He's a busy workaholic with a focus on financial wizardry. I'm the woman he hired to make sure he takes his vitamins and remembers to exercise his (incredibly fine) body. I'm also his friend. As his friend, I'd never ask him for more than he's willing to commit.

As fun as our little excursion has been and probably will be, once I bequeath my virginity to him—I'd be insane to say no—he'll cease seeing me as a dating option. New rules will have to be made. My duty is to take what I want, but not to involve my feelings. I can't take another gut-punch scenario like the morning I spotted him hugging Trish at Grand Marin.

No matter what, I have to let Benji be Benji. He grows tired of every woman he dates—I've watched it happen from both afar and up close—and I won't be an exception. Hell, his *laissez-faire* attitude toward commitment was one of the foundations on which we built this agreement.

I walk into the kitchen, notice his water bottle on the counter, and shake my head. I know he's done a hard workout because he's been down there for nearly an hour. This is why he needs me in his life. He's too scatterbrained and distracted to take care of himself.

In the gym I spot a discarded towel thrown over the weight bench and hear the water pounding the wall in the attached shower. I set the water bottle on the bench and open my mouth to tell him he's welcome and I deserve a raise when I catch a blurry image of him through the glass shower wall.

A breath stutters from my lips.

He's naked, obviously, in the amazing stone-walled shower. His round ass is visible without obstruction, but the front half of his body is blurred by partially steamed glass.

One of his arms is anchored to the wall, his head down as the spray beats the back of his head. Below the neck is a tantalizing, wavy view of his naked chest and, where the steam is most prevalently blocking my view, I notice his arm moving at a dizzying speed, his hand fisted around his—

I slap my hand over my mouth. I fully intend to dart out of sight behind the wall but remain frozen in place, mesmerized by what he's doing and how beautiful he looks while doing it. He lets out a grunt I hear over the pounding spray and then tilts his face into the water. Droplets hammer his cheeks. His movements below the waist increase in both speed and ferocity.

My breasts grow heavy, my belly drops, and I become aware of a throbbing heat between my thighs. I spin around to leave—I have no prayer of concentrating now—when I hear him call my name.

Praying he didn't catch me ogling him during an intensely private moment, I shield my eyes with one hand and call out, "It's just me. I left your water bottle on the bench!"

No return greeting comes. I peek through my fingers to find his head poking around the stone wall. His hair is dripping, his eyelashes are spiked and wet, his mouth is smiling. His bare shoulder and buff chest are dotted with water. He's an undeniably sexy sight. I might come in my panties without him touching me.

"Get your ass over here."

They're the most erotic words I've heard in my life. Helpless, I drift into the steamy room, and when I'm within arm's reach I say the only thing I can think of. "Did you need a towel?"

"I need a hand. Care to help me out?"

My lashes flutter as I try to process.

"And I don't mean I want you to wash my back." That grin again. It's going to be the death of me. "You get in, you'll be glad you did. I have some fun planned for you too."

He steps into the spray again and his, "Hurry up!" echoes off the walls. Before I can reason my way out of what I'm doing, I shakily strip out of my clothes and join him.

CHAPTER THIRTEEN

Cris

Arms hiding my breasts, I step deeper into the shower with a completely nude, completely wet, completely buff Benji.

Hard bumps of muscle stretch his taut skin. From his back to his arms to his chest to his abs to his fantastic butt. His legs are strong and long. He has nice feet. I've seen them before, but never with the rest of his naked body. It's an entirely new experience.

"How was your workout?" As icebreakers go, it's a lame one, but he doesn't take me to task for my inquiry. He reaches for my hips and tugs me under the warm water. The shower-head is high on the wall. I've always loved this shower. I've always wanted to use it, but on the days I worked out here, I made sure to do so in the evening and then went straight home to shower. Being naked in Benji's space seemed awkward before. I don't feel awkward now, which is unbelievable. Or maybe it's a testament to how easy it is for him to help me relax.

"It was good. Exhausting. But didn't keep you off my mind, which is why you saw me in here trying to divest myself of my current...situation."

I hazard a glance down at his "situation." His penis is standing straight and proud between us. One word flits through my addled brain: *mouthwatering*. Granted, I've never had a penis in my mouth before, but it wouldn't take much for me to offer to go down on him. I am not typically plagued with thoughts of blowjobs, but I am curious to learn what he tastes like.

Heaven, I imagine.

"You're not helping," he rumbles, his voice tortured and low and lined with his ever-present amusement. His joy has always been my kryptonite. How anyone maintains happiness after losing what he's lost and starting over at such a young age is beyond me. Money may solve a lot of problems, but it can't replace a loving family.

"Are you uncomfortable?" He traces one of my forearms, still crossed over my breasts.

"I'm curious. I want to touch you."

His grin widens.

"I also want to kiss you. Down there," I finish on a whisper.

His smile is gone, his grip on my arm tight. "That's not why I asked you in here, Cris. You're supposed to be learning how to take. How to accept what you deserve. Find out what you've been missing."

"That is something I've been missing. I just didn't realize it until now."

He presses my back against the cool, slate blue shower tiles. His body is lined up against mine, every hard, wet plane, including the several inches jutting from between his legs now nestled at my middle. It's as unyielding as the rest of him.

I take his tongue on mine, giving in to the urge to make out with him while hot water pounds his back and steam rises around us. The deep exploration of our mouths is as amazing as everything else we do together. No surprise there. My body is humming in anticipation. I know what he's capable of with his mouth. I'm curious what I can accomplish with mine.

"I can't let you do it," he says between kisses. "Fuck, but I want to."

I love how desperate he sounds.

"Let me," I beg.

"No." The word comes from between clenched teeth.

I reach between our bodies and palm his length, my grip slippery. "Please."

His eyes open lazily, but the rest of him is strung taut. "Cris, this isn't the way I planned—"

I press my finger to his mouth to stop the words trying to come out. I trust him. He should trust me. It's in the unwritten best-friend codebook.

"I want to." I run my finger down his chin to his neck and chest and finally drag it along his stomach. I stroke his cock and watch my own movements, the way the water trickles over the inches of him embraced by my curled fingers. I am nothing short of delighted when I notice he's watching too.

His hands were gripping my elbows but they loosen, giving me permission to explore him further. I don't hesitate.

I lower to my knees on the tile floor, the water blocked by his body. Rivulets form a Y and pour off his chin, run down his chest and legs. I like how he watches me. I watched him go down on me. I remember how turned on I was.

I lick the tip of his cock, which is velvet soft. A tight hiss of air escapes from between his teeth. I close my lips over the head and he moans. *Oh, yes.* This is going to be fun. Now I know why he looked so damned pleased with himself when he went down on me. I feel powerful enough to conquer the world.

I set my pace to stun, licking and sucking with renewed fervor. I experiment with swirling my tongue over the head, running it along his length, and cupping his balls in my hand. So into what I'm doing and the heavy feel of him taking up my mouth, I barely hear him over the spray when he commands me to stop.

He doesn't say it again. He hoists me to my feet and plunders my mouth with his tongue, and then reroutes my hand and motions for me to stroke him. As I do, he dips his fingers into my heat, finding me warm and wet. What I was doing didn't only turn him on. I'm right there with him. He maneuvers us out of the shower spray and we continue stroking each other.

"Dammit, Cris, come," he growls into my mouth. "I'm dying here."

On his command, an orgasm stampedes through my body, leaving wreckage in its wake. I drop my head back against the tile, squirming against his magic fingers. I remember at the last minute to watch as I stroke him to completion. Making sure to absorb the awed expression on his face, the way his eyebrows pucker. He bares his teeth and his eyes squeeze closed like he can't take another moment of pleasure. He's never been more attractive. A low groan echoes from his throat and then spills into my mouth when he kisses me. His hands go to my back and he pulls me close, every inch of our bodies stuck together beneath the warm water for several heart-pounding moments.

"How'd I do?" It's as easy to smile at my best friend as it is to tease him. I already know how I did. *A-plus.*

His grin is sated and slightly dopey. "That was so much better than me taking care of myself. I'm glad you came to check on me."

Then he rears his head back to look at me, his eyes narrowed with suspicion. "You heard the shower. You knew I was in here, didn't you? You looked anyway, knowing what you'd see."

"I didn't know I would see *that.*"

"No, but you hoped you would."

My cheeks grow warm.

"Naughty girl. You keep this side of you well hidden, don't you?"

I like being accused of being naughty way too much. I never thought of myself as anywhere near naughty. It's exciting. *Invigorating.* He's giving me an opportunity to explore another side of myself—the side that embraces being sexually satisfied as well as yearns to sexually satisfy him.

"Thank you," I whisper.

"I believe thanks is owed to you, Firecracker." He pushes a few damp, limp curls away from my face. "If I knew how good you were at that, I wouldn't have argued with you about you doing it."

"Well, it was my first time. I'm sure I can improve."

"I sure as hell would like to see you try." His devious smile brightens. "I like being your first in so many things."

"You would." I quirk my lips. "Your ego."

"It's not about ego. I mean, okay, it's a little about ego," he amends. "But it's mostly about you. I like knowing I can deliver firsts you won't regret later. You won't, right? That's a requirement for this arrangement."

I nod exuberantly and hope it hides my distaste for the word "arrangement." It sounds so impersonal and, as I'm learning, everything between us ends up feeling personal. But I'm completely capable of compartmentalizing, or so I have to keep reminding myself.

I totally have this.

"No regrets on my end," I say, feigning confidence. "This is different and unexpected, but we've figured out how to do things together before. Like when we were making the team schedule and two employees had too many hours. We didn't know at first prioritizing tasks based on each individual's strengths was going to be the key to... Why are you grinning?"

"You're so fucking cute. I always knew you were. I always saw it. Maybe it's your nakedness"—he runs his hands over my breasts and around to my back again—"but it's painfully obvious how fucking cute you are now."

"I'm talking about staff and scheduling. How can I be cute?"

"You're naked and talking about staff and scheduling after sucking me and tongue-fucking me. That makes you cute *and* hot."

Now my cheeks are burning. With an airy laugh, I ask, "Do I want to know what else you're thinking?"

"Definitely not. My mind has traveled down an unbeaten

path. There are some visuals along the way that violate decency laws in at least four states."

I hug his neck to bring his lips closer to mine. "Sounds tempting."

"One step at a time, Firecracker." He's adorable and sexy, and suddenly I understand what he means about me being cute and hot. I never imagined he would be as attracted to me as I was to him. It's jarring, and sort of throwing me.

I smile instead of letting him know I'm thrown. I'm working my way down a first-time list and doing pretty damn well, if you ask me. I've never showered with a naked man and I've certainly never gone down on one.

Check and check.

Out of the shower, I pull a towel off the towel warmer and snuggle the terrycloth to my nose. Benji grabs his towel and swipes it efficiently along his limbs, down both arms, down his legs, and over the part of him I just had in my mouth. When he turns, his back is speckled with water. I towel him off, being sure to dry his fabulous ass while I'm at it.

He turns and snatches the towel from my hand. "Taking care of me as usual. You have to learn to think of yourself first."

He dries me next, spending more time than is necessary on my breasts. Finally, I'm dried to his satisfaction.

"I hate to say this but you should get dressed," he says. "I'm starving. I can pick up dinner if you tell me what you want. Or we can go out."

"I have chicken thawing in the refrigerator at home, pre-chopped green peppers and onions at the ready. I'm making fajitas." I lick my lips, feeling as if I'm breaking a

121

rule that didn't exist until now. "Do you...want to come over?"

"Yeah. Hell yeah." He gives me a quick kiss, one he didn't have to think about. I return it and I don't think about it either. It's natural. Easy. Just as easy and natural as us enjoying dinner together at my house.

After we eat, he announces he has to go home. When I ask if he wants to watch TV instead, he gives me the most inviting, wicked smile.

"No," he says, hovering over my lips for a lengthy kiss. "If I stay another minute, you'll lose your virginity tonight. And that's not the plan."

I've never been so flattered and sad at the same time as when I stand in my doorway and watch him walk to his car. He sends me a knowing smile before turning over the engine and driving down my street.

CHAPTER FOURTEEN

Cris

I'm packing my suitcase and feeling frazzled thanks to my late start this morning. The past week has been gloriously distracting, but each time I resurface from touching Benji or remembering touching Benji, I'm greeted by a glob of to-dos I worry I might've forgotten. Currently, I'm trying to decide on a decent dress to wear to the fundraiser dinner tomorrow night, and also trying to locate my charger for my laptop, which I've never *ever* lost.

Mid-cramming clothing, along with a few options for shoes, into my suitcase, I realize I'll probably need a swimsuit in Florida. I sift through a dresser drawer and shove aside the sexy string bikini I bought when I purchased a tanning bed package (like, three years ago) and then hold up the scraps of material and consider taking them with me on my trip. Benji would like it.

"I borrowed your charger, by the way." My brother Manuel appears in my bedroom doorway, cord in hand. He stopped by, having no idea I was here. It's Friday at ten a.m.— a workday—so I normally wouldn't be. Once he learned I was here, he decided to hang out.

"I was wondering where that was." I swipe the cord from his hand and he, in turn, catches one of the strings of my bikini top and tugs it from my grip.

"What the hell is this?" Miniscule strips of flame-orange fabric dangle from his fingers.

I snatch the top from him and cram it, along with my cord, into a corner of my suitcase. "I'm flying to Florida."

"For a work trip." He's frowning. At age twelve, Manuel always wanted to know what was going on, so the fact that he's just as nosy at age twenty-four isn't surprising in the least.

"What else?" I answer. Before he can comment, I go on to say, "I'm putting together a care package for Timothy. I won't have a chance to drop by the post office. Can you go for me?" I zip my suitcase but before I can haul it off the bed, my brother has it in hand and is walking down the stairs.

"Where is the package?" he asks.

"It's not done yet. I have to add a few more snacks and tape the box closed."

A knock at the door startles me. I'm more startled when I see it's Benji. I glance at the wall clock. He's early, which is good, because I am so *not* early.

"Hi." I open the door.

He moves in like he might kiss me, then notices Manuel. "Oh, hey, man."

My brother smiles. "What's up, Benji?"

Manuel worked very briefly with Benji for a college assignment a few years ago. Some job shadow thing. Benji in my house, picking me up for a trip to Florida, doesn't look remotely out of the norm to my brother. Nor should it. I've gone on trips with Benji before and have attended this fundraiser in particular for years. Though it's usually in Ohio, not the Sunshine State.

"You might want to review the dress code with her," my brother says as he sets my bag by the door. "She packed a bathing suit I'm not even sure you can consider a bathing suit. It's scandalous."

One of Benji's eyebrows wings upward. The look he gives me says everything but "dress code." I wonder if he's picturing me wearing a *scandalous* bathing suit. We smile at each other before Manuel interrupts.

"Where's this box?"

"One second," I tell Benji as he lifts my suitcase by the handle. I race into the kitchen and grab a few processed, prepackaged snacks Timothy loves. I stuff a few hot chocolate packets in the box as well. I'm tearing off a sheet of paper from the magnetic pad on the fridge when my cell phone chimes.

"Hello?" I answer.

"What's up, sis?" Dennis says into my ear. My other younger brother's timing isn't great.

"Hey! How are you? What's going on?"

Before I can answer, he launches into a story about a guy he knows who works for Owen Construction who knows Nate. He's chattering about how that made him think of me but doesn't connect those dots to any one thing in particular. I "uh-huh" my way through the conversation while trying to write a legible note to Timothy. I manage to write something that makes sense (I think) and sign it. Manuel takes the paper, puts it in the box, and then takes the tape roll out of the junk drawer.

"Den, I have to go. I'm so sorry. I have a flight to catch." I put my hand on my forehead, having the sneaking suspicion I'm forgetting something.

"Where are you going?" Dennis asks.

"Florida." It hits me just as Manuel pulls a strip of tape over the box's top. "Wait! When he was home on spring break, he left one of his books here."

"Why are you going to Florida?" Dennis asks into my ear as I reroute to Timothy's bedroom.

"Uh, a fundraiser. Benji and I are about to leave for the airport."

"Boss man picking you up?"

"Yes." I sort through the books on Timothy's bookshelf and grab the book he needs for class. "And I don't want to miss our flight."

"Impossible," Benji says as I race by. Whatever that means.

"That book isn't going to fit," Manuel tells me as he winds the tape back onto the roll.

"It'll fit. Can you overnight the box? I'll get you some money," I tell him as I grab my purse. "Is twenty-five dollars enough?"

"Cris." Dennis sounds frustrated.

"I'm sorry, Den. I'm not trying to ignore you. I just have a few things going on. What about your friend, again?"

The phone vanishes from my hand and Benji says, "Dennis, Benji. How are you, man? I'll have Cris give you a call when we're in the air. You going to be around for a while?" A pause and then, "Yeah. You got it. Thanks."

Call ended, Benji slides my cell phone into the front pocket of my jeans and tucks my wallet into my purse. He follows me to the kitchen where he holds the box flaps down as Manuel applies the tape.

"We have time to drop this off," he tells my brother.

"We do?" I ask.

"Yeah, Firecracker. We do."

Manuel jerks his gaze from Benji to me and back again, processing the nickname. I give him a tense smile. Box tucked under one arm, Benji places his hand on my lower back. "Say bye to your brother. I'll be in the car."

He then sets a kiss on the corner of my mouth and walks out the door. Now I'm left in my kitchen facing my brother's narrowed gaze. He doesn't look happy.

"Don't." I point at him. He wants to know everything, but this might be too much to know. Especially when I don't have time to explain. Not that I would share details. "I love you."

He's normally recalcitrant, so I'm surprised by his returned "I love you too." At least he sounds sincere when he adds, "Have a nice trip."

Benji

Two hours later we've landed in Florida and a car is taking us to the hotel. I surprised Cris with a private jet rather than flying commercial. As she boarded our airliner, her cheeks tinged pink and her eyes crinkled at the sides. Totally worth it.

We made a quick stop to drop the package at the post

office before a cozy flight south. We didn't have sex on the plane, but I'm not going to say it didn't cross my mind. I want her losing her virginity to be right. Unfortunately, doing things right means not inducting Cris into the mile-high club on the first go-round. On the flight home, however, anything goes.

I put a pin in my libido and hand the valet the keys. The hotel I booked is a ritzy, modern-day masterpiece. Nothing's nicer than a Crane hotel.

We check in amidst white and glass and sleek, modern furnishings in the lobby and then take the elevator to the top floor. I booked a suite, and while it's not a honeymoon suite with a chincy, heart-shaped bed or a champagne-glass hot tub, they do have a bottle of champagne on ice and a vase filled with an assortment of flowers next to it. Nothing but class, which is exactly why I chose this hotel.

"Mr. Owen," Cris reads from the card. "Enjoy your stay at the Crane Hotel." She bends to touch her nose to a delicate flower petal and inhales. "Mm."

The throaty sound reminds me of the shower we had together a few days ago and wow, does that reroute my thoughts. I adjust my dick but don't linger the way he'd like, before blowing out a calming breath as I take in the view from our floor. I was promised oceanfront. I am not disappointed.

"Amazing," she says from beside me. "A few hours ago I was in my house, and now we're overlooking a blue ocean. Isn't life incredible?"

I smile at her simple yet poignant observation. "Want to dip your toes in?"

Her face lights up. "More than anything." Then she frowns. "But I can't. I have to finalize a few things for the event tonight. We're registered as VIP guests, but Marla asked us check in the moment we arrive. There could be a photo op. If so, we need to know where to show up and choose what you're wearing. You might want to coordinate with your dad and brothers, but I imagine everyone will wear suits." While she's talking, she flips open her suitcase and drags out her laptop. Shoving the flower vase and champagne aside, she opens the computer on the table and bends over it. "And then we'll have to—hey!"

Her exclamation was due to my shutting the laptop before she could log in.

"Beach," I instruct.

"Just because we are in an enormous, beautiful suite overlooking the blue water and white sand of the Gulf Coast doesn't mean we don't have work to do. Last I checked, I'm still employed by you. These events don't exactly run themselves."

See what I mean about her not letting people take care of her? I palm her arm.

"As my life assistant coach, you should recognize I need a little vitamin *sea* right now. As in water. As in ocean. This weekend isn't going to be about you corralling my schedule. I didn't invite you to work your tail off doing the usual administrative duties."

"Work hours, remember?"

"We're in neutral territory. Work hours aren't written in stone this weekend." I wrap my arm around her shoulders and walk her to the window again. "Think of them as written in the sand."

Just when I think she's taking in the spectacular view, she sighs.

"If I could send one email..." She gives me a slightly guilty smile. "You can't keep me from working."

"Wanna bet?"

"What about you? You're the workaholic. Is it killing you not to check in with Josie?"

A little. But I'm fighting the urge with both hands.

"Of course not. I'm here with you. What else is there to do?"

It's the right answer. She smiles at her shoes. "I guess I can email Marla when we come back to the room."

"Nate's assistant has handled everything. If I'm supposed to show up for a photo opportunity, or a speech, or a fucking parade, she'll let me know. Your only job while you're here is to have a good time on my arm and by my side."

"We should probably talk about that." She worries her bottom lip with her teeth. "I can't literally be on your arm. Not with your family here."

While I agree it might require explaining, I also don't plan on groping her in public. "Trust me, Cris, they're not going to notice. You come to almost every event I attend as it is. Nobody expects me to drag a date to Florida for a fundraiser. They're going to look at you and see my best friend. My coach. And if they ask why you're not running around working your fool head off, tell them I gave you the weekend off. After all, it's the truth."

Fluorescent orange strings spilling from her open suitcase capture my attention. I pluck the teeny-tiny bikini top and dangle it between us. "Is this the swimwear your brother warned me about?"

She grabs the bikini top and slams the suitcase shut. I wrestle with the lid of the suitcase while she makes a meager attempt (while giggling) to keep it closed. My strength bests hers. I pull out two scraps of fabric. Tiny triangles make up the top and bottoms of a bikini I absolutely cannot wait to see her wearing.

"You're going to need a lot of sunscreen if you wear this." I grin.

"Maybe I should buy a new one. I forgot how much daylight is out there."

"Over my dead body." I toss the bikini on the bed and rub my hands together. "The best way to ensure we don't miss an inch of skin is for you to get naked. I'll apply the sunscreen and then you can put on your bathing suit."

Hands on her hips, she cocks her head to one side. "Oh, is that how it works?"

"Totally how it works," I say as earnestly as I'm able. "*Strip.*"

CHAPTER FIFTEEN

Cris

I'm sun-kissed and smiling after having bought a dress on a complete whim.

I packed a simple black frock I've worn over and over again, but it didn't feel like the right dress to wear to the event. Even though we haven't gone "all the way," being physical with Benji has made me more aware of my body. After he applied the sunscreen in our room, watching unabashedly as I tied the strings on my teeny bikini, I realized I finally have someone to dress up *for*. A plain black dress wasn't going to cut it tonight.

I hug the dress bag to my chest and smile to myself as I step into the elevator. I can't wait to surprise him when I show up in this hot little number. A woman steps in after me, and it takes me all of a nanosecond to recognize the director of the event: Marla Hearst.

"Cris!" She regards me from her height. But then, I'm petite, so everyone is tall to me. It's no wonder why he went out with her casually once or twice. She's beautiful and professional.

"Marla. Hi. I didn't expect you to be at the Crane Hotel." I expected her to stay where the event was being held. Or maybe *hoped* is a better word.

"Ugh. No. I prefer to stay offsite. It's so wonderful to see you. Looks like you've been enjoying the sun. You're almost sunburned." She wrinkles her pert nose. "I hope the garment in that bag isn't red or pink. It'll make your face look the same color."

I try to hold my smile while my stomach flips. The dress I bought for tonight is red. I glance down at the opaque bag in my arms and pray she's wrong. *Steamed lobster* wasn't the look I was going for.

"My dress is cool blue," she continues with an elegant sweep of her hand before pressing the elevator button for her floor—one below mine. "Cool tones of blue and green are the rage right now. Who decides this stuff?" She laughs heartily. I echo her laughter, or try to anyway. It's hard to be jovial after learning I dropped way too much money on a dress that isn't "all the rage" this season.

The doors slide open and she leaves the elevator, turning to wiggle her fingers in a wave. Before the doors shut, she catches them with manicured fingernails and pokes her face through the gap. "I have a few things for you to handle if you're available. As Benji's assistant, you're always so organized. I'll email you! See you tonight."

She's gone before I can argue I'm not working tonight. I frown down at the garment bag, feeling like a soot-covered Cinderella who's been swamped with menial tasks moments before the ball.

With a sigh, I step out of the elevator on the top floor and angle toward the suite. Benji is sliding in the key card as I approach.

"How did I beat you up here?" His eyes go to the garment bag in my arms. "Shopping spree?"

"Something like that. I'm going to return it. It was spur-of-the-moment, anyway." I turn on my heel for the elevator, but he catches my elbow.

"Not before I see it. You almost didn't wear the bikini, and you looked amazing in it."

I admit, that was nice to hear.

He pushes open the suite door and gestures for me to walk in ahead of him. I do, unsure how I feel about tonight. About being his date. About Marla. About the red dress or my red skin. How did a run-in with someone he had a romantic encounter with throw me off so completely? It shouldn't matter. There's no reason to behave like a jealous girlfriend when I'm not his girlfriend.

Neither should it have mattered when I saw him with Trish. And that mattered way too much. I need to screw my head on straight before I let what we're doing mean something it shouldn't. It's as easy as making a decision.

And so, I decide.

"Honestly, this dress is a tad fancy for this event."

"What color is it?" He hoists an eyebrow, which makes him look rakish.

"Red."

"Do you like it?"

"Well, yes, of course. That's why I bought it."

"Then wear it. Tonight's special. Or have you forgotten?"

Rather than admit the surrendering of my virginity was

the last thing on my mind when I ran into his supermodel ex who was content to treat me like I was "the help," I say, "Of course I haven't forgotten."

He crosses his arms over his chest, widening his stance. "Let's see it."

I press the plastic closer, shrugging nonchalantly. "It's just a dress."

"It's a red dress. A woman buys a red dress because she's feeling sexy. Why don't you try it on for me? I'll give you my honest opinion."

"Then you would see it before the fundraiser and ruin the surprise!" I'm smiling as I reprimand him. I love the way he justified my purchase. That he's encouraging me to wear a dress I love. His slow grin also tells me something else. I just revealed I bought the dress as much for him as I did for me.

Benji

I left the hotel room before Cris to give her time to dress up for me. I know that's why she bought the dress. She can't convince me otherwise. Plus, she kicked me out, claiming she couldn't concentrate while I was hovering. I wasn't.

Much.

My mind is plagued with memories of watching her strut along the shoreline in naught but a scrap of spandex. Her bright orange bikini was as "scandalous" as Manuel suggested. Her sunscreen-slicked skin was luminescent as she unknowingly rocked her petite curves. There's something about having seen every inch of her already and then her hiding bits from me that drives me wild.

As I sip my scotch and walk around the bar area next to the ballroom, where the event is going to start in an hour, I let my mind wander to what sort of dress she may have chosen. I know it's red. I don't know if it's short. I don't know if it's long. I don't know if the back is out. I don't know if it's strapless. I don't know if she'll be wearing a bra underneath or if she'll forgo all undergarments. What I do know is she'll be on my arm while wearing it, and then back in our shared room where I'll slip her out of it.

Our teasing and flirting about tonight being The Night has me excited for the main event. I'm not sure I've ever been this eager to have a woman in my bed. And it's not like I get off on going "where no man has gone before." This is Cris we're talking about, and the fact that a firecracker is hiding underneath her official exterior intrigues me.

The hotel's ballroom is decorated in tropical hues of soothing greens and creams set against the backdrop of pale wood flooring. Cane pole chairs ring tables draped with linens and set with shining gold cutlery and glassware.

When I was first introduced to this sort of wealthy lifestyle, I was perturbed by how much trouble a dot-org went through to squeeze money out of the rich. The entire process seemed pointless at the time. Why spend a ton of money to thank donors for making large donations? Not to sound cheesy, but isn't giving supposed to be its own reward?

Alas, the pomp and circumstance is customary. Separating the rich from their money takes a bit of finesse, and after it's done you can't palm them cab money and shove them out the door in their socks. The Heart-to-Teen group has seen to it to make us feel extra cozy, and those warm fuzzies help us loosen the hold on our money clips.

"Hey, baby bro." I hear the unmistakable baritone of Nathaniel Owen over my shoulder. Oldest and also adopted child of the Owen clan, and one of the best humans on the planet.

I turn to find him standing next to Vivian, who is dressed to the nines in a plum-colored gown. Her hair is twisted at her nape and diamond earrings dangle from her earlobes. The hand draped over Nate's arm boasts a chunky engagement ring.

"Nate. Vivian." I nod around the room. "Are you taking notes for the wedding reception? This place is fancy."

"You know Vivian. She's going to have something far more overstated than this."

Vivian clucks her tongue at his joke. "You know Nate. He wants to get married in a replica of the Empire State Building with the President of the United States officiating, with bears in tutus dancing at the reception. Over-the-top planning is squarely in his wheelhouse, not mine."

"I would never have dancing bears. It's cruel. Those beautiful animals forced to wear tulle."

She beams at him, the love in her eyes so bright it's blinding to us commonfolk. "That's why I love you. Always thinking of how others are impacted."

Their kiss goes on longer than is comfortable for a bystander. I finally look up from my shoes when Nate speaks again. "Where's Cris?"

"She'll be down in a few."

"You didn't escort her?" Vivian's eyebrows center over her nose, her frown accusatory.

"She asked me not to."

This seems to appease my future sister-in-law. "As long as you're being a gentleman."

"No promises." I vowed to show Cris the time of her life tonight and take her virginity like a confident man should. I never promised to be a gentleman. I'm hoping like hell she doesn't want me to be one. Once I buffed the first layer of paint off my little life coach, I found the naughty streak she'd hidden. I'm not nearly done exploring it.

Just as those thoughts go dancing through my head, not unlike the bears in tutus Vivian and Nate were arguing about, I see a flash of red out of the corner of my eye. My date has arrived.

She spots our trio and instantly gives a cheery wave, her walk not exactly elegant, making her stand out in the best way possible. Cris is always Cris. Whether wearing Chuck Taylors and ripped jeans or in a smoking-hot dress I cannot believe she nearly returned. She's so gorgeous my heart stops before kicking into gear again and hammering my ribs. Trying to school my expression in front of my brother is a challenge I lose.

The second Cris is close enough to touch, I wrap my arm around her waist and take in every inch of her from tip to toe. Her freckles are out but so subtle no one would notice unless they were standing close. Her blond hair is pulled back like Vivian's but unlike Vivian's, unruly ringlets curl at her temples. Wide gray eyes take me in, dark lashes and subtle eye makeup making them appear almost chrome in color. And her mouth. God, *her mouth*.

Glossy red lipstick I want to kiss off and damn the consequences...and our company.

That's just the view above the neck. Below gets even better. The dress is cherry red. There are sparkles and straps. It's formfitting in the most complimentary way. It's short, but tasteful. Before I can arrange any of those observations into a halfway appropriate compliment, Vivian speaks for me.

"Cris, your dress is exquisite!" She steps between us and touches the delicate material between finger and thumb. "You are absolutely ravishing. What a perfect choice. Is there a special occasion I should know about?"

Vivian sends me an evil-sweet look only she can pull off, Nate smirks, and Cris bats mascaraed eyelashes like a cherub with a pitchfork.

I slide a derisive glare to Nate. "Does Archer know?"

Nate's eyes go over my shoulder and he grins. "Ask him yourself. What's up, Arch?"

"Do I know about what?"

"Benji and the life coach," Nate says, as easy as you please.

Now let's get one thing straight, I don't care what my brothers say about me and Cris. But I *do* care what Cris thinks about her reputation where they are concerned. I don't need them dabbling outside her comfort zone, especially with what we have planned tonight. Luckily, Archer doesn't let me down.

"How you doing, Cris? Tell me you haven't taken to shacking up with this idiot." He flicks his gaze at me, and his lips twitch in what might be an attempt at a smile. He's one stoic son of a bitch.

"Men," Vivian huffs, rolling her eyes. "Cris and I will be at the bar refreshing our champagne."

Vivian's glass of champagne is full but Cris could use one.

"See you." Cris waves at us collectively, but her red-lipped smile is just for me.

"I could use another scotch," I murmur to my brothers as the ladies walk away.

"I bet." Nate laughs. "You two."

"It's about damn time," Archer says.

If they had any idea what it was "about time" for Cris to do, they'd be shocked down to their shiny shoes.

CHAPTER SIXTEEN

Cris

At the bar, Vivian accepts a flute of champagne from the bartender and puts it in my hand. Her eyes are wild when she says, "Okay, what is going on with this dress and Benji drooling all over himself?"

I smooth one hand along the bodice of the dress I nearly returned. I'm glad I didn't. It's a stunner, and I wouldn't dare wear it anywhere else. But, as Benji reminded me, tonight is special, and not because of the fundraiser.

"The dress I packed was drab. By the time I saw this one in the window I figured, why not?" I smile at my friend. She's studying me like an algebra equation where x equals "Cris is lying through her recently whitened teeth."

"Things have progressed between you and the smiley Owen, haven't they? He's bringing you dinner. You're ignoring my calls."

"I'm not ignoring you," I bleat. But I sort of am. I don't

know what to make of what's happening in my own head. How can I explain it to someone else?

"You'd better give me deets," she hisses, sounding a little scary.

"This is hardly the place for details the likes of which I have to share." I raise my eyebrows meaningfully as I take a sip of my champagne. This delights my friend, who is back to grinning like a madwoman. Excited by her excitement, I whisper, "Tonight's the night."

"You're finally going to let him work his magic. You might combust when he kisses you. You two have been flirting around touching each other for so long."

"We've already..." I take a furtive glance around the room. Benji and Nate and Archer are standing in a suited-man circle, each looking like different cuts of the finest beef on the menu. I turn back to Vivian. "We've already done some stuff."

"What stuff?" She leans in.

"Sexy stuff," I say, almost defensively. "Just not *it*."

"Oh. Oh! You mean tonight is the night you cross a certain act off your bucket list." Her face melts and then she coos, "And with Benji."

"Shh!" I warn.

"I want to tell everyone. But I won't. I didn't tell Nate. Do you know how difficult it is not to tell him things?"

I wouldn't mind if she did. I trust Nate. But it's sweet she didn't rat me out.

"It's none of my business anyway," she lies.

"Liar," I remind her.

"I know. I made it my business, and I'm not sorry either. It's the best news *ever*."

"It's risky. This is my job we're talking about. And he's my best friend." Could I have made the stakes any higher? And yet, I can't blame myself for wanting to indulge.

"It's past time for you to take a risk. Nate and I balance the friend and sex and work thing. You can do it too."

Happily changing the subject, I ask her about working at Grand Marin. She shares how she's learning the ins and outs of property management and quickly segues into how she wants to build her own shopping center or live-work. "If I can find a decent location, which is key. I'm finally starting to feel like my old self." She pauses. "Actually, that's not true. I don't feel like my old self. I feel better than my old self. Confident. Certain. I have no idea how things will go, but I know I can handle what's on the other side."

I'm happy for her, and at the same time slightly envious. I want to feel certain. "Of course you can, Vivian. You're the strongest woman I know."

"Thanks, hon." She spares me a smile. "It's a small matter of naming what I want and going after it. Back when I worked for my father, I was hustling and racing around trying to make every hoop jumpable. And setting most of them on fire in the process. Self-sabotage is totally a thing." She touches my arm. "Don't sabotage what you and Benji have. You two are good together. You're about to make it better."

I smile and nod, not sharing my worries about the future. Living in the present moment is really freaking hard sometimes.

"Are you nervous?"

I have to think about her question for a second.

"You know, I don't think I am. We've eased into this by doing a host of other things." I think back to the shower and taking him into my mouth and blush. "I imagine he'll be as great at sex as he is everything else."

My eyes flit across the room to study his lean, fit build in a streamlined, expensive dark suit. His hair is styled to perfection, his smile infectious.

"I'll hand it to you, Benji's a good choice. He draws people in. He's instantly likable. Charming to the nth degree."

"Prince Charming," comes another female voice over my shoulder.

I turn to find a stunning woman standing in our midst. She's wearing black pants with a barely-there gray pinstripe design and a white button-down shirt open at the collar. A haphazardly knotted loose black tie hangs from the neck of the shirt. Her hand is bedecked in platinum rings, her finger-nails painted black. She's very tall, with a pair of high-heeled shoes helping her out in the height department.

She sips brown liquid, scotch or whiskey, from a rocks glass. When she lowers it, the ice clinks against the side. "I don't suppose Archer Owen shares his brother's disposition?"

Vivian bursts out laughing but sobers quickly, like she remembered the other woman is an interloper. She blinks back to her serious self. "I'm sorry, can we help you with something?"

Her response sounds rude to me. I resist flinching. The woman doesn't so much as bat an eyelash. "Talia Richards."

Vivian shakes Talia's hand and introduces herself. I do the same.

"I'm opening a spa soon, and I'm interested in attracting celebrity clientele. I heard the Owens were in town. I've also heard of Archer's ability to draw such attention. I apologize for the interruption, but I recognized you from across the room. You're Nathaniel's fiancée."

"You've done your research." Vivian's narrowed eyes hint she's suspicious of Talia's motives, but Viv's tone is almost impressed. "Have you contacted Owen Headquarters?"

"Not my style." Talia shakes her head, sending her long, chestnut-colored hair swirling around her. "I find I make a better impact in person."

I bet. She's gorgeous, sharp, strong-willed. But her take-charge attitude can't mask the tenderness emanating off her. She's intriguing. I won't forget her when she walks away, and if she does talk to Archer, neither will he.

"Would you like me to introduce you?" Vivian offers, proving my theory—she's impressed. "It's a bit selfish on my part, I admit. I sort of want to watch him react to you."

Talia grins, her green eyes crinkling prettily at the corners. I sort of want to watch too. Her wide mouth and layered dark hair are definitely Archer's style. It's rare, but I've seen him with women over the years. Unlike Benji, he has a type. Talia is it.

"So, he's not like his happier brother or your genial fiancé?"

"Nate has his moments, but no, Archer's not going to be as cooperative, I'm afraid," Vivian answers.

"We'll see," Talia murmurs, shooting a glance across the room at where Archer and his brothers are standing.

"We really don't mind making the introduction. He might be more receptive," I tell her, meaning it. Archer's not an asshole, but he can be intimidating to people who don't know him.

"Also not my style." Talia's smile is friendly before she

looks over her shoulder at Archer once again. Like he feels her gaze, he turns his head, notices us, and then does a double take at the woman standing with us. After a lingering glance I know Talia doesn't miss, he turns back to his brothers, pretending as if he didn't react.

"That," I tell Talia, "is his style. Good luck."

"I'll approach him after dinner. Lions are grouchier before they eat. Lovely to meet you both. Cris, Vivian."

She walks away and joins a woman and a man on the other side of the room.

"I've never been one for voyeurism but I *really* wanted to watch." Vivian finishes her champagne.

"Same," I agree, and then finish mine as well.

Cocktail hour drags on, which was surely determined ahead of time. The more the guests drink, the more money they'll donate to the cause. I don't expect dinner to be satiating. These events tend to serve tiny portions on tinier plates. It's all about bite-sized hors d'oeuvres, not a filling dinner. Someone's going to give a speech later—probably several someones—and carb-loading guests will guarantee at least a few of them nod off.

The mingling continues, and Vivian and I have been working the room. Like me, mingling comes as naturally to her as breathing. I just wrapped up a conversation with a statesman when I detect the scent of delicate, expensive perfume. I half expect to find Talia, thinking she's changed her mind about an introduction to Archer. When I turn around, I regret the smile I pasted on my face. It was too genuine for the likes of Marla Hearst.

"What an absolutely beautiful dress." Her cartoon-villain smile prevents the compliment from sounding sincere. "I take back what I said about the color red. You're gorgeous wearing it. Especially with your pale blond hair. I wish I could pull off my natural hair color. These platinum and caramel streaks come with a hefty price tag." Her laugh is less evil now, almost desperate.

Maybe that's why I don't care for her. Beneath her shallow surface, she has no confidence in herself. When I ran into her earlier, my own confidence flagged, but with good reason. She was very clearly putting me in my place. A woman of her stature and wealth should hold herself like... Well, she should hold herself more like Vivian. Or Talia. Talia, I liked immediately. Marla, I disliked from the first time I met her. Admittedly, that could have had to do with her flirting with Benji. Later, she asked me to set up a drink for them at a cozy bar so they could "talk." I wasn't thrilled at the idea of her seducing him. Even now, the memory sours my stomach.

Her dark eyes sparkle as her gaze wanders over my shoulder. "Benji! There you are. I have been looking everywhere for you. Where have you been hiding?"

She's plastered against his side so fast I have to move out of the way to keep her from stepping on my toes. He catches her slim waist beneath one palm as she lays a kiss on his cheek. If he hadn't turned his head, she could've easily placed that kiss on his lips. I feel my blood boil at the same time I remind myself there's no reason to be jealous. Especially when he sets her at arm's length and greets her professionally.

"Marla. How have you been?"

"Better now that I'm looking at you." She smooths one eyebrow with her left ring finger. Her *bare* ring finger, making it obvious she's unattached. "Actually, I was looking *for* you. I thought we could bail on this whole affair and go somewhere more private."

I blink. Forget Cinderella with her arms full of her stepsisters' mending, I feel more like I'm sitting in a pile of stringy pumpkin innards.

She turns and smiles a very stepsister-like smile. "Could you be a doll and find a quiet corner for Benji and me?" To him she says, "I noticed you didn't bring a date. It's like we both knew."

Oh no she didn't. I'm fairly sure my face is turning the same color as my dress. Even my ears are hot. I'm not sure where to start, but telling her to go to hell crosses my mind. I tried to compartmentalize. This is too much.

Before I can speak, or explode, Benji wraps his arm around my waist. Unlike with Marla, his palm slides around my hip and he tucks me against him.

"My quiet time is spoken for. I have a date tonight. You're looking at her. It should have been obvious I'd be with the most beautiful woman in the room."

I'm not sure which of us you could knock over with a feather but judging by Marla's expression, and a strange effervescent sensation in my chest, maybe both of us.

"Oh." Her smile twists into something less lecherous but more sinister. "I had no idea you were seeing each other."

"It's an honest mistake. We're finding our way, aren't we, Firecracker?" He hugs me close, and the nickname has me taking my finger off the red button. Marla shall live to see another sunrise.

"We are," I tell him, soaking in the warm intent lurking in his eyes.

"That's... How great for you. Both." Marla sounds a bit breathless. I know I shouldn't delight in shocking her but, well... Is a little delighting too much to ask for? "You two have fun tonight. The dress ended up being lovely."

By the time she walks away, I feel the weight of Benji's gaze on the side of my head. It's not hard to guess what he's thinking.

"What did she mean by 'ended up'?" he asks and then answers himself correctly. "You bumped into her earlier."

"In the elevator before I met you at our suite door."

He nods slowly, maybe coming to the correct conclusion that she was the reason I considered returning the dress in the first place. Or maybe not coming to any conclusion at all.

"Let's take our seats and find out what bizarre, minuscule exotic foods we'll be served tonight." Arm snuggly at my waist, he leads me across the room to a table teeming with Owens. Lainey and William, Nate and Vivian (she's not an Owen yet, but close enough), and Archer, whose attention is on the other side of the room. As I take my seat, I casually look over my shoulder and notice that, surprise, surprise, he's checking out a certain long-haired woman wearing a loosely knotted tie.

Talia flips her hair and doesn't look over, but I can tell she knows he's looking.

CHAPTER SEVENTEEN

Benji

Y ou know how when you're excited about an upcoming event you can't concentrate on anything else? Like Christmas, or those great seats behind home plate?

Tonight's like that. Multiplied by a thousand.

At this point, I've surmised the fundraiser might never end. I'm regretting coming to it. Or at the very least, regretting making tonight the night I divest Cris of her virginity. Why didn't I pick an evening during which we had control of the timeline?

Super fail.

While I'm tempted to blow off the remainder of this tedious event, a sense of duty keeps my feet rooted to the floor. Dad and Mom are here, and my brothers. There was a photo op earlier, by the way. We posed together in front of a backdrop with the Heart-to-Teen logo printed on it while camera flashes blinded us. Cris watched from behind the photographer, unvarnished pride gleaming in her eyes. She's the best.

I'm still pissed off at Marla. She had no right to slither over and claim me, which is a nice way of saying she behaved like a presumptuous bitch. Has she always been that way and I've been blind to it? My gut answers with a stern *yes* and I know I only have myself to blame. In the past I've rewarded those sorts of antics. What can I say? When my dick is running the show, I make bad decisions.

Tonight I'm the one in charge. Not that I have to delude myself when it comes to Cris. There's no reason to worry our evening together won't turn out exactly how I planned. I smirk, preferring this line of thought to the previous one. So I've made a few mistakes of the female variety in the past. It doesn't mean I can't learn or grow.

Cris is chatting up an old guy in a suit, her smile warm and genuine. Damn but she is wearing that dress, isn't she? She's been blessed with a hell of a lot more patience than me. I can't let her have too much more champagne, though. Her conking out after one orgasm isn't going to inspire a salacious Dear Diary entry. We need to get out of here *pronto*. Or faster than pronto, whatever word that would be.

"Tonight's the big night." Vivian materializes at my side, the picture of a woman who has drunk too much champagne. She's not sloppy, just giggly. Which is adorable on her, as she's not the giggly type.

She was doing her best to be unapproachable the first time I met her at Nate's house. I invited her to brunch with our family, unsure if he was going to or not. She looked surprised and didn't quite know how to respond. Luckily, she agreed and came with us. She met the whole family that day.

I could tell she was nervous. At the time I had no idea she was Walter Steele's daughter, but as I got to know her I understood why she was protective of her identity. Her dad was a piece of work.

"I don't know what you're talking about." I take a sip of my water. I abandoned the scotch after my second glass, not wanting to dull a single one of my senses tonight. I wasn't kidding when I told Cris I would remember everything. I'm going for a record on snapping mental photographs. I'll keep them tucked away in a private album for years. Mine, mine, all mine. My first mental photo? That luscious red dress. I'm going to take a hell of a lot more after we escape this endless shindig. I don't want to miss anything.

"I didn't tell Nate. Or anyone," Viv stage-whispers. "Cris and I were chatting about it earlier. I am really excited for you."

"You are?"

She nods, her grin wonky and adorable.

My chest puffs at hearing Cris was sharing details with Vivian, but I cover with, "It's a favor. She's a good friend."

"You can't believe that's true. That there's nothing else underneath the attraction other than her need to be rid of her pesky virginity?" She whispered that last word, but I peek around at the crowd anyway. No one appears to have overheard, which is a good thing. I'm sure Cris wouldn't appreciate her secret being advertised.

"We know who we are. That's what matters." There's nothing complicated about sex for me. There never has been. It's a way to have a release, reclaim the happiness and joy that eluded me as a kid. I lost my virginity at age seventeen, which might be young in retrospect, but I'm glad for it. Having sex was like discovering a new world. I had somewhere to go that wasn't mired in grief. I was granted a much-needed break from constantly trying to fit in with a family that wasn't really mine and none of whom looked like me. Plus, I was a nerdy kid. A mathlete. Thank God Will pushed me to play sports. Soccer put me in the same circles as the jocks, which kept me from being shoved into my locker on a daily basis. Turns out nerdy kids with decent physiques have no trouble winning the girl.

"You'd better not run her off. I love her." Vivian pushes her bottom lip into an exaggerated pout.

"Cris isn't going anywhere. We talked about it. We're not going to suddenly *not* be friends. I'm teaching her how to be treated well." The guys she dates in the future better step the fuck up. God knows those dopes from the dating app can't tell caviar from Rice Krispies.

"Well I, for one, am glad she doesn't have to lose her virginity the way most women do—to someone with zero skill who didn't deserve it." She grips my forearm and regards me earnestly. "I'm glad she chose you. It's a big responsibility and you won't let her down."

Is she trying to put extra pressure on me? Don't get me wrong. I'm fantastic in bed. I'm great at giving and pleasing. Her vote of confidence adds steel to my spine. I cannot fuck this up.

"Have you ever taken someone's..." She looks around furtively before deciding not to finish that sentence the way she'd originally planned. "Have you ever been someone's first?"

"No, but I remember my first time. I felt like an idiot. I'm sure I felt that way my second and third time too. Luckily, I knew the secret to becoming really good at something." I give her a grin. "Practice, practice, practice."

"What is my brother telling you? He looks full of shit." Nate slings an arm around Vivian's neck and kisses her temple. "Actually, he always looks like that, so never mind."

"Oh, just our usual chitchat at these boring-ass things. Can we leave now?" She exaggerates her request by sagging under the weight of his arm. "Please?"

On this, she and I are on the same page. "What a great idea, Viv. We can leave Archer here to handle anything Owen-related."

"Archer is busy with future prospects." Nate tips his head toward the bar. A stunning woman wearing a necktie and slouchy white shirt is sitting sideways on the barstool, facing our brother. She's wiggling one foot, a black high heel dangling from her toes, while twirling her hair around one finger. Archer watches her, his neatly-trimmed beard shifting subtlety.

"Damn. He's in trouble," I blurt.

"That's Talia. She introduced herself to Cris and me earlier. She asked if Archer was as friendly as you." Vivian pokes my chest.

I burst out laughing.

"Exactly," she agrees. "Anyway, she's opening a spa. She wants Archer to help her attract high-end clientele."

"He's done it for bars and nightclubs. I don't see why he couldn't help a spa, or its owner." I study their body language. Hers doesn't broadcast she's looking for more than a business deal. His, on the other hand, is reading a little 007.

Listen, I know the way Archer is around women. I've seen him on enough dates to understand when it's *on*. This

Talia woman may think she's propositioning him for a job, but my brother has something more nefarious in mind. I wonder if he'll succeed. I would stay and find out, but I have better things to do tonight.

"Bet they end up in bed together." I turn to Nate to see if he'd like to take that bet. He narrows his eyes like he's considering it.

"Don't you dare damn her to that fate." Vivian is so sincere, I find myself chuckling at her comment.

"If Archer has a hard-on for anything, it's his next business deal," Nate comments. "He was already looking for something to do in Miami, so I'm sure he's planning to piggyback the spa onto the other project to save time and money on travel."

"He's looking to piggyback all right, but I don't think it's with the spa," I say. Vivian emits a delicate snort.

Nate watches Archer for a beat. "You're wrong. He's got her on the hook. This is all business, Benj."

He might be right. Nate's a workaholic, but he tends to be out in the field with his guys, taking out walls or doing site visits. Even when he's meeting with the mayor, they're usually outside of an office. Nate is a noticeable guy with his sheer size and that crooked nose of his. He's a big teddy bear, though. He's good at a podium.

I've always been a behind-the-scenes guy. I work my magic with numbers and run my life as efficiently as possible.

Archer is a blend of Nate and me. He has our father's work habits (falling under the Why So Serious column), and nearly every biz deal is life or death to him. William doesn't approve of the bars and nightclubs Archer builds, but that doesn't stop Archer from building them. Pissing off Dad might be what fuels his productivity.

Whenever I've suggested Archer hire an assistant like Cris to help him with his schedule, he makes a joke about his phone being "slim, quiet, and never talking back," or some shit. Half of me always thought that was his shtick whenever we were in a crowd, but the other half of me considers he was sincere.

And yet there is a part of me wondering if this woman could break him. Like Nate said, there might not be anything going on between them other than Archer's hard-on for a shrewd business deal, but I don't think it would take much to escalate it into personal territory.

"No way will she allow herself to be wooed into his bed," Vivian comments. "She's going to eat him for dinner."

"Don't be so sure," I say, eyeing Nate as he slips his arm around Vivian's waist. "Archer is an Owen, and Owens have a way of landing the girl."

She rolls her eyes but her smile is unstoppable.

"He has moves," I say, baiting her.

"They won't work on Talia Richards." A devious smile curls Vivian's lips as a trickle of fear slips down my spine. Her hand lashes out to take mine. "Shall we wager an even three thousand?"

"Sure, if you want to be cheap about it." I smirk.

"Talia's going to come out on top." She squeezes my hand. "And *not* in Archer's bedroom."

"I love when beautiful women lose money to me," I say as I shake her hand. "Though you might be right since he'll probably go to her room."

Cris approaches and stands between us. "What did I miss?"

"My future wife and your...Benji made a bet about Talia and Archer."

Her Benji. I like that.

"What are the parameters?" Cris asks, interested.

"Three grand," I tell her. "I say Arch is going to romance the brunette. Viv thinks Talia is completely in control of her faculties."

Cris looks over her shoulder at the couple in question and then back at me. She shakes her head before echoing Viv's earlier sentiment. "He might try, but she's all business. You're gonna lose, Benji."

Everyone chuckles at her assessment. Even me, even as a frisson of fear follows the first trickle. If Cris can tell Archer's fate at a single glance, what does she see when she looks at me?

I have a premonition I'll live to regret her deductive powers. I've never been a fan of people seeing through me. It's why I keep a smile on my face. The idea of her detecting what's beneath my veneer, and excavating something I didn't know was there, is downright terrifying.

CHAPTER EIGHTEEN

Cris

Vivian, Nate, Benji, and I make the unanimous decision to leave early. We can't stand another second of this event. My feet are killing me and all I want to do is get out of this dress. Vivian too, though she announced it while her hand was wrapped around Nate's tie. I love that woman.

The event coordinators, including Marla, are still managing the event. She appears to be ignoring me, but the uncomfortable prickles on the back of my neck tell me otherwise. I can almost *feel* her watchful gaze. As agreed upon, Nate and Vivian leave the room behind William and Lainey.

"We're next." Benji scoops me against his side and murmurs into my ear. "I have plans for dessert and they involve you." Before I can accuse him of being cheesy, he adds, "I figured you'd be hungry after the paltry amount of food they offered us tonight."

"Do you mean literal dessert or...me *for* dessert?"

He winks. "I mean both."

My virginity went from something I didn't often think about to an albatross tied around my neck. I'm at once looking forward to ridding myself of it and anxious about letting it go. I shiver as his fingers trail up my bare arm. I know he'll be gentle, incredible, wonderful. In short, he'll be Benji.

For whatever reason my mind returns to Marla. Maybe because he had sex with her. I have felt the sting of jealousy at seeing him with another woman but never before has it felt this sharp.

He must catch me scanning the room. His warm breath coasts over my ear, his deep voice zapping my every nerve ending. "You have to know she isn't half as beautiful as you are."

"I have eyeballs," I tell him. "She's not exactly Billy Goat Gruff."

He doesn't laugh, which is perplexing. That was a good one.

"I'm sorry she treated you the way she did. It was rude. It was indicative of the kind of person she is and didn't have anything to do with you. The jealous glances she keeps darting your way, though, those are deserved."

"You think she's jealous of *me*?" A doubtful smile curves my lips.

"Of course," he says so sincerely I have no choice but believe him. "She can't touch you. You're poised and honest. Damn distracting in red." He nips my earlobe, and a jolt of awareness shocks my limbs. "Incredibly distracting. Let's get out of here."

"Okay," I breathe.

He takes my hand and tenderly weaves his fingers between mine. And just like that we're on our way. Marla is forgotten. Archer and Talia, if they're still here, off my mind. There is only Benji's hand warming mine as we cross the street to the Crane Hotel, walk through the lobby, and slip into an elevator. He presses a button.

Once the doors close, he leans down and places a kiss on my collarbone. He then drags his lips across my exposed neck. "Cris."

I can't breathe, let alone speak. I tip my head. He kisses my throat before licking a trail to my earlobe, suckling, and then taking my mouth. The kiss is deep and hard. I swear there are sparks behind my eyelids.

The elevator dings and the doors slide aside.

We're here.

On the top floor.

At our suite.

He opens the door for me and I walk into a fantasy.

Benji

"Is this the same room?"

She's impressed. I can hear the awe in her voice.

"Benji." My name is a faint whisper. The look on her face is at the top of the list of things to remember about tonight. I take a mental photograph. *Click.*

She glides through the suite, taking her time to admire the many, many changes since she left. Starting with the vases of roses—red, because my goal is over-the-top romance.

I tipped the concierge generously, and he didn't disappoint. Crystal vases, with two dozen fragrant buds in each, are stationed in various parts of the room. Ten in all, one for every year I've known her. A bath is drawn in the large free-standing tub next to the window, rose petals and flickering candles floating on the water's surface.

Cris walks to the bathtub, gazes out the window at the dark ocean, and then turns to me, a curious smile on her face. From there she checks out the sofa and a low coffee table where there is another vase and the dessert I promised.

"Donuts?"

"Chocolate-covered strawberries are cliché. Plus"—I join her—"these are not merely donuts. These are brioche donuts filled with vanilla crème."

"They sound amazing. And unhealthy." She bites her lip.

"You're off the clock, coach." I thumb her lip from her teeth. "Tonight you are my Firecracker."

I take her hand and we sit on the sofa. I lift one of the donuts, crème filling dolloped on one end, to her mouth. Powdered sugar dusts my suit pants as I instruct, "Lick."

She doesn't hesitate, her eyes on mine when she sneaks out her pink tongue for a taste. My pants grow tight when she closes her eyes and lets out a low "Mm" sound.

"I hope to hear more of that tonight," I tell her before taking a bite of the dessert I special-ordered for the evening. More powdered sugar falls on my pants. She tips her head back, spreads those lush lips, and laughs softly.

I take another mental photo. *Click.*

She swipes her fingers along the corner of my mouth. "You're really something, Benjamin Owen."

"I'm whatever you need me to be, Cristin Gilbert." I offer

her the donut, and rather than take a bite, she dips her finger into the crème and sucks it off the tip.

Sucks.

It.

Off.

Click.

And here I thought I was the one in charge tonight. She's doing fine without my direction. I polish off the donut, and offer the plate holding the remaining four. She shakes her head and the curls framing her face, more having fallen out of her updo as the night droned on.

I set the plate aside and scoot so close our hips touch. My upper body facing hers, I tuck my hand under her jaw and tip her lips to mine. Our sugary kiss turns sensual and deep a moment later. The rustle of her dress against my shirt reminds me we have too many clothes on for my plans.

Before I'm done kissing her, she pulls away to ask, "We don't have to take a bath first, do we?"

"We don't have to do anything you don't want to do tonight. This is about you. This is all for you."

Her smile is appreciative. She stands and takes my hand. I stand with her and allow her to lead me across the room. Three wide steps lead up to a bed covered in a white bedspread. Rather than rose petals, I asked the concierge to leave something else for her. Something unique. Something she's going to love.

She picks up the box, wrapped in white paper and tied with red ribbon. Her head snaps over to me as she clutches the box in both hands. She grins, her eyes flashing with gratitude, and she hasn't even opened it yet.

Click.

"What are you waiting for?" I ask.

"You—"

"If the words 'you didn't have to' come out of your mouth, I'm bending you over my knee. And trust me, Firecracker, that's a few levels up from where we are."

I wink. She blushes.

Click.

She tears open the box and lifts the lid, revealing a rectangular red velvet box. Inside is a delicate gold chain, and dangling on that chain a golden compass pendant with a diamond at the top. It's timeless, delicate, beautiful. Like her.

"It's...it's... I don't know what to say." She blinks rapidly, her gray eyes misting over.

"Turn around." When she does, I reach over her shoulder and remove the necklace. I drape it around her neck and snap the tiny lobster-claw clasp.

"This is your reminder that whenever you need guidance, you can trust yourself. You never let anyone down, Cris. Time to prioritize your own needs for a change." I kiss the back of her neck. "You are your own true north."

Fingers touching the compass, she faces me. "You know what I need, don't you?"

Like she transferred her emotions to me, a lump forms in my throat. I swallow past it, which takes some doing. Steering us from the emotional quicksand and into sexier territory, I blink my eyes slowly and add gravel to my voice. "I do. Which is why you've chosen me for this particular expedition."

I make an obvious show of checking her out, my gaze wandering down her body and up again while I rub my hands together. "I can't decide which part of you to kiss first."

CHAPTER NINETEEN

Cris

Benji has given me plenty of gifts since I started working for him, but never jewelry. Now, he's draped me in gold and diamonds moments before he plans to strip me out of my clothes and make love to me for the first time. The necklace, the roses, the bathtub, and the dessert... It's all too much.

If I'm not careful, I'll lose more than my virginity tonight. Time to shore up the walls of those "compartments" before my heart escapes and goes streaking through the nearest open field.

I forbid myself to fall in love with him.

Tonight is going to be special. Unforgettable. I can't allow sex or this gift to ruin our strong friendship. A real and lasting, meaningful friendship. With my mind properly reconfigured, I drop the compass pendant against my neck and tug at Benji's tie. Specifically, the knot.

He smells good. As I inhale, I recall Marla and her very

wrong assumption that he would be spending time in her bed tonight. The memory of him claiming me makes me feel powerful, so I use it to my benefit.

"Tonight," I tell him as I undo his tie, "the only thing I want pointing north is your"—I am a breath away from his lips when I whisper—"big, hard cock."

He crushes my mouth to his, and I giggle against his firm lips. Not because the kiss is funny, but because I had an inkling my talking dirty would turn him on. I'm feeling my power twofold.

"God, I love it when you talk to me like that." Breathless is too delicate a word for how he sounds, but I've definitely robbed him of some vital oxygen.

Wide, warm palms skim my arms before reaching for the zipper of my dress. My bare back is introduced to the cool air when he drops the dress to the floor. He stares at what he's revealed—my lingerie. This, I brought from home. I bought it specifically for this trip. I nearly died of embarrassment buying it. I boldly walked into a shop with mostly nude mannequins and heart-shaped tables and shiny black floors and chose this particular set.

"Is this for me?" His voice is choked with lust.

"Just for you," I tell him. "I didn't own lingerie before we made our plans tonight."

He cups my breasts over the see-through black lace and thumbs my nipples. They peak greedily, begging for more attention. He ducks his head and grants the wish, his tongue swirling over my sensitized flesh. He leaves the lace damp. Heat gathers into a warm pool at the apex of my thighs.

He takes my hands and helps me step out of the circle of my dress.

"Shoes too?" I ask.

He blows out a tortured breath. "I want you to keep them on, but I think for tonight you should leave them off. We'll save the dirty stuff for later. Tonight's about one thing and one thing only."

I raise my eyebrows.

He dips his chin. "You."

I try not to let that mean everything as I toe off my high-heeled shoes. Before I know what's happening, I'm off my feet and cradled in his arms. He steps around to the side of the bed and places me on the white bedding. Somehow—and I honestly have no idea how—when he lets me go, my bra is in his hands and I'm topless.

"How did you do that?"

"Skills, honey." He tosses the garment over his shoulder. Suited, suave Benji undressing me isn't a moment I'll soon forget. He peels my panties away, his eyes flaring as he takes in what he reveals. His voice is tight when he says, "These are very nice, but you won't be needing them either."

I make a "gimme" motion with my hands. "Lose the shirt, buddy. I'm not letting you stay clothed tonight."

"You're bossy. That's not part of the plan."

"I'm your life coach, Mr. Owen. I make the plans."

"I'm going to let you have that one, but only because you're naked and spread out on my hotel bed. Which, by the way, is a surefire way for you to get away with anything."

"Anything?"

"*Anything.*" His eyes flare, and a happy zing dances in my stomach.

"Something to remember for the future."

He slips the buttons through his shirt with nimble fingers

and then it's gone. In the flickering candlelight surrounding us, I admire the subtle shift of the muscles of his torso as he unbuckles his belt. I take inventory and catalog each detail, filing them into a secret place in my memory. My eyes zoom in on the carpe diem tattoo he designed himself. I've always loved the sturdy curl of his letter Cs.

Once he's gloriously naked, I stop thinking about his handwriting and focus on the feel of his warm flesh against mine. He's lying on his side, pressed against me. He teases my nipple with his tongue and then trails his fingers to my center where he finds me soaked for him.

"So wet," he praises, his breath beading my nipple. I feel a nudge against my thigh, something hard. Something mouth-watering—I know for a fact. He steers my hand to his length, and my fingers coast over coarse, manscaped hair. I tug on the part of him I've never admired so much or so often, and match my strokes to his.

My body recognizes the familiarity of his touch and relaxes, my legs falling open. I've arrived at a state of arousal so sharp, so hyper-focused, I lose myself in it. My orgasm builds, but slower than any one before it. And since he knows when I'm about to come, he times his strokes accordingly.

He reroutes my hand to his hair and then ducks his head to kiss my belly button. Then he slips between my legs and delivers a leisurely, devious lick to my swollen clitoris.

My hips tilt to meet his tongue. Soon I'm moaning and pulling his hair. I force my eyes open to take in the scene of his head bobbing, his amazing face framed by my parted legs. My fingers in his hair. The erotic scene is backlit by candle-light, the only music the sounds of his intimate kisses as he bathes me with his tongue.

Overcome by the intensity, I clutch and come. While I'm coasting on a wave of utter bliss, warmth blanketing me despite the cooler air of the room, I lose track of him. Eyes closed, my breaths lengthen. I feel his open mouth on my throat as he kisses me. More kisses trail over my ear and then to my mouth before he issues a command.

"Look at me."

My lashes flutter open. He fills every inch of my vision, and an unwelcome sensation clutches my heart in an iron grip. The predicament I've fervently been trying to avoid has been here all along. It's so painfully obvious I can no longer deny it.

I'm in love with Benjamin Owen.

Not a crush. Not lust. Not friendly love. In. Love. I probably fell in love with him a long time ago, but denial was the most self-preserving course of action. Tonight is going to encase him in an amber chamber of my heart.

I give the thought a violent shove. I am a damn good organizer. A good organizer knows how to prioritize; knows what to keep and what to throw out. What to hoard in a decorative box in the corner of the closet to be opened at a later date. I tuck my feelings for Benji into the box and vow not to reach for them. Not now. Not later.

"I'm looking at you," I say, my voice raspy.

"Are you sure about this? Really, really sure? This is it, Firecracker. You give me the green light, and I'm going to send you over again and again. Which I hear is not typical for a first time for a lot of women."

"Did you take a poll or something?" I tease, the joke hitting its mark. He smiles down at me easily, his thumbs at my temples stroking. I commit to not analyzing further. I don't want to miss anything.

"Unofficially. I've heard a few bad stories. You're going to have a good one."

I'm going to have the *best* one. I wrap my arms around his neck and tip my hips, bumping my softness against his hardness. His mouth drops open. He's the picture of turned on. I love the picture so much I frame it and tuck it into the box too.

He drops his forehead on mine and shuts his eyes. "I have to put on a condom." He delivers the news wrapped in disappointment.

"Do you?" I whisper against his waiting lips. I've already thought this through. Many, *many* times.

"Don't I?" Hope hugs every letter.

"I've been on the pill for five years. And you are a master of safety. I assume that extends to the bedroom." He would never forget a condom and risk an accidental pregnancy or an STD. "Plus, you've been single for a while."

His laugh ruffles my hair, which is a wreck. I can't muster up the energy to care. "That's a big gift for me, honey."

"Very big." I grind against him again. "Do you accept?"

"Fuck yeah, I accept." He kisses me again, and this time he doesn't hold back. He nudges my entrance with the velvety tip of his cock. He lifts his head and zeroes in on my face, his shallow breaths mirroring mine.

He tilts his hips and eases into my folds ever so slowly. His expression is awestruck but confident. Encouraging, even. "Walk me through it."

"I thought"—I gasp and curl my fingers around the back

of his neck when he eases in a bit more—"you were supposed to walk me through it."

"I don't know how you feel." He drops a kiss to my mouth. "Tell me."

"Eager," I whisper.

He gives me a million-dollar grin. "You're not the only one. You're also strangling me. I don't mind," he adds when I loosen my grasp. "But that's a sign you're not relaxed, and I need you to relax. I'm going to gauge my every move on your satisfaction. You say back off, I'll back off."

"Keep going." No way in hell am I telling him to back off. I'm a space shuttle before blastoff, all fire and smoke as I prepare to hurtle into the great unknown. He sinks in another inch and I hold my breath. A sharp pain pricks me deep within and I bite my lip.

He doesn't take his eyes off mine as he rolls his hips. The sharp spike dulls, and before he can slow down, I beg, "More."

He gives me what I ask for, his expression morphing from cocky confidence to positively tortured. His eyebrows are bent, his mouth grimacing.

"Fuck." He exhales harshly before brushing my cheeks with his thumbs. "Fuck, you feel good."

"So do you," I whisper.

"I have to move or I might die." He sets a slightly sweaty kiss on my upper lip.

"Please, Benji. Please move." I close my eyes as he eases out. He glides in and shockingly, there is less pain than before. I'm shocked further when my knees lift of their own volition, my heels gripping his ass cheeks to pull him closer. Then there's no talk of slowing down or speeding up. He sets a rhythm I match with my hips, angling so he hits a spot—*that* spot... Right...*there.*

"Oh!" Eyes wide, my hands wound in his hair, I stare at him in awe. He appears concerned for a second before his expression slips into arrogance. A grin takes over his face.

"Well, well. Look what I found."

"Is it good?" I choke out.

"Did it feel good?" he asks, but he knows.

"So, *so* good," I admit, a little afraid of my own body. It's reacting in a way it never has before and surprising me at every turn.

He hoists my leg up, placing the back of my knee in the crease of his elbow. "Stretch time." He gently lifts my ankle and rests it on his shoulder. Then he follows suit with my other ankle. This time when he sinks inside me, the heat within has nothing to do with pain and everything to do with pleasure.

Each deep glide hits the bullseye of a hidden target. I've given up holding on to him to twist the comforter in my fists instead. Anything to anchor myself to the earth and keep from flying into a gravity-free spin into oblivion. Each thrust sends me up an invisible incline I never knew existed. Up, up, until I have no choice but to go over.

My orgasm grips me tightly. It's all-consuming. My eyes close, my worries vanish, my thoughts break into tiny pieces. I float in sensory overload on the highest of highs. I gradually become aware of an increasing fullness followed by a stickiness inside me. Of him releasing my legs to rest on either side of his prone body. His weight presses me deeper into the bed as he fights to support himself with shaky arms. He's still inside me, thick and pulsing.

His lips kiss my eyelids once. Twice. Through sheer force of will, I lift the sandbags weighing them down and focus on the man above me. His fantastic eyebrows wing upward in an unasked question. He wants to know how he did. And damn him, he did excellent. He did *perfect*.

"I'm not sure who made out better in that transaction," he informs me gruffly. "I feel almost guilty for how much fun I had."

"I can't remember how much fun you had because I was on another planet," I murmur. And then I laugh. He laughs.

This is so...easy. Even if I've only lived a third of my life, I know this moment is one of the best moments of the rest of it.

Hands down.

CHAPTER TWENTY

Benji

Cris is lying on her belly, the sheets pooled at her waist. I have no idea what time it is, but we've been at it a few hours. We paused to warm up the bathwater and slide in. I extinguished the flames on the floating candles first, but we left the rose petals. Sitting across from her in the wide tub, the moonlight streaming through the window and hitting her fair hair, I couldn't help thinking how much time we've wasted together not having sex.

Because, fuck, are we good at it.

When she stepped out of the tub, some of the rose petals stuck to her naked back and legs. I carefully removed them, kissing the skin behind each red petal. When I led her back to the bed, she dropped to her knees and took me in her mouth before I could lay her down again. As good as that felt, having sex with her was ten times better.

Now, after we've both spent ourselves again, she's

propped up on her elbows, her fingers clasped together, her blond curls a riotous mess surrounding a cherubic face. Only she looks less angelic since I know what she's capable of.

I decide to pose the question I've thought at least one hundred times since I first kissed her. "Why haven't we done this before?"

She laughs, adjusting her position and revealing creamy breasts with pink nipples I can't resist touching.

"What's so funny?" I ask as I brush one of those nipples with the side of my knuckle.

"When would you have had the time?"

"Meaning?" I'm not offended. I actually have no idea what she means.

"Come on, Benji. We both know you date a lot. I'm not sure when you would've slotted me in between all the women you were wining and dining." She gestures around the room at the roses and vases, and the remaining two donuts (we stopped for a snack after the bath and round two). "Evidently —*obviously,* this isn't your first rodeo."

Now I'm offended and uncomfortable but unsure why. It's not like she's wrong. I date a lot. Not constantly, but often. But she's wrong about part of her observation, and I feel the need to point that out. A little in my own defense, but mostly so she doesn't underestimate her power.

"I'll have you know, this entire setup for the hotel room is completely unique to *you.* I've never treated a woman to such decadence. At least, not all at once." Jewelry, roses, candle-light, and a night spent steeped in romance is a recipe for a woman having the wrong idea about where we're headed. I've never put on a show for anyone for just that reason.

"No VIP treatment for *Marla?*" Under the guise of

teasing me, she's concerned about how she compares to the women in my past. Her mouth is a cupid's bow of impishness, but insecurity shines in her eyes.

"We've already discussed how she doesn't measure up to you. I'm not going to lie, I've sent flowers to the women I've dated. I've given them gifts. Never jewelry," I add, realizing that *damn*, I never bought a woman jewelry until Cris. Except for Lainey, but moms don't count. "The roses and the candles were for ambiance. The necklace was for..." I'm suddenly weirdly embarrassed. I lick my lips and will myself to finish the sentence. "The necklace was because I want you to know how strong and capable you are."

Something warm and gooey seeps into her expression before she wills it away and rolls her storm-gray eyes. "And it had nothing to do with my *state* before tonight?"

"Your virginity was a big consideration." How could it not be? "That you're my best friend is another. If I would've booked a cheap motel and bought a heart-shaped box of chocolates, you wouldn't have let me live it down." She laughs, and the tension in my chest uncoils. "The event gave us an excuse to fly down here, away from who we are at home. I thought it'd help you relax."

She props her jaw on her fist and leans her head to the side, studying me. I'm having trouble meeting her eyes, my gaze skittering over her bared flesh and wild curls instead. As I mentioned earlier, the idea of her assessing me makes me nervous. She knows me well. It wouldn't be hard for her to come to whatever conclusion she's trying to shake out of the tree.

But I know myself well too. I'm in charge of what I show and what I hide. Normally. Naked and under her scrutiny, my cloaking mechanism is not working as well as it should. Sex has a way of leveling my brain cells. My guard has dropped. God knows what I've revealed without knowing it.

But this is Cris, I remind myself. The one thing she needed from me happens to be the only thing I have to give. She lost her virginity in an elegant, satiating, body-melting dance.

"You are one of the most sincere, genuine people I know," she says. I start to sweat, worried she can tell I've been sitting here trying not to be either of those. "Why all the dating? I don't get it. I was certain you were going to keep jumping from one relationship to the next like a rock skipping across a lake, until you met Trish. Then I worried—I mean, wondered —if you two would last."

The mention of my ex-girlfriend startles me so much I'm unable to hide my shock. *Thanks, sex.* "Why did you think that?"

"That was a long relationship. Longer than any other relationships you've been in. I mean probably." She picks at a loose string on the blanket. "I wasn't like, tracking it or anything."

"What does length have to do with it?"

"I didn't have much experience before, but after tonight I'd say length matters quite a bit." Her eyebrows lift into a saucy wiggle. Then the beautiful smartass lying across from me lifts up the sheet to inspect my naked body. That earns her a kiss. I can't help myself. I've always enjoyed my ego being stroked, in addition to other parts.

She drops the sheet. "Most people measure successful relationships by how long they last. You dated her several months. Didn't you think it was going to turn into more at one point?"

I'm already shaking my head. "No. Trish and I got along, but neither of us were anxious to take it further."

Absently, Cris picks at the string again. Or maybe not absently. I have a feeling she isn't meeting my eyes on purpose. "Why did she end it?"

"She didn't. I did."

She frowns, head cocked. "Really?"

"Sometimes things don't work out. All the time, in my case." I press my lips closed, willing myself to shut the fuck up.

"How is her mom?"

Sweet Cris. Always thinking of everyone else.

"Is this really what you want to talk about tonight?" I sure as hell don't.

"Not Trish, no. I'm curious about you."

Danger! Danger!

"Well, I'd rather talk about sex." Sex, I can hide behind. Sex, I'm confident I can deliver to a round of applause. Sex... masks the unpleasant feelings fermenting in my gut. I shake off that disconcerting thought and shoot her a smarmy smile. "Do you have any sex questions I can clear up for you?" I deliver a smacking kiss to the center of her lips. She turns her eyes to the ceiling in thought.

I've successfully distracted her. Thank Christ.

"I have one," she announces. "Now that I've experienced sex for the first time—"

"You're welcome." That earns me a poke in the stomach.

"I admit it's mind-blowing. But..." A slightly embarrassed smile crosses her lips.

"But what?"

"Does it..." She wrinkles her cute nose. "Lose its excitement later?"

A disbelieving "ha!" leaves my lips because the first thought that lights my brain like the bulbs on a marquee is *of course it never loses its excitement!* Except I can't say that. It's not true.

The first time I had sex I was understandably nervous. I knew the basic mechanics but wasn't ready for everything that came with it. The awkward closeness. The strange silence as we pulled our clothes on afterwards. The next time, or maybe it was the next, *next* time, I tried to avoid the awkward and the silence. Then sex became nothing short of awesome, which made me happy. Happiness doesn't come easy to a kid with two dead parents and zero family members in this country. Granted, sex is a different sort of happy, but it sufficed. It was a duct-tape solution to a problem requiring complex machinery, but I accepted it at face value.

I lick my lips, debating how to answer. I sure as hell can't say any of *that*.

"I imagine starting over with a new person each and every time would be strange," she presses, not leaving room for a graceful exit out of this conversation. Her eye contact is unwavering. The walls surrounding me are more like mosquito netting. I have the uncomfortable feeling she can see straight through them to the ugly bits I've been trying to keep hidden. "Granted, your body is perfect, so maybe it's not strange for you. I've been worried about how imperfect I might look to you. How much shorter and rounder I am than some of the women you've dated before."

"What?" I shake myself out of my terror to address the very wrong impression she has of herself.

"I'm a woman. I have body issues."

"Your body is perfect. Lush hips, beautiful breasts. Flexibility is important," I joke, and she cracks a smile. Success.

Click.

"Well, no matter how 'perfect' you think I am, the idea of being naked in front of a veritable god"—she gestures to my body, and a choking laugh erupts from my throat—"has been overwhelming. And the idea of doing this every couple of months with someone new is a frightening prospect."

She's right. Picturing her naked with a different guy every few months is pretty fucking frightening. I don't want to picture her naked with anybody but me.

"Women do not corner the market on body issues," I say instead. "But you have a point. Intimacy comes with familiarity."

"And so when it starts to become intimate, you leave?"

My head jerks back, but her shocking comment hits lower than that. Somewhere in the vicinity of my gut, like I was sucker-punched in the diaphragm and I'm struggling to catch my breath.

I've never thought about it in such precise terms before. It's not a pretty picture, is it? Do I bail out of relationships when they become intimate? Do I make my escape before we get to the good stuff?

I'm nowhere near ready to admit that, even in question form. Instead I go with, "I've always seen sex for what it is. A physical release between two people. It's up there with the basic needs in life. Shelter, food, water, sex."

"Sex is needed to populate the planet. If you're not populating the planet, why do you need it?" she challenges.

I lean in and murmur, "Why did *you* need it?"

She blushes. "To be honest, I didn't know I did. You make a compelling point. I'm not sure if I can live without it now."

I'm halfway to punching the sky in triumph. What stops me is the realization that the intimacy she spoke of, the intimacy I may or may not be trying to avoid, is filling every corner of this room.

I've never had a conversation like this. With anyone. Long relationship or short, the topic of intimacy never came up. I'm not sure if that speaks to the shallow relationships I've had, the women I've been with, or my own warped ideas about how relationships work. I'm torn between being relieved and pissed off. Nobody bothered to do a deep dive on Benjamin Owen before tonight. What gives?

I roll to my back and study the ceiling. I'm not sure how much of what I'm thinking I should reveal, if any of it. Since she keeps revealing things without my permission, I guess it doesn't matter at this point. Cris is a safe space. She is my life coach. She's my assistant at work. She's my best friend. Just because I've never shared the ins and outs of my relationships with her doesn't mean I can't.

So why didn't we talk about them? Why didn't she ask me about Trish when clearly, she must have wondered? Why was she so careful to stay out of the way? I could blame professionalism, but her work attire of tattered jeans and Chuck Taylors are proof professionalism isn't top of mind for her. Still studying the ceiling, I ask, "Why the sudden interest in my relationships?"

When no answer comes, I roll to my side and prop my head on my hand again.

Her mouth frowns as she shrugs. "I was curious."

Curious because we slept together? Curious because I took her virginity? These are the kinds of questions I don't typically have to contend with since the women I sleep with are experienced. Cris is the very definition of *inexperienced.*

"There's no reason for you to be twitchy," she states, confirming she can read my mind. If I was twitchy before her observation, now I'm twitchier. "Normally we talk about whatever interests us."

"Yeah, *normally* we do. You've never asked about Trish or why we broke up before."

"You never offered to tell me," she snaps. "I may have phoned in a few reservations for dinners, but you kept me in the dark about the women you were dating."

I open my mouth to tell her she's wrong, but she's not wrong. That's the thing about Cris. She's always fucking *right.*

"I'm sorry. I didn't mean to start an argument." She tears the sheet off my body and hers and climbs on top of me. I'm covered in petite blonde, her feisty smile and perceptive gray eyes going a long way to helping me forget this conversation.

Her breasts are between us, the perfect handfuls. I focus on them rather than the jittery feeling that I'm overlooking something really obvious. So. Breasts. I love the way they taste on my tongue, and she loves the way I love the way they taste. On that, we agree. Wholeheartedly. We should focus on what we agree on tonight.

"Let's not spend the rest of tonight arguing," she says,

again echoing my thoughts. "I'm sure you can think of a dozen things we can do instead."

"Honey, I'm game for whatever you want to do." As much as it pains me to say it, there is a "but" coming. "But this is your first time or technically, your third time tonight. I don't want you to be sore tomorrow. We can take it slow. I can do a lot of completely satisfying things with my mouth without the sex."

She looks almost hurt. "Is that what you want?"

"No! No. Not even a little. But it's not like this expires when we check out of the hotel. We can have sex at home."

"Really?"

That's the second time she asked, and I admit I'm almost as surprised as she is that I offered. I wasn't planning on dumping her on her ass after this trip, but I was expecting her to want to wrap things up. I thought after she'd taken what she needed from me, she'd be ready to go back to the way we were. I hadn't thought that far ahead until now, but damn, why would we stop?

Answers line up to shout at me. Answers like "the intimacy," "the questions," and "because she's your best friend." I ignore them. They don't know what I know. They don't know Cris the way I know her. She's cool. As evidenced by her suggestion to stop arguing and have sex instead. How many women have said that to a guy in the history of the world?

Exactly.

Zero.

She doesn't want to march the debate to its inevitable end, but that isn't the only reason I'm continuing our affair after we leave Florida. I cup her breast and lean in for a kiss.

"I won't stop you if you would like to use me for my body some more tonight."

She smiles so big I accidentally kiss her teeth. That moment is as memorable as the rest of them. Cute. Sweet. Sexy. Erotic. I'm not sure I've used those four words to describe one woman, but here we are.

What was I saying earlier? Oh right, the reason I'm continuing our affair after we leave. The main reason—I deepen the kiss as I roll her onto her back—is I'm having way too much fun with her to stop.

CHAPTER TWENTY-ONE

Cris

I'm sitting across from Benji at the Thai restaurant, Muse Elephant. It's trendy and delicious, and I'm damned relaxed considering the circumstances. I've been sleeping with my best friend/boss for over a week now, and things are going really well.

Like really, *really* well.

He was right about my being sore after that first night. The day we returned to Ohio, muscles I didn't know I had were aching between my legs. Not that he was rough in any way. I was the one on top when I talked him into having sex before we checked out of the hotel. On a high from the night before, I didn't hold back. Being in charge of his pleasure was both exciting and enthralling.

I couldn't imagine doing any of it with anybody else. Or maybe I don't want to. There's a comfort level with him I don't have with other people. I've seen him day in and day out consistently for the last year and a half or more. I can tell him if he has basil stuck in his teeth without either of us being embarrassed. Sex with him is so...*easy*. I have a feeling if I were with someone else I'd worry myself silly over my partner's every microexpression.

We are doing remarkably well. I don't have much experience, but I've offered a sympathetic ear to my girlfriends. I've heard about their dating lives, and let me tell you, it's a lot of agonizing over "should I do this" or "is he doing that."

I haven't grilled Benji about his dating history since my rogue bout of curiosity at the hotel, but the women he's dated have crossed my mind. I've known him for ten years, albeit most of those years from afar, but he didn't date any of them long enough to know them as well as he and I know each other.

I sip my wine as he continues talking about work, silently wondering if his arms ever grow tired from holding up his guard.

His smile is hiding something. I assumed it masked stress at work. But what if it's covering something thornier? Does he have a problem with intimacy?

There is a compatibility factor already in place thanks to our friendship. He certainly didn't have friendship with Trish. I'm aware there was physical attraction between him and the women he dated, but it's clear we have that component as well. Benji and I are off-the-charts physically attracted to each other. Not only have we crossed a couple of firsts off my list, but I'm teaching him a few things as well.

Like: Women don't always like butt grabs as they're walking away. And we like to be told we're smart as well as hot. Oh, and having a ceiling fan on while he's going down on me makes me cold. In turn he's taught me if I bury him under the covers while he's pleasing me he's in danger of suffocating.

We're both learning.

"Leave it to Josie," he says, wrapping up his story. I was listening, partially. In my defense, I already knew what happened. I know everything going on in the office. I overheard his conversation with Josie this afternoon. "I figure you can iron it out on Monday. She likes you."

"Absolutely." I reach for my cell phone and open my calendar.

"No phones at dinner," he says.

"Now you're turning into your mom?"

"It's Dad's rule, but he made it for her."

"Will is a good husband."

Benji nods, his smile as warm as a mug of tea. "He is."

"How else am I supposed to remember I need to do something for you on Monday if I don't put it on my calendar?"

"One of the perils of mixing business and pleasure."

I press my lips together to keep from smiling at him unabashedly. The mix of business and pleasure between us is less fifty-fifty and more like thirty-seventy. I'm having trouble compartmentalizing like I promised myself I would. The lines between best friend and boss were easier to navigate than the lines between best friend and lover.

"I didn't invite you to dinner to talk about work. And here I am talking about work." He picks up his wineglass and promises, "No more work talk."

"Don't be silly. What else do couples talk about when they're on a date?" I lift my own wineglass as an awkward silence falls between us. Clarity dawns as I replay what I said. We're a couple in the most technical sense of the word. But we're not a couple by the standard definition. There will be no shared holidays. No snuggling on the sofa after a long day. No moment where he gives me his house key or we talk about how to navigate the treacherous waters of dealing with the in-laws.

I am saved from further dissecting who we are to each other by our server, who glides over to ask if we'd like dessert. She rattles off a long list of options. By the time she mentions "warm vanilla-glazed donuts" I exchange glances with Benji across the table. His eyes sparkle, a knowing smirk parked on his lips. I assume his mind returned to the memory of the donuts we shared the night I surrendered my virginity. If, like me, he's thinking how any donut, no matter how gourmet, would fail to stand up to the divine perfection of the donuts we shared that evening.

"Just the takeout boxes," I tell our server without breaking eye contact with my date. "We'll have dessert at home."

"Excellent choice," Benji praises after our server leaves.

"The takeout boxes?" I widen my eyes and try to look innocent.

"Pray tell," he says, holding my hand over the table. "What kind of dessert do we have at home? And are you now calling my house 'home'?"

"I... I guess I am. I've been at your house more often than mine." Lately especially. For good reason. My house is cavernous and lonely. There are no noisy brothers to keep me company any longer, and no luxurious bedding with Benji on top of it.

"Yeah, I guess you have." His eyes narrow in consideration. "I didn't notice. I'm so used to you being there. Huh."

"I can cut back if you like," I sort of joke as my hand grows damp in his.

"Don't be ridiculous," he reprimands gently as he pulls his hand from mine.

"I'm just surprised I didn't notice."

"Too busy having your mind blown?" I lob the brag at him, hoping he takes my cue. We can banter our way out of being uncomfortable if he's willing. He doesn't disappoint.

"I have created a monster."

"It's not nice to call a lady a monster."

"I can't say what I'm thinking here, Cris," he murmurs.

"Those damn decency laws," I whisper, noting the exact moment when the awkwardness dissipates between us. He leans in, taking my hand again. I'm warm all over, eagerly anticipating some signature Benji dirty talk.

Unfortunately, at that moment the server returns with our takeout boxes. Even more unfortunately, we are forced to sit back in our seats and wait while our server makes small talk and packs up our food for us.

When we finally make it out of there with our bagged goodies, we dash hand in hand to Benji's car parked on the edge of the street.

"I didn't think she was going to allow us to leave. It was the Heart-to-Teen fundraiser all over again." He's so sincere I have to laugh.

"She was schmoozing you. I think she recognized you and knew how deep your pockets went."

"I think you slipped her some cash to delay us so I'd want you more."

The compliment, along with the romantic evening, has hit its mark. I feel special and cherished and sexy and wanted. The glass of wine at dinner went a long way to helping me let go of the workday. He steps closer and tips my chin with one knuckle. I'm drowning in caramel-colored eyes with no desire to be saved.

"How am I supposed to concentrate on the road during our thirty-five-minute drive when I have a hard-on with your name on it?"

"I require a fact-check," I whisper.

"*Monster*," he teases before placing a kiss on the center of my lips. "I'm not obeying any speed limits on the way home."

Longing wraps itself around the word *home* and settles deep in my belly, its weight comforting. Which doesn't make a lot of sense. To me, home has only ever been a place to manage. A place to organize, pay for, and maintain. Benji's home is different. His home is welcoming and comfortable. A lot like him.

A warning burbles to the surface of my mind, cautioning not to allow his version of home and mine to become synonymous. He might appear to fit seamlessly into every single part of my life as I do into every part of his, but it's a mirage.

My mother has been married seven times. I'm getting married one time. *One*. I decreed it when I was fifteen years old and feeling particularly despondent about the permanence of anything. She'd already had a number of men in her life, and I refused to let myself get to know any of them. They never stuck around. I noticed she was always the one who asked them to go.

Even if I never ask him to leave, I know Benji isn't interested in marriage and family. As comfortable as we are with each other, and as many naked moments as we've shared together, I can tell he's holding back. Protecting himself, similar to the way I protected myself years ago. He's been hurt before and doesn't want to risk being hurt again.

The worst part is he's right to hold back. He must suspect I want more. He doesn't want to ask me to settle for less than the future I envisioned for myself. And, more importantly, if we try to appease the other and each become people we're not, we could risk everything.

A friendship ten years in the making, meant to last a lifetime, is a high price to pay no matter how good we are in bed together.

The thought of us becoming bitter and not speaking, the way my mom refuses to speak to any of her exes, hollows out my chest. I recognize the irony, but it doesn't make it any less true: I love him too much to lose him.

"Who says we have to wait until we get home?" I reach up to play with his hair. The streetlight overhead bathes him in warm light. He's so freaking gorgeous it's criminal. And for tonight he's mine. Which is probably why I boldly add, "Find somewhere dark where we can park. Your backseat looks roomy."

He studies the sky as a laugh bobs his throat. Then he takes my hand and kisses my palm. "Lesson number...whatever we're on: Never *ever* let a guy take you to dinner and then do you in the car. No matter how much of a hurry he's in."

I grip his tie and tug his lips to mine, delighted to have the freedom to touch him the way I've wanted to for years. Delighted further when he bends to my will. It's heady, this power. "What if I'm in as much of a hurry?"

His eyes darken to deep brown. His arm lashes around my waist, and I'm pressed against his firm body from breasts to hips. Part of him is quite a bit firmer than the rest.

"Much as I want to give you your way, Firecracker, I'm committed to treating you to more than hurried, backseat sex. But there is another option." He turns his head. I follow his gaze across the street to where a Crane Hotel towers over the surrounding buildings. Its glass reflects the moonlight boldly, brilliantly, and beautifully. "If you don't want to wait, you shall not wait."

I want to argue, but the word "hurried" stalled the idea of car sex. I want to take my time. I'm not sure how much more we have left. I'm learning to put my needs first. He's a good teacher. I arc my neck to take in the glass and metal shrine that is the hotel. As much as I shouldn't want to relive the first night I spent with him, especially with hectic feelings swirling around me like debris during a hurricane, I can't deny myself.

"Lead the way."

He takes my hand and we jog across the street, the paper bag holding our takeout crinkling against his leg with every other footfall. We're laughing when we enter the lobby, the heady anticipation of what's to come having overtaken us.

"Your best room," he tells the front desk clerk. The Crane Hotel is not a place you rent a room by the hour. My stomach flutters with excitement at the idea of breaking an unwritten rule. While the clerk finds us a room, Benji turns to me and asks, "Maybe we should order donuts from Muse Elephant after all."

"We can have those delivered for you, sir," the clerk gleefully informs us. "Shall I add a bottle of champagne to your order?"

Benji shrugs with his mouth, impressed.

"You shall," he answers her, then he pulls me in for a quick kiss.

CHAPTER TWENTY-TWO

Cris

The eldest of my three younger brothers is sitting at the head of the kitchen table, his hand wrapped around a bottle of beer. Manuel has been trying to pin me down for over a week, but I've been busy doing...well, Benji, quite frankly.

Finally, Manuel and I carved out time to have dinner together. It involved me leaving work instead of going on a run with my boss, but Benji understood. I came home and cooked a simple dinner of macaroni and cheese and tuna steaks. I also steamed a large side of broccoli both Manuel and I ignored.

"I love you," my brother tells me.

"I love you too," I respond brightly. I suspect that's not the end of his sentence. I'm not sure I want to hear the rest of it. Regardless, I prompt, "But?"

"No but, Cris. I love you. You're my sister. Half-sister, but you know that shit doesn't matter to me."

It doesn't matter to me either. Not that his skin is darker than mine or his father is crazy wealthy or Manuel has the worst habit of leaving his socks scattered through the house. When he lived here, anyway. I miss him.

"It threw me seeing Benji kiss you." He makes a face like he ate a stalk of disregarded broccoli.

"I know." I try not to cringe, but I'm not sure I'm successful. "I didn't mean for you to see that."

"You've been spending a lot of time with him."

I nod. That's true. I have always spent a lot of time with him, but it's been more than usual lately. Since Manuel has been visiting me more often, he's noticed when I'm not here.

"I didn't intend for you to know," I tell him. "I've always tried my best to set a better example for you and Dennis and Timothy than Mom did. Which is why I haven't dated much. Like you needed one more woman bringing men into your life and then taking them out again."

It wasn't lost on me that the boys suffered, if not more than I did, through each of those transitions. I tried to help them withstand the blow, but I also knew my limits.

He leans forward on his chair. His fingers curl around mine and gently squeeze. "You're not Mom. Will you let me finish what I have to say?"

I nod, making a motion like I'm zipping my lips.

"I'm happy for you." He grins. Big, bold, and so unexpected.

"You are?" My shoulders drop a few inches.

"*Yes*," he says patiently. "You sacrificed your twenties for Dennis, Timothy, and me—"

"It wasn't a sacrifice."

"Cris."

"Sorry." I press my lips together again.

"I'm twenty-four and I can't imagine taking care of three kids while trying to work and have a personal life." He shakes his head. "I took you for granted when I was younger. Den and Tim still take you for granted, but they'll come around. I'll see to it. What I'm saying is you deserve some time for yourself to worry about yourself instead of worrying about everyone else."

"That's what Benji keeps telling me."

My brother nods, so young and yet so wise already. Tears threaten as pride engulfs my being, but I stamp it down.

"Benji's smart," he says, serious once again. "Worrying about her kids was supposed to be our mother's job. And our fathers' jobs. There should be more people dedicated to the survival of our little family than the four of us."

Ain't it the truth. My nose tingles as emotion surges up my throat.

He lets out a sigh and sits back in the chair once again. "She called me."

"Mom?" She rarely calls anyone.

"Yeah."

"Wow. I can't remember the last time I talked to her. It was a holiday, I think, but not a big one. Labor Day or something." I shake my head, figuring it doesn't matter. "What did she want?"

"To tell me she and Todd have been married for a year and it's going to last. And..." He takes a very deep breath. "She's pregnant."

"What?" My voice is a desolate whisper. While she is mathematically able to be pregnant, she's nowhere near emotionally capable of dealing with a baby.

"My first question was who is raising it," Manuel says.

"Did you ask?"

"Yep. She said she was, then made excuses about how and why she moved to Vegas. She swore she loved me, loved all of us, and promised her having this baby won't take away from the love she has for her other children." Arms dangling at his sides, he sits back in the kitchen chair and regards me dubiously.

It's the same chair Benji repaired after he came over for fajitas not so long ago. He drilled a screw into the leg and *voila*, the frame didn't wobble anymore.

"Can you believe that shit?" Manuel says, bringing my attention back to the news I didn't want to hear. "I want to understand her, but in so many ways she's a stranger."

"I know, honey." Guilt pierces my heart. I tried to make up for her absence. I tried to involve my brothers' dads and their extended family members as much as possible. Other than a random visit from an aunt here or a cousin there, everyone seemed content to leave us on our own. "I tried to make your lives as normal as possible."

"Our childhoods were not normal."

I wring my hands. "I know. I'm sorry."

"No. Don't be sorry." He shakes his head. The smile he gives me is amused. "This is what I'm talking about. You need to stop worrying about what you could have done better, or what you're doing now." There is a pause before he says, "You're seeing Benji."

I give him a pained smile. "I am."

"And he's making you happy."

"He is."

"For the first time in your life you're doing what you want regardless of what anyone thinks. Enjoy it."

My shoulders sag further. Not from relief this time, but from more guilt. Manuel believes Benji and I are in love. My brother knows me, and he knows I vowed over and over again to never be like our mother. I will get married once. Monogamy, I've said on numerous occasions, many of them while I was vocal about how Mom had let us down, is my middle name.

"Benji is a good guy," Manuel continues. "And he has money, which isn't the end-all, be-all, but it's better than you dating a broke dude."

I laugh.

"I hope it works out. Seriously. Stop hiding or trying to act like you're not happy." He slaps my knee. "Lighten up. Life is good."

My smile is brittle. I can't tell him the truth. That my relationship with Benji is as temporary as one of my mother's many husbands. I suppose it's possible the odds are in her favor this time. Maybe this Todd guy is cool and excited about having a baby, in spite of having it with a woman who abandoned four of her children already. I somehow doubt it.

"I'm going to mow the lawn while I'm here." My brother stands. "And do the dishes."

"You don't have to do that."

"Yeah, I know." He chucks his empty beer bottle into the recycling bin. "But you have a boyfriend now, so you don't have time to do as much around here."

"I was planning on hanging out with you, not putting you to work." *Plus he's not my boyfriend,* I mentally tack on.

"You also said you had 'a million' errands to run and had

no idea when you'd run them. How about now? I'm giving you the night off. I owe you a few."

I'm moved by the offer and so proud I could burst. All my efforts to help my brothers become good humans are paying off. They're not perfect, but they're trying. What more could I ask for? Rather than be mushy and possibly discourage any further heart-to-hearts with the eldest of my younger brothers, I slip into parent mode. "If you have a second beer, no driving."

"Yes, Momma Cris." He bends and puts a smacking kiss on my forehead. "Where's your list of shit that needs fixing? Wasn't there a leak in the roof?"

"You're not climbing on top of this roof without supervision," I tell him curtly.

"I am a grown man."

His words hit me in the solar plexus. I vividly remember him as a little boy. I'll always see him as a boy. Which is probably why I snap, "Yeah, and your bones are as breakable as any other grown man's. The answer is *no*."

He finds the list on the fridge as I carry our plates to the sink. "Well, am I allowed to pull a box out of the attic for you?" He holds up the paper. "And change the batteries in the smoke detectors?"

"Both of those require a ladder." I gnaw on my bottom lip, aware I'm being ridiculous.

"Worst-case scenario, I sprain something. Besides, weren't you going to be the one up on the ladder? How's that safe?"

I hate when he makes a good point.

"Promise me you won't climb on top of the roof," I say as he folds the list and tucks it into his pocket.

He makes a scout's honor sign while rolling his eyes.

I shouldn't smile, but I can't help myself. My brother is an adult. And he's taking care of me for a change. He's grown into such a good person, I'm tempted to get misty-eyed over it, but I resist.

As I gather my purse and keys, I can't help thanking him. He shrugs off my gratitude, but I can feel how much he appreciates it when he hugs me goodbye.

Benji

At a somewhat spontaneous Owen family gathering, on the balcony at the back of our parents' house, I admire the trees and the lush green grass in the backyard. Mom's roses have started blooming. Soon the entire garden will be filled with their sweet, unique fragrance.

"Thinking of a special someone you'd like to make a bouquet for?" Vivian lowers onto a cushioned chair next to mine. "Your dad and Nate sent me to inform you they're smoking a cigar in celebration of Nate's latest project."

"I thought you were Nate's latest project." I slide her a smile.

"You have that backwards, buddy."

"You don't have to tell me. I grew up with him." I'd ask her if she gave Archer this much crap about the mysterious woman he met at the fundraiser, but I was witness at the dinner table tonight where she did just that.

So, tell us more about the feisty brunette who wants you to make her famous.

Archer, predictably, was not rattled by her prodding. He sipped his scotch and answered, "I know about the bet, and I'm not giving you anything."

Our money's held up until he lets down his guard.

William and Nate asked a few follow-up questions, but they were business related. Arch ducked and dodged like a practiced politician.

"Before you smoke with them, will you level with me?" The teasing quality is gone, and now I'm facing a sterner version of Vivian. "About Cris, I mean. How is she?"

"I thought you two talked all the time," I hedge, not sure what she's asking.

"I'm trying to be respectful and mind my own business."

"Present moment excluded?"

"I like you, Benji. Don't make me change my mind."

I laugh at her signature sass, but she doesn't laugh with me. Her mouth is tight at the corners like she's legitimately concerned.

I lean forward in the chair and prop my elbows on my knees, considering her question. "How is Cris? She's...Cris."

"So she's adorable, accommodating, reliable."

"And a lot of other adjectives I won't share aloud." Like hot. Sexy. Sensual. Insatiable. Surprising.

"And how are you with everything?"

I sit up and force a shrug so big my shoulders almost touch my earlobes. I drop my arms and say, "Fine. Great. What would I have to complain about?"

Honestly, what *could* I complain about? I'm getting laid on the regular by a woman who is so sexy I can't think of anything else. Whether she's across the hall working, or having dinner with her brother, she's rarely not on my mind. I almost invited her tonight, but Manuel beat me to the ask. I hope he's not there to break difficult news, like his girlfriend is pregnant or he wants to move back home. Cris is just now learning who she is without taking care of her brothers full-time.

"It's not that you should have something to complain about," Vivian tells me, her eyes turned up to the starry night sky. "I was curious if you had any sort of epiphany about you *and* Cris."

"Excuse me?" I ask, even though I know exactly what she's saying.

"You. And Cris. Together." Her eyebrows climb her forehead.

"How would you have felt if I sat you down and asked you to describe your feelings for Nate when you two were first together?"

She rears back and frowns. "That's different. I didn't know you back then. You wouldn't have sat me down and talked to me about anything. You were too busy trying to make me feel at home, which is its own form of meddling, by the way." She pats my hand to soften the blow.

I exhale through my nose. "I can understand how Cris's...*circumstance* makes you concerned, but we very carefully crossed that bridge."

"And she enjoyed the *crossing*?" Viv's chin dips, her eyes widening meaningfully.

"Immensely," I say, but that's all she's squeezing out of me. "I'm doing my damnedest to teach her everything I know."

"Well, let's hope not everything. I'd rather not see her serial date men the way you serial date women."

This again? Jee-*zus*.

"There's nothing wrong with serial dating as long as it's mutual," I defend, feeling prickly. But it's not my own reputation I'm thinking about. It's the idea of Cris with another guy. Dating. Kissing. Her stripping for him and letting him sink deep inside her while she's making those panting noises I've grown so fond of. I grind my back teeth to dust to keep from admitting the jealousy kicking up around me like sand in a dust storm.

"Are you planning on serial dating again?"

I make a sound between an offended grunt and a disgusted laugh. "Not right now."

"But eventually."

"Look, even if—when—Cris and I wrap this up, it's not like I'm not going to be in her life." As I explain, my chest constricts. I have been trying not to think of the future, but it's hard when Vivian keeps bringing it up.

After Cris and I finish our sexual quest, then what? I assume she'll keep working for me. She'd better. But what happens when she inevitably lands a boyfriend? Some guy who's decent to her, albeit far less smooth and charming than me. Am I going to have to listen to her talk about him during our runs? Will she still go running with me after moving on?

An ache forms between my eyebrows, and I realize I'm frowning hard enough to pull a muscle.

Like she reads my mind, Vivian presses, "How are you going to feel when she starts seeing someone else? Or when she falls in love? Or when she gets engaged?" She wiggles her left hand at me. The diamonds sparkle in the flood of moonlight painting the house lunar blue.

I stand, frustrated and more than ready for a cigar with my dad and brothers, if only to escape Vivian's interrogation.

"Benji." She stands too, nowhere near giving up.

"Fuck, Viv, I don't know!" I try not to shout too loudly. Her fiancé's the protective sort. He'd have no problem pummeling me for merely raising my voice at her. "I guess I'll be happy for her," I lie through my teeth. I force a smile to sell what I'm about to say, ignoring Vivian's suspicious glare. "And when she invites me to be part of the wedding party, I'll say yes." I touch her shoulder. "I know you're gunning for maid of honor, so I'll settle for walking her down the aisle."

My heart clenches at the picture I've painted. The visual of a faceless groom at the end of the aisle looms like a bad omen. In my vision, my steps falter, my hand over Cris's squeezing to warn her, but she's too in love with her future husband to pay attention to me.

Damn, that's dark.

"And you would be *totally* okay with that?"

"Of course! She's my best friend. I want her to be happy forever."

"What about you?" she asks so sincerely, I'm thrown. What about me? No one ever asks about me. I take efforts to prevent anyone from worrying about me. And since old habits die hard, this one in particular resurrects itself like Lazarus.

"I'm already happy. I couldn't be happier. Look around." I gesture at the utopia that is our parents' property. "I was raised here. Happy Central. You've seen my house. You've seen my car. You haven't seen my bank account, but you've seen Nate's. I don't want for anything, Viv. Are you honestly worried about me, or are you dancing around something else you're hesitant to admit?"

Like Cris deserves better. Or that she deserves more from me. Or I should let her go, so she can find that bad-omen husband and let things unfold the way they're supposed to.

I lick my lower lip, fold my arms over my chest, and brace for hearing any or all of that.

Vivian is uncharacteristically silent. She fiddles with her ring, as if debating saying what's on her mind. Miraculously, she doesn't say more on the topic of Cris or me. She employs the tactic I've used often and to great success. She gives me a dazzling smile and backtracks.

"I didn't mean to pry. I wanted to make sure you were good." She cups my arm and rubs a few times. "I'm glad to hear you have it all figured out."

I tell myself I'm satisfied she stopped prying, but when she turns and walks away, I'm irked that she gave in so easily.

Also, is it me or did that bit about her being glad I had it *all figured out* sound a tad sarcastic?

CHAPTER TWENTY-THREE

Benji

"Slower," I hiss between my teeth as I try to endure another stroke.

I make it. *Barely.*

Cris is perched on top of me, gliding back and forth, her inner thighs clamping my legs, her hands on my chest, her plush bottom resting on my thighs. Her blunt fingernails dig in, the bite welcome. And Christ, is she tight. *So fucking tight.*

"Like this?" A devil's smile clashes with her sweet voice, but hell if I mind. She rotates her hips, lifting up and slamming down to take every inch of my cock. Her perfect breasts jiggle with each smooth slide. I tease her nipples, lifting my hips to meet her each time she's seated. I'm pleased to see she's losing her concentration. Before I have to employ the thumb-to-clit move, she finds her release. She's clenching around me and moaning my name, her hips moving in jerky starts and stops.

I help by holding her in place while her orgasm racks her. Another few intimate strokes and then I lose track of time, space—everything. My eyes slam closed and I clench my jaw. Lightning streaks up my spine. I spill into her tight channel, my fingers gripping her hips with enough force to leave bruises. I'm fairly certain I finished on a shout. I'm not a shouter, but *fuck*, that was good.

And so I say, "Fuck. That was good," when she collapses in a boneless heap on top of me.

Her cushiony breasts press against my chest. She sighs and the soft exhalation tickles my collarbone. When she kisses my neck, her hair tickles my chin. Blindly, since I haven't found the strength to open my eyes yet, I wrap my arms around her and silently beg her not to move. She doesn't. My heart pounds, communicating to hers without my permission—tapping out its own Morse code—for what, I have no idea.

She hums, places another kiss on my neck, and pushes off me. I swear I'm trying to let her, but my hands clamp her middle. I lift my hips, still trapped in her warmth and not wanting to leave. She laughs, wiggles back and forth, and eventually wins the fight. I blame my orgasm for zapping my remaining strength.

She returns from the bathroom, her petite yet curvy body gliding across my bedroom. I decide I've never seen a more beautiful sight.

"From now on, will you work naked? I'll close all the blinds," I vow.

"No." She lies next to me on her back, her head turned, her eyes on mine. "That breaks my rule."

She's broken a few of mine and I didn't think I had any.

Granted, "don't fuck your best friend" should be a given, you know?

"You already broke that rule." I tap the turgid tip of one of her nipples. "It's nearing two o'clock on a Tuesday. That is very much a workday."

"How was I supposed to react?" She clucks her tongue like she's mad at herself for capitulating. She hates when I'm right. She lifts an arm and drops it, explaining with two words. "The roses."

I grin. She went for a walk after lunch. While she was gone I filled her car with pink roses from Mom's garden. I mean, it was *packed.* I idled the engine and turned on the A/C so they wouldn't wilt, then waited outside for her to come back. The awestruck, flattered look of disbelief on her face when she stepped onto the driveway and encountered a car full of flowers was priceless. I immediately snapped another picture for my mental scrapbook.

Click.

Vivian put the idea in my head a few nights ago when she asked if I was considering putting together a bouquet. While having a cigar, I decided that since I vowed to teach Cris how to be treated well, I was going to make damn sure I treated her like gold.

"Did you like them?" I'm shamelessly fishing for compliments. I know she did. When she opened her car, she pulled an armload of the bouquets against her chest and looked over to where I was standing in the garage. Wetness shimmered in her eyes, and sweat glistened on her forehead as she regarded me over hundreds of pink petals.

Click.

Instead of worshiping me, she let out an exasperated

207

breath and then asked, "Where am I supposed to find vases for this many roses?" I told her she could use the bathtub. She rolled her eyes but instructed me to grab an armload of roses and meet her inside. From there I was thanked with many kisses. I returned the gesture by plucking her clothing off piece by piece.

"Mom called Manuel the other day," she says, sounding contemplative. I find it odd she didn't tell me this morning. Her mother calling is big news—that woman never calls. Out of everything Cris shares with me on any given day, I would think a call from Lina would be the headline.

"She's pregnant."

The blaring horn of a freight train sounds inside my head, sending my heart into a full gallop. I blink rapidly at the spinning ceiling fan, my own head spinning. My hammering heart returns to normal as my brain sluggishly processes her words. Apparently, the mere mention of the word "pregnant" has the power to send me into a panic. However, the "pregnant" person in this scenario is not the gorgeous, naked blonde I am sleeping with, but instead her mother. Still alarming, but nowhere near deserving of my Code Red reaction.

"You're kidding." I clear my throat when my voice sounds strangled.

"I'm not kidding." She sounds exhausted. I can imagine why. The news carries with it a hell of a lot of weight—way more than the sum total of pounds and ounces of a newborn baby boy or girl.

We are talking about the woman who was too irresponsible to raise her own kids, so she heaped that responsibility onto the oldest of them. If Cris was a different person and reported her mom, the state would have seen to it that Lina (or other available family members) performed her parental duties. But Cris didn't want to upset her brothers. She refused to risk them being taken and relocated. I remember my family being ripped away, what it was like to start over. The brothers I'm insanely grateful to have in my life were strangers to me back then. It was terrifying. How'd she know exactly the right thing to do for Manuel, Dennis, and Timothy when she was so young herself? I don't know, but she did. God, she's incredible.

"Manuel was almost robotic when he told me the news," she says. "I wish he had a better relationship with Mom. He had more time with her than Dennis and Timothy, which is alarming because it still wasn't much."

"Lift up," I instruct, unwilling to have this conversation without holding her. She snuggles in, and I wrap an arm around her shoulders. "Listen—"

Downstairs a desk phone rings. Her body stiffens against mine, her abs tightening like she is about to rise and run to answer it.

I squeeze her against me. "We're having an important meeting. Ignore it."

"Is that what this is?" She side-eyes me, but settles, her head on my shoulder and her arm draped over my middle. Idly, she strokes my chest. I ignore the flare of heat there, my normal reaction to her touching my body.

"Your brothers consider you a queen, Cris. They know you didn't have to do what you did. And if they haven't figured that out yet, you can rest knowing you loved them harder than anyone else in their lives. They know that, even if it's deep down."

It's what the Owens did for me. I didn't know what to make of my childhood. The grief overtook me at times. But when I was lost in the storm, I had Archer and William and Lainey and Nate. My ports. I struggled with grief for a while, but then it had no choice but to leave. There was too much in my life to be grateful for—so I hung on to that instead.

"I could have done more," she says. "I should have called Mom more and updated her on her sons, on their lives. Maybe if I would have tried harder, I could have pressured Timothy's and Manuel's fathers into taking them on the weekends or something."

"You were eighteen. And in no way responsible for the actions of divorced adults. That was on them."

"I was an adult."

"You were an adult in the eyes of the state, but you weren't prepared to raise three tweens."

She sighs. I'm right and she knows it.

"I don't wish Mom and I were closer," she whispers like she's ashamed to admit it. Her voice drops almost too low to hear when she further admits, "I... I don't like her."

I kiss her forehead. "Understandable."

"After losing your parents, who you loved more than anything, how are you this understanding when I say I don't like my mom?"

I pull in a deep breath. I don't talk about my birth parents often. Ever, really. Cris knows what happened to them as she and I have known each other for years. Every so often, she asks about Mom's paintings or lingers in the garage where I keep my woodworking tools to watch me build another frame. She's noticed the photos sitting around the house, most notably the one where I'm wearing Dad's white coat and oversize glasses. It's my favorite, even though I had no interest in becoming a doctor like him.

"She hurt you," I say. "She left you behind to raise your brothers, of which you did a spectacular job."

Cris told me Manuel checked off a few items on her honey-do list and mowed the lawn while he was there. If I knew she had more repairs or tasks other than the wobbly chair in the kitchen, I'd have done them for her. I suppose it turned out for the best. Manuel, a stubborn kid who has grown into a completely awesome guy, stepped in. I'm glad he has her back.

"She left you in charge of bus schedules and cooking dinner and helping with homework. You were both Mom and Dad to those boys and they won't forget it, honey." I hug her close when I share, "We don't forget the people who loved us when we felt unloved."

I feel her gaze on me, questioning, heavy, so I shift back to talking about her brothers. "Lina let you shoulder the worry of keeping those kids safe, of making sure they weren't pulled out of your care and rehomed. She gifted you with nothing but cares and worries while she lived any damn way she pleased, not giving a rat's ass about the family she should have been there for."

Cris sniffs. I'm not sure if she's crying. I hope not.

"You did a great job is what I'm trying to say." I hug her shoulders again.

"It's unfair your parents were taken away when mine walked away." Her voice is thick. Every instinct in me screams to lighten the conversation, but I don't want to brush it off since she started it. If she needs me to listen, I'm here for her.

"Did you ever meet your dad?" I bristle as I ask, realizing I've never asked before. Talking about family is a sensitive, intimate topic. And discussing it after a particularly sensitive, intimate act tempts me to flee the room in search of solace far, far away. But this is Cris, and like everything else she and I talk about, somehow this hallowed ground isn't so sacred.

"He left when my mom was pregnant with me. He never came back. He rode a motorcycle and had blond hair. That's all I really know."

"Explains your wild streak," I tease, unable to help myself. I'd do anything to erase the melancholy from her voice.

"Was it hard acclimating to the Owen household?" I'm not sure she's asked me that before. It seems we're both drifting out to sea and ignoring the buoys warning us we've gone too far.

"Yeah. I mean, I was ten. I wasn't sure where I fit in with the world, let alone with a family I didn't know. When I was adopted, there was just Archer and William and Lainey. I was an interloper. Then came Nate a year later, and I remember feeling this massive sense of relief. I was no longer the only kid who didn't fit. And he *really* didn't fit."

She laughs softly as her fingers dance over my skin.

"He was a big, rough kid. He scared the shit out of me at first. I stuck close to Archer for a few years and then Nate ended up being my best friend. My other best friend," I correct, placing a kiss on the top of her head. "We fought and played the way brothers do and eventually, an unbreakable bond formed."

"You three are inseparable. It's sort of awesome." Her voice is as soft as her touch. Her fingertips trail over my chest hair and tiptoe down my torso, tickling a path to my belly button before repeating the pattern. It feels good to be touched this way—to be touched by her.

"Sometimes I find myself wishing my parents were alive," I admit. "Then I feel like a traitor, because if they were I'd never know Nate, Arch, William, or Lainey. Or you. That is some fucked-up thinking. Knowing if I could turn back time and prevent the accident, I'd lose all of you. I think that might be worse than losing them. Now there's something to feel bad admitting."

"No, it's not." It's her turn to give me a comforting squeeze. "My life would suck without you in it. And the Owens." She shakes her head against my chest. "I don't want to think about it."

"You don't have to, Firecracker. I'm not going anywhere."

Two things happen then. First, Vivian's question from a few nights ago pops into my head. The one about how I'd feel if Cris were to marry someone else. Devastated. That's how I'd feel. I'd be a miserable, sorry sack and virtually inconsolable. Even now, the idea of her leaving me carves an ache deep in my chest.

Second, the phone rings again, bursting our bubble. Reality barrels in on our fantasy world. There's work to be done. A job we do together. We pull on our clothes in our respective corners of my bedroom and barely make eye contact while doing it. She answers the phone, first putting on her "work voice." I smile sadly as I realize I know she has a "work voice" to put on.

Reality is a world away from where we were an hour ago, shucking our clothes and our inhibitions and talking about the things you talk about when you're lying skin to skin with someone you care for very much. Caring for her was never up for debate. I adore her. But there's something different about the way I care about her since we started sleeping together.

When I propositioned her, I told her, as well as myself, that it was just sex and I was providing a service. Once she gave me the go-ahead, I dove in tongue-first, content to give her everything she wanted out of her first time. Her third. Her *tenth*.

I sit at my desk, frowning at the screensaver on my laptop —photos of me with Nate and Archer on a golf course. One of William and me shaking hands after I accepted my high school diploma. Another of me kissing Lainey on the cheek on her birthday while she holds a giant bouquet of flowers.

Cris's musical laugh from the other room slices me open and reveals the ugly parts I've been trying to keep hidden for decades. I haven't successfully relegated what we're doing to "just sex." I can't categorize what she means to me as "just" anything.

When this ends and she's here every day, clothed, and *not* kissing me by the coffee pot or flirting with me when she strolls by my desk, how the hell am I going to handle it? Before we had sex, I thought we could chalk it up to fun and move on. Now, though... Knowing what I know...

How the hell am I going to let her go?

CHAPTER TWENTY-FOUR

Cris

I'm at Club Nine, Archer's nightclub, for Nate and Vivian's engagement party, toddling along in a pair of borrowed shoes—one of the many pairs of Christian Louboutins Vivian owns. I'm doing my best not to resemble a newborn foal on shaky knees attempting to stand for the first time. Apropos, considering I'm navigating new territory tonight.

"How do you walk in these things?" I ask as Vivian and I come to a stop at the bar. I rest my hand on the surface, relieved to have something to lean on. My toes hurt. Like, every one of them.

"It's all in the calves," fabulous Vivian answers. "Takes quite a bit of willpower too. You don't want to think about it too much. Actually, it's a really good practice in mindfulness." She says it so sincerely I can't help laughing.

"It's sweet of Archer to throw you guys an engagement bash." Especially since he shut down the club to do it. I can't imagine how much money he's losing by closing the doors on a Saturday night. Nate mentioned the high demand to book the VIP room for next weekend. Archer evidently knows what he's doing. He made his club more in demand by closing it to the public for one night. He does things his way and doesn't apologize for it. It's admirable.

That said, I also noted how happy he looked when Nate thanked him during a quick speech after everyone arrived. Archer has a head for business, but he's not only business. He loves his family and would do anything for them.

Benji and I arrived together, but I noticed a gap between us as we listened to Nate gush over his bride-to-be. Nate held Vivian's hand, thumbed her engagement ring, and promised to love her for eternity. My romance-loving heart did cartwheels.

There's nothing official left on the agenda for this evening. Nothing to do but drink, dance, and be merry. Common for an Owen get-together, but my being here with Benji is new.

As in *with* Benji. As in I'm his date. He said he was sick of pretending nothing was going on. That if anyone could understand why he and I were here together, it was Will and Lainey. So, we entered the club holding hands. It felt like a finale of a romantic comedy. My arm in his, a frozen smile on my face, as I worried about what the world would think.

His dad was polite and nonchalant. Lainey pulled me into a side hug while giving Benji a "we'll talk later" look.

"There he is!" Vivian exclaims. I jump, startled by her outburst. She rushes from the bar to embrace her younger brother, Walt, and crushes him into a bear hug.

It wasn't long ago Walt showed up on her doorstep,

preceded by an urn full of their father's ashes, no less. He's a recovering alcoholic. Viv says he's doing well working for Nate and living in the Windy City. The pretty, tattooed brunette on Walt's arm must be the woman he vowed to marry. Vivian has mentioned her. I can't remember her name, but I know her own lapse with addiction landed her back in her home state of Georgia for a stint.

Vivian leads them over, her holding Walt's hand, his other hand in the tattooed woman's hand. When they're close, Viv gestures to her brother. "You remember Walt."

"Of course. How are you?"

"Hi, Cris." He has a big smile and an angular face. He looks well. "This is my girlfriend, Dee."

"I love your curly hair." Dee is as wide-eyed as I was the first time I was steeped in Owen wealth. Walt appears less impressed, I assume because he came from Steele money.

"This place is amazing!" she calls over the music. "Are you Archer's girlfriend?"

I open my mouth to correct her assumption when someone else does it for me.

"Hell no," the slightly possessive voice behind me affirms one second before a strong arm wraps around my waist. Benji tugs me to his side. "She's too classy to hang out with the likes of Archer."

"How's it going?" Walt asks before shaking Benji's hand.

"Good, Walt. You?"

"Good." Walt doesn't answer like it's a passing thought. He holds Benji's gaze and nods while folding his hand into Dee's once again. "Really good."

Aww. I'm such a sucker for a happily ever after. I hope they find theirs.

"I'm going to show them around and introduce them to a few very important people, namely my future in-laws." Vivian's smile is contagious.

"Go, go. Benji can look after me." And keep me from falling on my ass when I attempt to walk in these shoes again. I hold on to him for purchase just in case.

Vivian, Walt, and Dee walk through the club. Nate intercepts them and reclaims his future bride. He bends to kiss her before he shakes Walt's hand and kisses Dee on the cheek.

"Was that a deep sigh of longing I heard?" Benji murmurs into my ear.

Busted. "I was standing in this club, at this very bar, when I asked Vivian to indulge me with stories of her and Nate. I'm a sucker for romance."

"You never told me that."

I blush. I can feel my face flame. I glance down at my borrowed shoes before tracking my gaze up his black jeans and black T-shirt and finally land on his eyes. He looks amazing. With all his thick, dark, perfectly styled hair and shoes that cost even more than the ones I borrowed this evening.

"Why would I tell you?" I ask, not knowing what else to say.

"What do you mean?" His smile is intact, but he doesn't sound happy. "We talk about all sorts of things."

"I know." We argue rarely, if ever. Tonight isn't the time or the place to have a spat. I wrap my arms around his neck, which admittedly feels strange knowing his family could be watching, and distract him the best way I know how. I lean in and kiss his mouth. His hands cup my hips, which I've draped in a classy black dress. It's new. And so is what's underneath it. I have a surprise for him tonight.

"Maybe we should sneak out early and have our own private party." Climbing to my tiptoes, I place another kiss on the center of his mouth. "Wait'll you see what I'm wearing under this dress."

"You can't keep me chained to the bed, Cris. You have to take me out and show me a good time on occasion. I'm starting to feel used." Despite the complaint, he lingers over my lips for a lengthy kiss. "How about a drink?"

Once a short glass of scotch is in front of him and a tall glass of chardonnay is in front of me, he gives me a look I can't classify. His smile seems to be hiding something.

I take a fortifying sip from my wineglass. "What's on your mind, Benjamin Owen?"

"I'm glad you asked." He glances around the club before sipping his scotch and then pinning me into place with his gaze. "I've been thinking."

"About what I'm wearing under this dress?" I lean in, giving him full view of my cleavage revealed by the low cut of the bodice. I'm almost desperate for him to keep things light, but I can tell by the serious set of his eyebrows he's not going to.

"About us. About what we're doing."

A chill skates over my skin. I knew this conversation was coming. And I knew he would be the one to start it. "What we're doing" was always going to end. I knew from the beginning, and I knew no matter when it ended, the end would come too soon for me.

If there's one thing I know for sure about my best friend, it's that he ends relationships before they become too close. I'm well-prepared for this moment. Sure, I might have accidentally fallen in love with him, but I'm a grown woman. I can handle whatever he's about to tell me. Though an engagement party is a particularly bad place to break up with me, maybe sooner than later is best. I ignore the cracking sound of my heart and give him a smile, telling myself I'm ready. Then I betray my own sound and steady advice and try to postpone his announcement.

"Why don't we wait until we're somewhere private to talk?" I hold up a hand like a stop sign. He touches his palm to mine and weaves our fingers together. Then he rests his elbow on the bar and we sit there, hands intertwined, eyes on each other.

"I don't want to wait any longer to say this, so it's going to have to happen here. In the midst of this noise and my family."

I swallow thickly. He so...resolute. I nod and wait for the words I've been expecting since the night he made me the craziest offer of my life. I take a hearty drink from my glass, awkwardly maneuvering around our joined hands to set it aside on the bar.

"I'm ready," I say, but I'm not.

"Let's keep doing this."

"Holding hands?" I frown, confused.

"This. Us. It's working. You like it. I like it."

True story. I do like it. But that's not what I thought he was going to say.

"Uh... Until when?"

"Why set an end date?" He shrugs. "Why not keep..." He grins and waggles our hands. "Doing what we're doing until we stop liking it?"

So many reasons. The primary one being my heart and how every other beat has Benji's name tattooed on it.

"My family likes you. They like seeing us together."

I'm still not sure how to respond. I didn't expect a proclamation of love, but him pointing out how well-received we are as a couple is somewhat hope-dashing in light of the intense feelings I have for him.

"People like what's familiar." That was my careful way of not agreeing or disagreeing.

"We're more than familiar. We're good together."

"Maybe so, but—"

"Definitely so."

"Okay, definitely so." My mouth is suddenly dry. I lick my lips. "We both know there is an expiration date coming, and to pretend differently is...unwise."

"Why?" His terse question has a knife's edge.

"Why?" I laugh the word. I don't want to do this, and I especially don't want to do this now, but he hasn't left me much choice. "Benji, when are you going to throw a party like this one?"

His eyes sweep the room as a perplexed expression takes over his handsome features. "A private party at Archer's club? Whenever. What kind of party do you want to have?"

Oh, Benji. I sigh as I untangle my fingers from his. I pray the smile on my face will gentle the blow of my words. "I'm talking about an engagement party. To the woman you're going to marry."

His head snaps back. He's no longer perplexed. He's alarmed. "Never, if I'm lucky." He blinks, then his shoulders sag a bit. "Don't tell me you're planning on having an engagement party here in the future. That would be weird for everyone."

"What are you—?" Then it dawns on me what he means.

"How could I be engaged? As long as I'm spending time with you, I won't find anyone else to marry. And you are never getting married. I've heard you say so yourself on many, many occasions. Marriage and children aren't in your future." Not only has he said that to me, but I have also overheard some form of that argument come out of his mouth when he's talking to one of his brothers.

"It's settled then," he says, and I chuckle again.

"Nothing is settled." I break it to him gently. "I *am* going to be married one day. And unlike my mother, who seems to think marriage is like having a birthday and she has to have one every year, I'm only doing it once."

His mouth slides to one side at my joke. But I'm not through yet.

"I don't hold it against you." I knew the score from the beginning. What we have was supposed to be temporary. He can't give me what I want—permanence, and I can't give him what he wants—a shallow relationship with no end date. It was never going to work out. There is no happily ever after for us, unless you count our friendship. I'd die before I let anything happen to that. "Marriage is not for you, and that's okay. But it's also the reason we need to set an end date on what we're doing. We can't let your family expect us to be together for an extended period of time when there's no future behind it."

What I don't say is that most of the expectations that need managing are mine. I'm the one who needs to keep my hopes in check. It hasn't been easy to give the man who has my friendship and my loyalty my body too. I have to be super careful not to toss my heart in with the pot. I've been double cautious not to tie the strings already connecting us into secure knots.

"What are you saying?" His mouth pulls into a deeper frown. "That we're breaking up tonight?"

"What? No. I admit I thought that's what you were going to say, and I wasn't ready to hear it."

"You thought I was going to break up with you?" Now he looks hurt.

"I'm not saying I'm in a hurry to end this." I take both his hands in mine. "I just want to make sure you've thought this through?"

It comes out like a question as I realize he *hasn't* thought this through. He hasn't considered who we are beyond moment to moment. He hasn't thought about what happens when we attend future events as "just friends" once again. He hasn't recited the explanation he'll have to give to his family about why he has a date and she's not me.

"You should be thanking me," I tell him. "I'm letting you off the hook. I am the ultimate *having your cake and eating it too*. And I'm so grateful. I have learned more from you than I've learned from anyone. I know exactly what to expect from a good man in the future. You taught me not to settle for less than the best."

As I'm talking, I cup one side of his face. My heart patters out an SOS. The big speech I've given both out loud and to myself a few times is kind of a crock.

Not even kind of. It's total crap.

My lie hits me with the force of a closed fist. I close my eyes and swear I see stars. When I reopen them I'm lost in the golden brown of Benji's stare. The truth is I *never* want this to end. Even though I'm sure about me marrying in the future. As sure as he is that he's not. Even though the cleanest way out is to cut our losses. Even though everything I told him is ultimately what's best for both of us, I don't want any of it to happen.

I love him too much to let him go. The idea of him with another woman is pure agony. I want to scream and beat his chest for asking to stay. I can't stay. Not like this.

If I do, I'll grow to resent him, even while stripping out of my clothes and riding his cock for the relief we both seek. Or maybe because of that, since I'll be falling deeper and deeper in love with him as he holds me at arm's length. He'll be embedded deep in my body, but he'll never let me into his heart. Not all the way.

There is also no way in hell he can know how I feel about him. His heart isn't mine for the claiming, which sucks, but I won't risk losing him entirely.

CHAPTER TWENTY-FIVE

Benji

Inf I haven't mentioned it a time or three already, Cris is absolutely right.

Her reminding me of our agreement at the beginning was brave and totally the right call. But she also agreed we didn't have to stop sleeping together right away. Thank God. My idea of never having an end date was kind of crazy. I'm not sure what I was thinking when I made that suggestion.

She's going to want to move on with her life. I can't monopolize her time indefinitely. Well, I *can*. Totally tempting given how I know I'll feel when she's with someone else, but shit. I'm not a total dick. What I am is a dedicated bachelor. Eventually she'll meet a guy who's not. Maybe have a few babies.

I hate that. But she deserves to be happy.

I'm half embarrassed to admit I was caught up in the

emotions bleeding out of Nate as he worshipped Vivian at their engagement party. His proclamations weren't made with sweat clinging to his forehead or with a shake of doubt in the hand holding the microphone. He was certain. How the hell does he do that? He's so damn transparent it's galling.

During his speech, happy tears shined in Cris's eyes. I wanted her hopeful smile to last forever. Then she admitted she was a romantic, and I started wondering why she never told me.

And then I started considering the things I've been doing for her. Like the rose petals and artisanal donuts the night she gave me her virginity. The fancy Thai dinner before I whisked her into a hotel room to blow her mind once again. The day I packed her car with pink roses and carried her to bed after.

Romance squared.

So okay, I was caught up before the party, but the party definitely put me in the mindset to suggest we don't stop. Nate's speech to Vivian was really something. Not the words he said so much as the way he looked at her when he said them. Like he'd reached up and plucked her out of the sky. Or maybe like she'd fallen and he caught her.

Ha. Actually, that did happen. Anyway, Vivian has changed since meeting Nate. She used to be guarded and hard. Careful and calculating. On Saturday night her smile was easy and her eyes only for him. I saw in those two something I swore I couldn't trust.

Permanence.

It looked damn good too. Easy, like Vivian's smile. I thought maybe I had it wrong. Maybe I could achieve permanence too. But, like I said, Cris was right. I was caught up, is all. Who wouldn't be? Nate and Vivian swept up everyone in their happiness whirlpool. Good for them. I mean that unironically, by the way.

Three days later, on a mundane Tuesday, I'm standing in front of the coffee pot in my kitchen waiting for my mug to fill. I've had a few days and nights to marinate on the idea of permanence. I came to the same conclusion I had before the engagement party briefly robbed me of my pragmatism.

Permanence is a nice idea, but it's a myth.

Absolutely nothing in life is permanent. Hell, life itself isn't permanent. Each of us will hang up our boxing gloves at the end of the last round, no exceptions. Nature isn't permanent. Trees drop their leaves every fall. Birds crash into windows and break their delicate necks. Gone in a snap. The pink roses I gave Cris withered and died within a week.

Sorry. That was bleak. But it's the truth. Pretending there is a never-ending daily rollover, or that there's a way to stretch the perfect now into eternity is a kid's dream. Being the kid I was, I learned at a young age dreams can turn into nightmares.

So, after a blip of irrationality appeared on my radar, I have once again come to my senses. I properly seduced Cris on Saturday night after we left the club—hey, she's the one who invited me to guess what she was wearing under her dress. I masterfully steered us out of the choppy waters of commitment and straight into my bed.

A good night turned into a better weekend. She stayed Saturday night. On Sunday, we woke up late and had more awesome sex before she headed home to do the requisite laundry and other unsavory weekend tasks belonging to those of us who practice regular "adulting."

A splashing sound yanks me from my thoughts. I blink at my coffee mug, currently overflowing onto the counter.

"Shit! Goddamn—" I muzzle the other swearwords I might have said. Cris is in her office and could be on the phone. Two seconds later she bursts into the kitchen, her hand over her chest, alarm in her wide gray eyes.

"I thought there was some sort of emergency out here."

"There was, but I'm handling it." I flash her a quick smile as I swap out one mug for another, carefully pouring the excess from mine so I can take a drink without spilling it down my shirt. I set both mugs aside and reach for the roll of paper towels, but she snatches it from me. "Sorry about the shouting."

She mops at the spill. "Everything else okay?"

Other than feeling totally and completely thrown off every day since Sunday? Everything is peachy. I smile and hope mine is more believable than hers. "Great. You?"

"Oh. Yeah. Great."

The silence that follows is stifling and for us, incredibly unusual. Maybe that's what's throwing me off. The sex on Saturday was amazing, and waking up to her on Sunday felt relatively normal—our new normal, anyway—but then Monday came and... Weird City, population: two.

I want old Cris back. The one I found attractive from afar but whose feelings I didn't have to worry about hurting.

Trish called yesterday. I didn't answer. I waited until Cris went home for the day and then I called Trish back. The bad news is her mom died. She was in tears when she told me. I guess there is no good news. The point I'm trying to make is, before Cris and I were sleeping together, I would've answered the phone call and not thought a thing about it. Now the idea of letting Cris make reservations for my dates is cringeworthy.

Which begs the question: Will we *ever* return to normal?

I need to talk to her about it, but not today. I'm too off-kilter today. I would probably make an ass out of myself. Correction: I *will* make an ass out of myself. The cosmic Magic 8-Ball has spoken. The universe is gleefully fucking with me, and the overflowing coffee mug is just one example of how.

"I knew things weren't going my way when that file was corrupted first thing this morning," I grumble, mentally cursing the universe as I help her clean up spilled coffee.

"Is Mercury in retrograde?"

"I can't blame Mercury for the coffee incident. I zoned out and pressed the brew button twice." I hold out my hand to take the soggy paper towel from her. "Stupid."

Our fingers brush and pure electricity skitters up my forearm. My chest tightens and expands before tightening again. I can't blame Mercury for that either. I don't know what the hell to blame. I don't know if there is anything to blame on anyone. She still works here. She's still my best friend. What the hell am I upset about? Like she said, I have my cake and I'm eating it too.

The thought makes me feel more confused and less grounded than before.

"If it doesn't stop raining, we're going to have to skip our run," she says. I turn to the window where the delicate summer raindrops fatten and pick up speed.

"I'm up for a skip day. God knows what'll happen if I go

229

outside. Twisted ankle? Heart attack? Sinkhole that swallows the entire park?"

"Very unlikely," she responds easily. I'm starting to think she's A-okay with everything and I'm the one wigging out. "As your coach, I will remind you that regular exercise is good for your heart and your mind." She taps her temple.

I can't resist pulling a reaction out of her. I wind one of her curls around my finger. "Coach? I thought you went by Firecracker now."

"Coach works too." Her smile wobbles, and it's not as sincere as she'd like me to believe. She's not A-okay at all. She's not herself, but to be fair, I'm not myself.

I'm not sure we can blame that on Mercury, either.

Cris

I have been wearing noise-canceling headphones for the last two and a half hours. I am working, but I definitely don't need complete silence to do it. What I need is a break from the strange vibe buzzing between Benji and me.

I'm not sure where it came from. Sure, the discussion at Club Nine wasn't the most comfortable one, but afterward we found our rhythm fine. The sex was great that night and the following morning, no surprise there. I didn't plan on staying over, but once we were snuggled in bed after wearing each other out, and Benji had turned on the TV hanging over his dresser, I couldn't motivate myself to leave. Especially knowing I would have to put on those damn shoes to do it.

Leaving on Sunday wasn't like I imagined. I didn't expect to do the walk of shame, but I did expect to feel at least slightly uncomfortable. Not so. We lay in bed, he brought me coffee, and then I drove home to do some housework. Come Monday I was convinced my worrying was for naught. Until I showed up and said hi to Benji. He was sitting at his desk like normal, but the way he looked at me before jerking his gaze away and mumbling "good morning" was anything but normal.

The awkward trend is continuing today, and for some reason it's making my skin itch. Well, not for *some* reason, but for a very *obvious* reason I'm trying not to acknowledge. Even noise-canceling headphones can't shut out the worry that I let the proverbial Siamese out of the sack.

Have I been acting like I'm in love with Benji? I have racked my brain and sifted through every conversation we've had over the last three days. Oddly enough, sex is the Switzerland of our relationship. The intimacy is there, but we transition out of bed and back in again without encountering any emotional landmines. Things just...go well. They start great and end phenomenally. I've had the orgasms to prove it.

So what's up with him being so not-Benji today? Yes, the corrupted file was irritating, but Josie was able to send most of the information in an older file, and he and I have been working all day to fill in the information we lost. I heard him on his video chat earlier. At one point he totally lost the thread of the conversation and asked Josie to repeat herself. He never does that.

Then there was the fleeting eye contact. More than once his gaze slid away from me only to return and slide away again. That wasn't normal for him. He likes eye contact. I like having eye contact with him. It's probably how we grew so close so quickly. There weren't a lot of boundaries between us in the beginning. How odd now that there are almost none, to have a gap the size of the Grand Canyon keeping us from relating to each other.

I don't get it.

I pull off my headphones and hear him talking on the phone in his office. His voice is low, gentle. Almost a murmur. Almost a *romantic* murmur.

I shouldn't listen. Eavesdropping is rude in any situation. Except for work, I justify. What if there is another problem with the file? As his life assistant coach, isn't it my job to anticipate his needs?

Yes. Yes it is.

I practically leap out of my chair and then linger in my doorway. His voice rolls down the short corridor between our offices. I quickly conclude he's not on a business call, but I can't make myself return to my desk.

"Of course I'll come. Was there ever a question I wouldn't?" Definitely his tender voice. I know it well as he's used it with me a lot. "You don't have to apologize for what happened last year." He pauses and then says, "I mean it, Trish. Don't think another thing about it. We were who we were. And now we are who we are. Sometimes things happen to bring people together. Maybe this is one of them."

My back hits the wall, and I have to fight not to sag down it and curl my arms around my knees. I was in his bed two days ago and now Trish is calling and he's speaking to her with his tender voice about...getting back together? Why is he being so damn nice instead of telling her no?

There's only one answer. Because he's *not* telling her no.

I was the one who drew the line between us very clearly. He's moving on. With Trish.

I'm trying not to hate her. And simultaneously trying not to cry. I should have known he couldn't stay out of the dating pool for long. That's not who he is. And wasn't my speech at Club Nine about how I knew who he was, and I knew who I was, and the best thing to do was to end this in a timely manner?

But that was before he took me home and made love to me and let me sleep over. That was before I let myself forget my righteous speech about how we should split up.

"I'll see you on Thursday," he says into the phone. "Seven o'clock. You too. Bye, Trish."

Ugh. I'm going to throw up.

I hustle back to my desk and put my headphones on. I try to look casual as I type on my keyboard, sending gibberish to the screen.

He steps into my office and waves his hand in front of my laptop to get my attention. Pretending to be surprised, I pull off the headphones and smile up at him.

He looks the same as he does every day. Painfully attractive in trousers and a button-down. His hair is perfect, his full lips—I know from experience—taste exquisite. He also looks different. He looks like he's no longer mine.

"I changed my mind about running." He holds up his cell phone. "Weather app says thirty percent chance of rain. I say we risk it. Why not, right?"

I can think of a few reasons why not to take risks. One being my stupid heart. Another being my misguided sense of optimism. I'm not sure if I'm more sad or enraged. Running with my boss/best friend/former lover would be the best way to burn off the confusing swirl of emotions clogging my bloodstream.

Twenty minutes later, I realize I'm dead wrong about that.

CHAPTER TWENTY-SIX

Cris

Benji and I are running in a veritable deluge.

I pause under a tree and then question my safety as thunder rolls by overhead, low and ominous. We're a few miles from the car, making this run an epically bad idea. Which seems to be the theme for my life lately.

"I guess a thirty percent chance is still a chance," my best friend calls over another peal of thunder. Rain is splattering his face and hair. We're soaked to the bone. I'm starting to get a chill from it. I didn't pack a coat since the sun was shining when we left. I should have known this was coming, which also mirrors my circumstance with Benji.

"I see we're the only morons here," I grumble. The park is abandoned. I turn to march in the opposite direction. It's going to be a long, wet walk but we don't have a choice at this point. I bump his arm as I pass him. "Meet you at the car."

"Hey, you all right?"

I shouldn't say anything, but as soon as he asks I know I'm not going to be able to help myself. My body has chosen a side in the sadness/rage debate. Rage won. "No, Benji. I am not all right."

"Aren't you supposed to find meaning in this?" He gestures to the sky as he blinks water out of his eyes. "You are a life coach."

There's a lightness to his voice like he's back to normal. And since my life isn't back to normal, that pisses me off.

"Oh, am I?" I shout over the driving rain. "Am I supposed to be totally *Zen* soaking wet and freezing my ass off? If you recall, I suggested we work out in the gym. The dry, temperature-controlled gym. You were the one who dragged us out here. Why don't you dispense the wisdom for a change?"

"What the hell's your problem?" he barks when I turn toward the parking lot again.

"I knew this was going to happen. I absolutely knew it." I also know I'm upset about way more than being caught in the rain or not bringing a jacket. I saw this coming and didn't do a damn thing to protect myself. Yes, the rain. Also, falling in love with my best friend. I'm officially an idiot. Someone buy me a jester hat. Believing we would somehow survive this experiment intact wasn't naive, it was grand-scale delusional.

"You haven't been yourself the last few days," he accuses.

"Me?" I stop walking. "What about you? You were the one who would hardly look at me on Monday. You were the one giving me forced smiles in the kitchen today. And what's up with that lovey-dovey phone call with *Trish* two days after I was in your bed?"

Oops. I wasn't supposed to bring that up.

His eyebrows crash together. "What are you talking about?"

"You didn't know I heard that, did you? I wasn't going to listen, but then you used *the voice*."

"What is 'the voice'?" He looks completely confused, and I can't decide if he's trying to avoid trouble or if he has short-term memory loss.

Memory loss is an outside possibility, but just in case, I explain. "I heard you on the phone saying you would meet Trish Thursday at seven o'clock. That's two days from now. What was your plan? Sleep with both of us? Or dump me before you crawl into her bed?" Steam escapes the fissure in my heart like a geyser might erupt at any moment. "I had no idea you would move on at lightning speed. I know I'm not supposed to be taking this personally, but it's kind of hard not to."

He has gone from confused to really, really angry. Adrenaline pours into my bloodstream, sending a thrill through my veins. He's finally as upset as I am, making him the perfect target for the accusation arrow I've loaded into my bow.

"You're mad about my plans with Trish. On Thursday. At seven o'clock."

It hurts to hear him state it so plainly. Nevertheless, I incline my chin. "Yes."

"You're invited."

My turn to be confused. "What?"

"To the viewing. Her mother passed away on Monday. She called to ask if I would come, told me I didn't have to, and then said to make sure to thank you for the flowers she knows you picked out and sent when her mother was sick.

And then she said, and I quote, 'I'd love to see Cris if she can make it too.'"

Rain splats the top of my head and tightens my blond curls into ringlets. I digest what he told me slowly. Shame creeps in as a low roll of thunder takes the worst of the storm with it.

I am a jackass.

A shiver climbs my spine. "I didn't know her mother passed away."

"So I gather," he says, his voice pure steel. "And yet it was easier for you to believe I was planning to have sex with her on Thursday night?"

It was. I'm not sure if that says more about who I am or more about who I think Benji is. I guess it doesn't matter. What we had was destined to come to an end. Why drag it out? Eventually he *will* call a woman and arrange a date, and it's going to hurt this badly or worse.

We shouldn't have slept together Saturday night. But I'm weak. My rain-soaked tirade proved how weak. He needs to move on. I need to let him. I need to move on too, taking the amazing memories with me. If we call a truce, maybe we can salvage the relationship we had before we had sex.

"I'm sorry," I say, willing to take the first hit. "Truly. Both for Trish and for accusing you of something you aren't guilty of."

"It's okay. For the record, I don't want her back. If you recall our conversation the night of the engagement party, it involved me asking you if you'd like to be the one who shares my bed."

"I recall." Vividly. It was everything I thought I wanted to hear. No end to Benji-and-Cris sex? Best news ever! Part of me still wants to yell *Cowabunga!* and leap into the unknown with him.

Stupid.

I've never had the privilege of being irresponsible. I've been raising kids for as long as I can remember. Similarly, Benji is my responsibility. My professional one and, as his life coach, my personal one too. Sleeping with him when we know it won't last is the epitome of irresponsibility.

"So. Are you going back to the car?" he asks carefully, his expression grave. I sense he's asking more than if I'm going back to the car. He's asking me if I'm turning my back on him too. Or if I'll continue on the path, weather the storm, and come back to him.

For now, anyway.

His wet T-shirt is molded to his chest. His running shorts are glued to his thighs. Raindrops trickle down his legs. I know what I want, but I also know what he needs. Even if he doesn't. He might not dive into a casual sexual relationship right away, but he's more than willing to have one with me.

I'm not a risk. I'm safe. And risk-averse Benji, who wouldn't dare dream of forever for fear of losing more than he already has, knows he can sleep with me and I'll still be his friend and coworker in the morning. Ironically, in his quest to teach me how I should be treated, the way he's treating me isn't good enough.

I can't go forward with him. There is no forward. I can stay and stagnate, or move on without him. I have to make the right choice for me, and because I know him well, I know what choice to make.

"It's time for me to go back to the car," I tell him, my heart breaking. The light drizzle of rain masks my tears. "I shouldn't have accused you of making me come out for a run. You didn't make me do anything. I did it to myself, even if I knew better deep down."

His eyebrows bend with sympathy. He's figured out I'm talking about way more than the rain or the run.

"I could've stayed in the gym," I continue, "where everything was familiar. I wanted to try something different. I don't regret it. I learned a lot about myself. Mostly that I don't like being caught in a downpour."

He looks around at the trees surrounding us, or maybe at nothing in particular. The smile returns to his face. The same smile he gave me the first time we met at his father's office ten years ago. The same smile he turns on to charm almost everyone he encounters. That smile doesn't set me at ease like it used to. It feels forced. Like a mask.

"Well, I'm obviously coming with you," he says, his tone jovial. "I can't let you walk through a soaking-wet park by yourself. Plus, I have the car keys." He offers his hand. "Come on."

Our fingers link together naturally as we walk the trail in silence.

I know what we've decided. He knows what we've decided. But neither of us talk about it. Not when we climb into the car. Not when we return to the office.

"I HATE THIS." Vivian is sitting across from me at a high-top table in a fancy wine bar downtown. It's Thursday night. I didn't go to Trish's mother's viewing. It was nice of her to invite me, but it's not my place to be there. Benji went as a friendly gesture, and I don't blame him. It was the right thing to do. He's a good person. And now that we have officially ended our sexual relationship, though we never said the actual words, it's time for him to do more things without me.

"Everything worked out for the best," I lie. "I had an absolute blast. I didn't lose my job or my best friend. You know Benji, he rolls with the punches better than anyone."

"I don't understand how he didn't fall for you. I've only known you a handful of months and I'm in love with you." She regards me tenderly.

"I love you too." Vivian and I have grown close. "But, hon, everybody knows you're in love with Nate. There's no room for me." I sip my wine. She doesn't smile at my joke.

"You can't be okay with this. It doesn't bother you that he let you go?"

Well, when she puts it that way, *yeah*.

"I'm the one who walked away."

"Yeah, I tried that too. I was hoping Nate would come for me, no matter what I said." She squints at me as if trying to see straight through to my soul.

"Our situation is not like yours and Nate's. It's been two days since the park, and everything is back to the way it should be. No more awkward standoffs at the coffee pot. Our jogs have been good, and dry." Still no smile from Viv. "We work together better than ever. We cohosted a video conference call and practically finished each other's sentences. Things are back to normal."

Except that I really miss him flirting with me, touching me casually, kissing me in the hallway. And the day we stopped in the middle of a workday to have sex wasn't bad, either. But what we had wasn't everlasting, and if I believed it was, I was lying to myself.

I take a gulp of my wine instead of a sip this time.

"Can you think of a better ending?" I ask, miserable.

"Yes. I can think of a lot of better endings."

I was afraid she'd say that.

"But." She takes in a deep breath and blows it out. "I support your choices. I always will. If this is what you want, then who am I to argue?"

From there she guides the conversation to wedding talk, and I, having become a master of compartmentalizing, lose myself in talking details and minutiae. I lean over her cell phone when she shows me photos of how her custom-made bridal gown will look when it's finished. I give her my opinion about the reception location and whether or not she and Nate should write their own vows. (Yes, obviously.)

"That leaves one question," she says an hour later as we each finish our second glass of wine.

"Which is?"

"Will you be my maid of honor?"

Gratitude thrashes inside me like a shark in the shallows. "Really?"

She nods, her smile wide and happy. Then, despite the promise I made to myself not to cry again this week, I burst into tears.

CHAPTER TWENTY-SEVEN

Benji

Down the road from Archer's fancy-pants condo is a community rec center complete with outdoor tennis courts, basketball courts, and a swimming pool with a diving board. His is a wealthy neighborhood, like mine, like Nate's. We opted to live around people who have healthy bank accounts not because we like rich people better, but because it makes us feel more normal.

Since the Owens built their empire while rearing Archer in his early years, Arch has admitted he doesn't remember doing without. My parents died when I was starting my fifth-grade year, and even though they didn't have Owen money, I didn't do without, either. Mom and Dad were professionals who put plenty of food on the table and lots of presents under the Christmas tree. Alternatively, Nate rode the struggle bus for most of his youth.

Before I lived in opulence, I imagined life as problem-free for the mega-rich. What a load of shit. Even if I only count the last week, my problem-free theory has been blown to smithereens.

I roped Archer into playing one-on-one today to mask my real reason for coming here. I need advice.

I lean on my brothers in a lot of areas. Work, predominately, but I talked to Archer and Nate about girls when I was a teenager. Especially when I was fumbling through first dates, first kisses, first time—condom use is a sensitive topic to bring to a parent. But I can't talk to Nate about my Cris issue. My Cris *nonissue*. He is a happy son of a bitch and doesn't need me weighing him down with my woman problems. And yeah, okay, I'm not totally philanthropical. I don't know if I can deal with his "up" right now. He asked me to be in his wedding. Archer and I are both best men. He said he'd fistfight either of us if we made him pick. He told us to flip a coin for who stands next to him—he refuses to choose.

Archer and I are smart, so we didn't fight him. Nate is a tank. Arch and I can hold our own, but neither of us are anxious to cross our Chicago-streets-raised brother. Nate's a guy you want on your side.

And *yes*, I did get fucking emotional when he asked me to be his best man. Luckily, we were at Club Nine. I downed a few tequila shots and danced it off. Fog machines are aces at masking tears.

Not that I cried.

Anyway.

Archer sinks a two-pointer without any defense from me whatsoever since I was lost in my head.

"You suck extra hard today," he tells me.

Nonplussed by being caught off-guard, I nab the basketball and dribble away from my brother, who doesn't catch me. I shoot. I do not score.

This dance goes on for fifteen minutes until sweat is pouring down our faces. It's too damn hot to do this today. I make one last attempt, swiping the slick ball from his hand. The ball hits the backboard, bounces off the rim, and... Nope.

Dammit.

Hands on my hips, I catch my breath. Sweat stings my eyes as I squint against the bright noonday sun. I'm considering going back to the office. Sunday or not, I could do the world and myself more good sitting in front of a spreadsheet.

"Seriously. Suckage." Archer tosses the ball at me and I catch it, cradling it under my arm and following him home like a sad-sack puppy. Rather than go inside, we collapse onto the chairs on his stone patio. It's cool under here, at least.

"Beer?" he offers.

"Yeah." I toss the ball onto the cushioned wicker chair next to mine. When an open beer bottle is offered to me, I slug back half of it, taking in the tiny yard behind his three-story condominium.

"Why don't I live here? It's fucking gorgeous. I have to mow the lawn today." On the top floor of his condo are bedrooms and bathrooms and a balcony. On the second, a screened-in porch leading to the kitchen and a living room with a half bath and a large office off to the side. Ground floor, where we are, offers the walk-out patio and a stone path cutting through the middle of a grassy area he *doesn't* have to mow. There is a fountain with flower gardens he doesn't plant or prune.

"You don't have to. You choose to," he states. Annoyingly.

I know I choose to. I chose familiarity. One of my favorite

memories is Dad mowing our backyard in Idaho. Sometimes he'd let me sit on the riding mower with him. Arguably not the safest thing to do with a seven-year-old, but he was a doctor and good at assessing risk. I am too. I used to be, anyway.

"What gives? You don't shoot the shit with me on a Sunday. Or ever."

I rest my beer bottle on my thigh and argue, "Yes I do."

"Not anymore." He slugs back half his beer in a few long swallows. Cheeks full, he raises his eyebrows and waits for me to tell him why I'm here.

"Cris and I broke up." I frown in thought. "Sort of."

"Sort of?"

"We weren't actually together, or well, we aren't actually apart." I shake my head, confusing myself. "Shit."

"Spit it out," my impatient brother snarls.

"Cris and I were, for lack of a better term, friends with benefits."

He grins.

"It's not funny."

"It's not funny at all. It's fantastic. A first for you."

This throws me. "What's that supposed to mean?"

"You prefer women who don't get close. Couldn't believe I saw you on an actual date with Cris at the fundraiser. Half of me thought 'finally' and the other half thought 'bad move.'"

I didn't think either of those things. I thought "awesome" and "what could possibly go wrong?" I'm beginning to think, of Cris and me, I'm the more naive one.

"If anyone knows about not getting too close, it's you," I lash out, slightly stung by his comment. It's true I have had a lot of brief relationships, but it's not like the women I've dated hate my guts afterwards. Look at Trish. That turned out fine.

"Women don't like my focus on work," Archer argues, stroking his beard. "If I found a workaholic who lived out of state, maybe that'd change everything." His eyes glaze over as he stares off in the distance, and I wonder if he's thinking of the brunette he met in Florida. I don't know if she's a workaholic, but she does live out of state.

"You hired Cris to be your assistant life coach," he says after a beat.

"Life assistant coach," I correct automatically, remembering how cute she was when she rolled her eyes the first time I used her title. I think briefly of my calling her "coach" and decide I won't do it anymore since she doesn't like it. The nickname Firecracker has to be retired, though. A damn shame. My stomach clenches, but I ignore the pain.

"Whatever," Archer says. "Point is, she knows what she's doing. She hasn't steered you wrong yet."

Did I steer her wrong? During our time sans clothing, I was the one doing the steering. Or so I thought. I feel less like the captain and more like I'm bobbing in the ocean in a life preserver. Or clawing onto the edge of a door while slowly freezing to death like poor Jack in *Titanic*.

At first, I was in charge and running the show, but since I asked for an extension and she refused, I've been rethinking. Overthinking. Questioning.

"Something feels off," I say, almost to myself. I set the beer on the patio. My stomach tosses, as if thinking about the ocean left me seasick. Maybe the heat is getting to me, or maybe alcohol after so much physical activity wasn't a great idea.

"You look off, man."

"It's the heat," I explain, unconvinced.

I say goodbye to my brother, who waves and tells me to feel better and "don't sweat the life coach. It'll work out."

On the drive home I recall many, many pieces of advice Archer has given me, all of them sound. He's older than me, so he walked me through my first richy-rich affairs and made sure I knew how to behave, where to sit or stand, what to say when meeting a family friend or a potential presidential candidate.

So why, when he laid it out for me just now, am I railing against his advice and my own? Could Archer be...wrong?

My stomach tosses again.

I reach for my cell phone as I maneuver into the left lane and brake at a stoplight. When Nate answers, I tell him, "I'm coming over."

I hear Vivian murmur, "Is everything okay?" and realize I'm interrupting.

"It can wait," I say, prepared to excuse myself. Next, I'm talking to Vivian.

"Benji, get your ass over here." I hear her tell Nate she's getting dressed and then I *know* I'm interrupting. By the time he's back on the phone, the decision has been made.

"See you soon," he tells me.

"SPRITE," Vivian announces, and I take the glass from her hand. I'm standing next to their dining room table where Odessa has left a spread of salad, fruit, and sandwiches for lunch.

"Thanks," I say. Nate offered me lunch and I nearly

hurled. Vivian decided Sprite would fix me right up. I kind of doubt it, but the gesture was nice. "Enjoy your food. I'm going to step outside."

She exchanges a glance with Nate that tells me at least one of them isn't going to leave me alone. Sure enough, when I walk outside my oldest brother follows.

The view from his back patio is very different from Archer's. It's similar to mine, but his backyard is larger without the addition of a swimming pool, heated or otherwise. Then I notice the hot tub. "This new?"

"It is. We've been in it almost every night."

"I don't want to know," I say. I really don't. If I had a hot tub at my house, I know exactly what I'd be doing in it with Cris "almost every night." Not that I have the option to do anything with her any longer. My throat grows thick, making it hard to swallow.

"What's going on with you, man?"

"Why does everyone keep asking me that?" I snap.

He doesn't so much as flinch. "You are typically a macaron."

He lost me. "A macaron."

"Yeah, light and airy. And definitely more upbeat than you've been lately. Does this have anything to do with the conversation Viv had with Cris?"

"What did Cris say to Viv?" My ears perk.

"That's a yes. And if you think I'm telling you, you're insane." He takes a pull from his water bottle and walks out to the yard to stand in the sunshine. I trail his steps, my feet sinking into the thick, plush green grass as I go. "Remember when you were thirteen and had that math competition? The televised one."

It's an odd turn of topic. I'd rather know what Viv and Cris talked about. If Cris is suffering from doubt and worry the way I am, or if she's living her best life now that she doesn't have to juggle me in another capacity other than boss/best friend. Did I make everything harder for her? I'd try and steer the conversation but I know instinctively I'd be wasting my time. When Nate digs in, he does so with an oak tree's roots. He's not going to tell me anything even if I do indulge him. But hey, it's worth a shot.

"What was that show called?" he asks.

"*Divide and Conquer*," I say.

"Right." He chuckles. "So fucking dorky."

"Hey, we were serious." I came alive whenever we practiced. I was the best on our team—the ringer by a long shot. Numbers make sense to me. Which reminds me of the conversation about numbers Cris and I had at the restaurant. The morning I tried out some dirty talk and was thrilled down to my Ferragamos when she liked it. My naughty Firecracker. Only she's not mine anymore. If she ever was. My shoulders sag.

"You don't have to remind me how serious you were," my brother says. "You made yourself so sick you didn't eat for two days before the show."

"Come on." That can't be true.

His eyebrows wing skyward. "Ask Lainey. She was finally able to coax you into having orange juice so you didn't pass out on stage. I heard Will tell her he was sure you were going to fall off your chair. I was in the audience with them, willing you to succeed. Your face was paste white. The show went on, and remarkably, so did you. Live TV, and you pulled it out in the clutch."

I feel a smile curl my lips, the first in days. I recall the weight of the buzzer in my grip, the way the answers flashed on the screen of my mind. We slayed it. The other team was fast, but we were faster.

My smile fades when he shakes his head and adds, "Before then, God, you were miserable."

"Is there a point to this tale other than my humiliation?" I sip my Sprite and my stomach gurgles in protest.

"What do you think's going on here?" He points at my glass. "You and Cris split up and you can't eat."

"That's ridiculous."

"Is it?"

"Yes," I say with a certainty I don't feel. Just because I skipped lunch and dinner yesterday and couldn't hold down the piece of toast this morning doesn't mean anything. "I have a bug or something. I'm fine. Cris was right. She's always right. She is my life coach, you know." I stare at him, silently begging him to share a snippet of what she said to Vivian.

"Yeah, and she's up to her eyeballs in you, just like you're up to your eyeballs in her. How can either of you see anything clearly when you're drowning in each other?"

Holy shit. I can't believe that worked. Before I can cling to hope, I shake my head. He can't be right. Maybe I need to point out I'm the one freezing my ass off while clinging to the door Cris is safely floating on. Somehow though, I don't think he'll understand. I could lose the *Titanic* references and try and explain some other way. Explain how she and I have everything under control and eventually life will return to normal. There may be dregs from our sexual relationship, but they won't last forever.

In the end, I don't explain. I tell him what's been looping

my brain like a stock car on a racetrack. "She's getting married once. I'm getting married never. That's what she told me when I suggested we keep doing what we were doing."

His eyebrows rise. "You wanted more."

Those words are a punch to the sternum. I fight for my next breath. "I don't want more. Not like you mean."

"You sure about that, Pukey?"

"I didn't puke on *Divide and Conquer!*" How many times am I going to have to remind him?

"Only because you didn't eat. And you didn't eat because you were torn up over the idea of losing the tournament. A stupid math tournament, Benj."

"It wasn't stupid," I grumble. "I know what you're angling for, but you're wrong. I didn't lose a tournament. And I didn't lose Cris."

"She might be in your office, but she's not in your bed. You lost her. Which would not be a big deal if you never wanted anything long-term in the first place. You just said you do."

"*She* doesn't!" My arm starts shaking, rattling the ice in my glass. I put my hand to my forehead. I need to get the hell out of here. "Thanks for nothing. I talked to Archer, and he wasn't a whole hell of a lot of help, either. The more I talk about what happened with Cris, the more lost I feel. I may as well be the center of the Bermuda fucking Triangle for all the help the two of you are being. I was looking for a tiebreaker."

"Kinda hard to have the tiebreaker when you don't know how you feel. Or rather, you *do* know how you feel but won't admit it. You want to know what I think? Really?"

At the idea of him sharing more hard truths, my stomach

does another barrel roll. Nevertheless, I need honest feedback and he'll never lie to me. So I say, "Yes."

He faces me, his crooked nose shadowing his frowning mouth. When he was at my house last year, he looked similar, more desolate, but similar.

"Do I want to hear this?"

"I don't know," he admits with a headshake. My hand automatically goes to my stomach at his bleak tone. He doesn't look happy about what he's about to say, but he lays it out. With the brute force you'd assume would come from a guy his size.

"You're in love, brother."

I try to laugh but the noise escaping my lips is more of a pathetic wheeze. Biting my lip, I scan the immediate area around me, the lush grass and the fence, the sun-dappled trees with mulch at their bases. There's nothing in my eyeline offering support, save for the man who just delivered a throat punch in a silk pillowcase.

"That's not..." Shrugging for effect, I try to sell it. He waits, eyebrows lifted. "She's not..." Another headshake from me. Nate slow-blinks, appearing slightly disappointed.

"Look. I understand with your upcoming nuptials you might think this is what is going on, but I'm telling you..." My throat constricts, cutting off my words.

"Like I said." He caps his water bottle and gives me a supportive slap on the shoulder. As he walks past me toward the house, he calls over his shoulder, "Better 'fess up and win her back or invest in a lifetime supply of antacids. Your call."

There in the middle of Nate's lawn, my stomach in turmoil and my Sprite fizzing audibly, I realize he might have a point. And that I am a giant fucking moron. Being with Cris was easy. Almost too easy. My whole adult life I've thought of relationships as complicated. *Temporary.*

My argument about permanence being a myth seems incredibly shallow when I remember our time together. She's my best friend for a reason. I trust her implicitly. She trusted me too.

She made a mistake.

Not in trusting me with her virginity, but trusting me with a tender part of her that I totally manhandled. We crossed a line, and in doing so, uncovered another layer we hadn't acknowledged until now. Is it possible our relationship was built to last? Is she The One? Who the hell knew that was a real thing?

I have my answer when I step back into Nate's house. Vivian is arguing with him about mayonnaise, of all things. He's gesturing with the butterknife in one hand, a slice of sandwich bread in the other, defending his position. They pause when they notice me in the doorway. Her face melts into a smile that is both sad and satisfied.

"Oh, Benji." Her arms close around my neck. I catch my brother's proud smile over her shoulder. No, not proud. Loving. He loves this woman and he should. She's a good person. A *great* person. At one point she didn't allow herself to have nice things, either. Nate loved her regardless. The same way Cris loved me.

"I think I fucked up," I say, my throat suspiciously tight.

She holds me at arm's length. I search her face for a reason to have hope, anything hinting I'm not too late to save what Cris and I had...if I didn't already annihilate it by being a selfish, clueless prick.

"I've never been in love before," I tell her.

Her smile widens. She pats my cheek. "It's easier than you think."

I cling to those words as tightly as Jack clung to the door. Hopefully, things turn out better for me than they did for him.

CHAPTER TWENTY-EIGHT

Cris

"**D**o you want me to kick his ass?" Dennis asks.

I was able to convince all three of my brothers to come home for a late Sunday dinner. I blamed my sadness on living alone. While cooking and baking in preparation for their arrival, I convinced myself that when the house was once again filled with their raucous, youthful energy, my sadness would magically vanish. It didn't work out that way.

Somewhere between saying "pass the salmon salad" and announcing we have a chocolate cream pie for dessert, the sadness hit me tenfold. I sobbed over my empty plate. Full-on ugly cry.

Six hands lifted me out of the chair and corralled me into the living room. Now I'm sitting on the sofa, Dennis on my left, Timothy on my right. Manuel, arms folded over his chest, is taking up a stuffed chair in the corner. His frown hints at the battle scene taking place in his imagination.

"Remember when I said I was happy for you?" he growls. "I take it back. I'll go with Dennis to kick Benji's ass."

Their rallying to my defense is sweet, but there is no one to blame. Benji was being Benji, and I was being myself. My own delusion made me believe I could have sex with a man I was already half in love with and not fall the rest of the way. Maybe I'm the one to blame.

I swipe my eyes with a tissue and give my brothers a watery smile. "Nobody's ass needs kicked."

"Needs kicking," Timothy corrects with a smile. He places a supportive hand on my knee.

"That too." I sniff. "I still love my job. He's still my friend. My heart was confused when we went back to the way we used to be. I just...have to sort it out. In my head." God knows sorting it out with my heart hasn't done any good. "I haven't sorted it out yet."

Understatement of the millennium.

At work I am plagued with memories of my orgasm on the couch or kissing Benji in the kitchen. I have to wind my hand into a fist to keep from reaching for him or blurting out that I made a giant mistake by telling him I didn't want to continue our relationship. Maybe we could keep our sexual affair and I could give up the idea of marriage altogether. Most marriages don't last anyway, right? I'm so damn miserable. I'm beginning to believe part of Benji would be better than none of him.

But I don't have "none" of him, either. I have him as a boss, as a friend. We work out, though I refuse to step foot in the downstairs gym. I fear my own volatile reaction if I even catch a glimpse of the stone shower. What happened in it will forever live in my memory as one of the best moments of my life. I keep telling myself the addition of sex into our stable relationship made us unstable. Like too much water in an overflowing stockpot, doomed to spill over and steam away on the cooktop.

Only the pot has nearly boiled dry. I've lost the intimacy we had when we were sleeping together, and I've lost the ease we had as friends. We can't seem to find the comfortable middle we so effortlessly carved out over the last year and a half. But I'm not going to stop trying. I treasure his friendship. Losing it is unacceptable. We shared things over the last two months we never shared before. We told stories from our pasts we never told before. We were different. We were good. Really good. Which is why this hurts so much.

I touch the compass necklace at my throat. I shouldn't be wearing it. It was Benji who reminded me I was my own true north. To trust my own judgment. I'm not sure I can. Look where my judgment landed me.

"What is there to sort out?" Manuel shakes his head. "You're clearly in love with him. And he broke your heart."

"He didn't break my heart," I say in my defense, the words etching my throat as if they're fighting being spoken. "Anyway, you don't know him. He doesn't have the same plans I have. Staying with him means relegating myself to dating without the promise of a future. I can't do that to myself. Or you guys."

In unison, Dennis and Timothy both say, "Us?"

Manuel chimes in with, "What does this have to do with us?"

"Everything has to do with you three. You're my brothers and I love you. I would die before setting a bad example for you guys. I want you to know what's possible in the world."

"That's a shit reason to get married," Timothy blurts.

"Hey—" But before I can remind him not to swear, Manuel cuts me off.

"What if one of us decides not to get married?"

"Or what if one of us ends up divorcing, or marrying two or three different people over a lifetime?" Dennis says.

"Are you going to disown us? Write us off because we're like Mom?" Timothy asks.

"Of course not!" My head swivels to each of them. Surely they don't think I'd disown them over something so trivial. "I love you too much. And that's hardly the same thing."

"It's exactly the same thing," Manuel argues. "You don't have to try to live a mistake-free life because Mom has made seven of them."

"And you wouldn't ask us to be perfect," Timothy says.

"You never expected us to be perfect," Dennis adds.

"Yes, but I'm the oldest and I go first. I have a responsibility to be a good role model."

"You are a human being first," Timothy says. Look whose psychology class is paying off. "We're our own role models. You can't control what we do, but you can be yourself, Cris. Who you *can't* be is Mom."

"She's cornered the market." Dennis smirks and then stands and looks to Manuel. "I still say we kick his ass."

Manuel stands.

"I'll drive." Timothy stands as well.

I need to put a stop to this before they stir up trouble for everyone. "Why don't we eat some chocolate cream pie instead?" I look around at my taller-than-me brothers and realize I'm addressing grown men. Not the little boys I helped with homework or bandaged their scrapes. They tower over me, unconvinced. "I promise I'll talk to him tomorrow morning. If he says something stupid, *then* you can kick his ass." When I'm greeted with stone faces, I add, "I'll drive you there myself. Okay?"

Manuel nods once. "Okay."

I start for the kitchen, but Dennis wraps his hand around my arm. Always the affectionate one, he pulls me into a hug first. Manuel embraces me next and then Timothy joins in. I sigh, not crying despite the urge to release the pent-up, confusing emotions swirling inside of me. Instead I soak in the moment and the love of my brothers who have my back no matter what.

I'm then told to sit down. Dennis asks if I want coffee or tea. Timothy and Manuel shove each other playfully as they walk to the kitchen and argue over who will eat the most pie.

Manuel shouts, "Ice cream too?"

"A lot of ice cream," I shout back.

I shouldn't feel better, but I do. The heartbreak—fine, I admit it's broken—will keep until tomorrow.

Hours later, I'm slouched on the couch watching *Friends*, not having bothered to change out of my jeans and T-shirt. I ate more pie and ice cream than I want to talk about. I don't want to go to bed. I don't want tomorrow to come. Not that sitting here watching reruns of my favorite sitcom is going to stop time. If anything the distraction is accelerating it. This episode is particularly funny, but I can't muster up the energy to laugh.

My cell phone rings. I recognize Benji's ring tone immediately. I blink at the clock, slightly worried he's calling me at eleven p.m. Snapping into assistant mode, I pick up, anticipating a work problem.

"Hey, is everything okay?" is how I answer.

"In life coach terms, no. I need you. Can you come over?"

"Of course." I'm already off the couch and sliding my feet into sneakers. "I'll be there as soon as I can."

"Thanks, Cris," he says, his voice scarily toneless.

"Are you sure everything's okay?" My heart is pounding, sending buckets of adrenaline to my bloodstream.

"Nothing's okay. I'll explain when you get here." Then he's gone.

Well, that was ominous. I grab my purse and dash out the door. On the drive to his house my mind concocts one worst-case scenario after another. Thankfully the rational part of my brain is functioning. If one of his family members was hurt, he would've led with that. If someone was in the hospital, I'd be heading there instead.

He said it was a life coach problem, which could still mean something happened with work. Maybe he has to fire somebody he likes and wants tips for how to handle it.

Except none of that makes sense, either. He doesn't have a case of nerves at work. That's the area where he absolutely shines. He's lost in work every day at his desk. Which is why I refill his water, bring him hot tea instead of a fourth cup of coffee, and schedule his workouts so he doesn't forget. That's my job.

No other reason?

No. None.

Mourning what could've been isn't going to help solve whatever problem he's having tonight. I'm sure he has a very good reason for calling me, and after time well spent with my brothers, I'm more than prepared to tackle it.

I park in his driveway and climb out of the car, my cell

phone in hand. He must've seen me coming. The garage door opens a second later. I see the shoes first. Shiny, expensive. Then dark trousers, a thick leather belt. By the time his checked shirt gives way to his handsome face, my knees are weak. I remind them to stay strong. *We can do this.*

Other than the weird garage-door reveal—I typically enter via the front door—nothing else seems out of place. His hair is fantastic as usual and, other than the dark hollows under his eyes suggesting he hasn't slept much lately, he looks good.

"Boy, am I glad to see you." He wastes no time coming to me, and my stupid heart, who really cannot take a hint, pounds mercilessly against the walls of my chest. I silently lecture her, a fruitless endeavor.

He takes my hand and pulls me through the garage, past a bench and his latest woodworking project, and finally into the house.

I gasp when I step into the kitchen. It's so bright that for one terrifying second I think the house is on fire. Lit candles dot nearly every surface. There are vases of roses everywhere—red ones. Red rose petals litter the floor, the furniture. He takes my cell phone from my hand, places it on the coffee table, and continues to lead me through the house.

"What's going on?" My voice echoes strangely in my own ears, as if I'm in another realm. Maybe I am. Maybe I'm still fast asleep on the couch not laughing at any of Joey's one-liners.

"Donut?" Benji offers.

"Huh?"

He points out a plate on the kitchen counter holding

what looks suspiciously like the brioche vanilla crème donuts we enjoyed in Florida.

"Are those...?"

"It wasn't easy with short notice, but there they are." He continues tugging me through the house. I quicken my steps to keep up. At the sliding door, he pauses and gestures for me to go out ahead of him.

There are floating candles and flower petals in the pool. The lights aren't violet like before, but pink. My heart is doing cartwheels, but she's been wrong a lot lately, so I'm hesitant to trust her.

"You said you weren't okay." My confusion gives way to denial. This can't mean what I think it means.

"I'm not. At least not yet." His palms bracket my hips as he stands behind me, his lips against my ear when he asks, "Do you want to swim?"

"It's eleven o'clock," I say numbly.

"It's later than that. Do you?"

"I didn't bring a bathing suit." I study the sparkling surface of the pool, a lump in my throat forming. He wants to have sex again. That's what this is about. I refuse to hope it's more. If he asks me to resume our physical relationship after he's romanced the hell out of his house, I'm not sure I have the strength to say no.

"No suits needed," he rumbles into my ear. "In fact, I prefer you without."

I turn to face him and see what, I'm not sure. Again I'm met with the sense I can't trust myself. He tips his chin. "You first."

"Benji..." I'm not sure what's going on, but I'm sure whatever it is will end badly for me. Say we do have sex—amazing, incredible, mind-blowing sex. Afterwards I'll go home and then what? *Die?* That sounds about right.

I search my brain for remnants of the speech I halfway prepared to give him tomorrow. I need more time. I'm not ready.

"Okay, I'll go first. But only because you're forcing my hand. I wanted to save this for last." He pulls his T-shirt over his head and tosses it onto one of the loungers next to the pool. Soft pink light glows warmly on his bare skin, shadowing the bumps of his ab muscles and the round firmness of his pecs. He's beautiful. A golden god. And for a brief moment in time, I could touch him whenever I wanted.

It's been a little over a week since I've seen his body, and already it feels like an eternity. I don't mean to, but my eyes feast on his torso. Halfway through their exploration, they snag on something new. He notices me noticing. He doesn't say a word.

"You have another tattoo." The fresh ink, so recent his skin is red, surrounds the carpe diem tattoo.

"I was lost," he says, his voice choked with an emotion I refuse to name. "Now I'm not. I have to cover it up before we get in the water, though. It's still new."

"It's a compass," I whisper, my hand going to the necklace draped at my throat. He touches the pendant before his glittering brown eyes hit mine.

"When I gave you this, I told you that you were your own true north. And you *are*. You always will be. No matter what happens in the future."

It's harder to ignore my heart when she's screaming at the top of her lungs, but I block her out and focus on Benji. Benji, who tattooed a compass onto his flank. I shake my head, unsure how to respond. He keeps talking and saves me from it.

"When you left my bed for the final time, and life was like it used to be, I didn't have any direction anymore. I have felt lost every day since. I don't ever want to feel that way again." He touches the tender skin around the compass tattoo. "I had this done as a reminder of my true north. There is a capital C where the N should be. It's for Cris. You're my true north too."

His smile isn't the confident, disarming smile I'm used to seeing. It's more hopeful, less sure, and a million times more genuine. Something has happened. I clutch hands with my heart and pray he gives us what we've longed for over the last year or two. Or hell, *ten*.

"Remember when you said I was never getting married and I agreed I wasn't?" he asks.

A rocky start, but I nod anyway.

"Marriage has always been a far-off idea attached to some faceless, nameless person. The idea of it is absolutely fear-provoking." He takes both my hands in his. "But when I picture marrying you, it's way less scary."

I don't want him to make promises out of guilt or to make himself or both of us feel better for a little while. So I say, "You don't have to—"

He interrupts me.

"Let me finish. I'm not saying you have to marry me. I'm not saying you have to marry anybody. What I'm saying is, I can't..." He licks his lips. "I *don't* want to let you go. And that's something I've never said to anyone. Because everybody goes, Cris. My parents left, and they didn't choose to. They left me alone, and I made myself sick over it. Did you know I had stomachaches every day for the first year I lived with the Owens?"

He never told me. Poor Benji. I hate picturing him as a sad kid—as a sad adult. Sad, period. His smile is my refuge.

"I have loving, kind adoptive parents who treat me like gold. Brothers who treat me...well, back then not like gold, but eventually they did when we grew up. And then when I was on TV on this show called *Divide and Conquer*. It was this huge math competition—"

"Divide and what?" I ask as a smile trembles on my lips.

"I know. Stupid." He shakes his head, embarrassed. He's so endearing, I fall in love with him a little more. "Anyway, before the show aired I thought I was going to die of a stomachache. I didn't tell anyone, but I was scared to death I was going to lose. Not just the competition but everything that meant anything to me. I latched onto that group, onto my friends. I was terrified I was going to bomb the tournament and then they'd leave too."

He moves his hands to my jaw and tips my head. I'm staring into his eyes. Those caramel-colored eyes. There's definitely something in them I've never seen before. It looks like what's in my heart. It looks like love.

"This last week I have been so sick," he tells me. "Terrified. It took me way too long to realize why. What I'm terrified of losing, Cris, is you. I worry I blew my shot at having a future with you because I was too stuck in my own head to take a chance. So this is me taking it. The night in the hotel room, with the roses and donuts and the candles, I told you I was going to make sure you knew how the man in your future should treat you. But you're not going to need that advice any longer. *I am* the man in your future, and in your past, and here, in the present. And I know exactly what you need."

I swallow thickly, my mouth dry and my eyes wet.

"All you have to do is give me one more chance. You can't pretend it's enough for me to be your boss or your best friend or your client. I need you to be all in, Firecracker. I need you to give us your best damn shot. If I blow it, then you can try and get rid of me. But I deserve a chance to love you the way I know I can. The way I already do."

Tears shimmer on the edges of my lashes and his face goes blurry. "You do?"

He gives me one of those melty Benji smiles—a real smile. A smile the likes of which I haven't seen since the night he suggested we didn't stop what we started.

"Duh. I was afraid to say it, and so my body made me say it. I'm torn up. A complete wreck. I don't know if I'll be able to eat or sleep or function if you tell me no tonight. But I love you enough to let you tell me no if you have to." He lets out a laugh that sounds the slightest bit unsure. "I'm really hoping you don't tell me no."

"Why would I tell you no when I've been in love with you for weeks—years, probably." I roll my eyes. "You're my ultimate weakness."

His lips cover mine, his arms wrapping around me and holding on tight. As I kiss him, I consider all the ways he's shown me he loves me without saying it. Without either of us realizing what he was doing.

"We wasted too much time," he whispers against my lips, his fingers diving into my curls. "I've been shortsighted. I've been selfish. I've been—"

I smother his words with another kiss he doesn't waste

any time deepening. I reach for his belt and he tugs at my clothes. Soon I'm no longer wearing my T-shirt. Then my pants are being pulled from my legs. He shucks his jeans next, and once we're both down to our skivvies, he's grinning, the happiest I've ever seen him.

He tips his head toward the pool. "Get in."

"You have more tricks up your sleeve?" I ask as he carefully tapes a plastic covering over his fresh tattoo.

He hoists one amazing eyebrow. "Not in my sleeve."

I dive into the deep end and then rise out of the water into rose petals, dodging the floating candles flickering on the water's surface.

He dives in next. When he pops up, he pushes his hand through his hair and blinks long eyelashes at me. Water rolls down his cheeks, his smile permanent. He leads the way to the shallower part of the pool and I follow. When I reach him, he catches me and locks my legs around his waist.

"This is what I know for sure," he tells me as I rest my arms on his shoulders. "I didn't know what love was until I found you. My true north. My Firecracker. A future without you—every part of you—isn't one I want to contemplate."

"Same," I say, my voice cracking.

"You're going to have to do better than that."

Through my own incurable smile, I oblige him. "I love you too."

He places a gentle kiss on my lips again. "I say we start with the donuts, take a shower, work our way to the bedroom, and then we can talk about when you're moving in."

My head snaps back and I blink at him. "Isn't that fast?"

"Is it? You've already raised three kids. You're an empty nester. What are you waiting for?"

I laugh. He makes a very good point. "I can't think of a single reason to say no. I mean, you were my first."

"Your first," he says, his voice a low possessive growl. "And your last."

We make out for a while longer in the pool. Until the thick ridge of his erection is nudging my center and we're both out of breath. We skip the donuts and shower and go straight to the bedroom. After a sweaty round of the best makeup sex ever, we circle back and check the other two items off the list at the same time.

While sitting on the bench in the stone-walled shower enjoying our crème-filled donuts, Benji talks about the way life will look once I move in. And the photos of us we'll take and hang on the walls.

He promises to make frames for them.

TURN THE PAGE FOR A PREVIEW OF
ONCE UPON A BILLIONAIRE

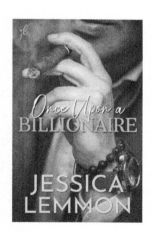

ONCE UPON A BILLIONAIRE [PREVIEW]

CHAPTER ONE

Vivian

Vivian Vandemark isn't my real name.

It sounds fancy, though, doesn't it? That alliteration of both Vs is to die for and reminds me of a classy label on clothing. Vandemark could have been the next Gucci. Maybe in another life.

I changed my name because my actual last name has been tainted by the man who gave it to me. My father is a criminal. Was. *Was* a criminal. It's hard to get used to the idea that he's no longer living. One would think since he was in prison for the last several years he'd be easy to forget, but that's only because I haven't told you who he is yet.

Walter Steele.

Yes, *that* Walter Steele.

The man who robbed his investors of millions and

millions of dollars to line his own pockets. That man is my father.

Was. Damn. That really is hard to wrap my head around.

The trial was bananas. It lasted one hundred days, and during that time my mother, brother, and I were harassed nonstop by the press. That was six years ago. Since then I've fallen off the radar.

My mother quite literally fell off the radar when she swallowed a lot of pain relievers and chased them with a lot of vodka. That was the day my father was sentenced. By then I was twenty-three and out of the house. My younger brother, Walt, was twenty. He's been trying to finish what booze my mother didn't since then. He'd been an addict most of his young life. I've never enjoyed escapism as a hobby.

Until now, I suppose.

Chicago is a far cry from Clear Ridge, Ohio. Clear Ridge has an unassuming Midwest vibe. The town is mostly shopping malls and chain restaurants, tall maple trees, and fences surrounding green, grassy yards. The live-work site currently being built is unique to this area. It's impressive, even if the company building it is the bane of my boss's existence.

I'm employed in a government office in this aspiring city. The building I walk into each day is half the size of my father's former summer home. *Half.*

I used to be a high-powered executive. All my faith, trust, time, and savings were wrapped up in our family's company. And then it all turned out to be a sham. On my watch, everything fell apart. Steele Investments toppled like a house of cards, taking my position with it. My father went down with the ship, the rest of my family "spared," if you could say that.

I've never felt more powerless. Watching my life crumble

reminded me of TV footage of the World Trade Center vanishing in a plume of smoke on 9/11. When I left that life behind, I swore *never again*.

I'll never again stand by, unwittingly, while someone steals (steal/Steele—how about that for irony?) people's life savings and retirement funds. I thought I was living the good life, but it was blood money.

Now, I buy my clothes at department stores or Target— they have some really nice clothes, by the way. I also cook at home a lot—not well, but I'm learning. And I endure the office coffee even though I pass a drool-worthy Starbucks each and every morning on my way to work.

I'm paying penance for a life I never chose. *Thanks, Dad.*

The second I set foot in the office, I'm met with raised voices. The loudest of the two is Gary, an otherwise mild-mannered inspector at our bureau. I don't think I've ever heard him raise his voice. My boss, Daniel, however, has a well-known temper. His blood pressure often runs high—you can tell by his reddened face.

Gary and Daniel are in Daniel's office, and while I can't make out what they're saying, it's obvious they're having a disagreement.

"Amber." I lean into my coworker's cubicle. "What's going on?"

She looks over her shoulder and gives me a smile that is half amused, half surprised. "Gary is fit to be tied."

"Yeah, I hear that. What's it about?"

"Who do you think?" She raises one prim, blond eyebrow.

"Nathaniel Owen," I answer. The billionaire in charge of

the live-work project has been mentioned about a *billion* times since I started working here, and never favorably.

"The one and only." Amber, still smiling, stands and leans a shoulder on the cubicle wall. We're both facing Daniel's closed door where the "conversation" is going strong. Nathaniel Owen's name is used like a curse word in this place. I've never interacted with him personally, but I'm familiar with the type.

Rich. Entitled. The kind of man who believes he's above the law.

The door swings open and Gary steps out, his mouth a firm line of disapproval. He huffs past Amber's cubicle and we brace ourselves for Daniel's wrath when he looks at us. No, wait.

Looks at *me*.

"Vandemark. Get in here." He vanishes into his office.

Daniel is in charge of my paycheck, a paycheck I need very badly, since I refuse to touch the money in an account I set up after Dad's trial. That money is for my brother's rehabilitation. Those places aren't cheap, and I'll drain every dime out of it if it makes him better. I failed him once—I won't fail him again. He's the only family I have left.

Anyway, my paycheck. It's all that stands between me and homelessness, so I tend to be more gracious to my boss than he deserves.

Amber whispers "good luck" as I leave her side and enter the lion's den, aka Daniel's office.

"Good morning." I try to sound breezy.

"Not even close." He's pacing the floor, hands on his hips, frown marring his receding hairline. "Nathaniel Owen is a burr in my ass."

That should be the motto of the Clear Ridge Bureau of Inspection.

"I need you to go to the Grand Marin site," he tells me. "Owen's crew is there today, and I have it on good authority he has a meeting with the mayor which means he'll likely be onsite. I don't care if the mayor is in Owen's pocket. We are not. At least we aren't any longer." He mutters that last part while looking out the window facing the alley.

"Not Gary?" I can't imagine a scenario where Gary would do anything short of aboveboard.

"Owen paid off Gary. He had to have." Daniel's face turns beet red. "That electrical inspection paperwork flew in here on wings for my approval. It was way too fast. Gary was bribed. Mark my words."

I'm not a conspiracy theorist, but in this case Daniel makes a great point. Nothing happens fast in our little government bureau, and it's particularly suspicious that Owen seems to make things happen at lightning speed compared to everyone else.

"Did Gary quit?"

"I fired him." Daniel puffs up his chest, proud.

"Seriously?"

"No one at CRBI accepts bribes and remains on my payroll." He ices me with a glare. "You'll do well to remember that since you're heading over there."

My blood heats. I'd never accept a bribe. Especially one from a stubborn billionaire.

"We have a narrow window to teach Owen a lesson. You're just the woman to do it."

"I hope you understand that I will not falsify paperwork

in order to shut him down, either. I respect your mission, Daniel, but I'm not going to stoop to Owen's level."

My boss's grin is a tad creepy, but approving. "I know you won't. All you have to do is ask Owen for proof of a passed electrical inspection. He won't be able to show you one because he doesn't *have* one—not legally, anyway. I never signed off on it. Therefore, you can shut him down."

"Wouldn't you be a better candidate?" I don't do site visits. In my six months as chief desk jockey, I haven't been to a single construction site. It's part of my plan to lay low. If I'm not in charge of anything I can't fuck it up. Not to mention I'd have no idea what to do once I got there. "We both know how much you'd enjoy nailing his ass to the wall."

"More than you can imagine, but my schedule is full. Since Gary was fired, the next inspector in line handles their shit-show. Our other inspectors are busy, and frankly, I don't want to wait another second. So, you get a raise. Congratulations. This project is a nightmare."

Did he say raise? My ears perk. Despite wanting to lay low, an increase in my income would be nice. Given that I refuse to touch my brother's and my nest egg, I have to keep the lights on at home somehow.

"If Owen isn't there when you get there, let the site manager know you mean business."

Nathaniel Owen has a reputation for completing projects on time, which is a rare and coveted quality in a builder. He also sidesteps rules and does things his way rather than follow the letter of the law. The city of Clear Ridge doesn't take kindly to rule-benders, and Daniel hates them. Look at that, my boss and I have something in common.

"No problem," I assure Daniel.

Maybe delivering justice will be cathartic. I can't go back in time and keep my father in line, or recoup the money of the people who trusted him, but I can prevent Nathaniel Owen from lining his pockets with even more money. The Owen name is stamped on nearly every new build within a thousand miles. How much more can the guy possibly need?

That's the thing about greed. It knows no bounds.

"I have a meeting in five minutes and they'll probably keep me for the afternoon." Daniel swipes his sweaty brow. He's a good seventy pounds overweight and even on his tall frame, it's too much girth. "Can I count on you not to fuck this up?"

I force a smile. His wasn't the most wholehearted vote of confidence, but I'll take it. "Of course."

"He's cocky, strong-willed and needs a knot tied in his tail," Daniel says, not quite finished with his tirade. "You're strong. Smart. The perfect candidate to take him on, Viv." His voice gentles, and I feel an odd catch in my chest at the compliment.

The last man who praised me was my father. When I learned I couldn't trust him at the end, I wondered if every ounce of praise he gave me before was a lie. There are two versions of him in my head. The man who encouraged me to believe in myself and never give up, and the man who told me those things while stealing money from innocent people.

Disgusting.

"Shut him down," my boss repeats. "Let's teach him a lesson."

I draw my chin up at those words. Owen needs taught that you can't do what you want and give the rules the finger.

"Grab a hardhat from the back. Don't want you busting that pretty noggin of yours and then suing me."

Aaaand...moment over.

"Sure thing," I reply blithely.

I grab a hardhat from the back and walk outside to my 2014 Hyundai the car salesman assured me was "reliable." I don't even miss the sleek black Audi RS I used to own. Okay, I do *a little*. But a car is a car. This gem will deliver me to Grand Marin just as well as that Audi.

Grand Marin is a soon-to-be massive live-work community. An open-air style shopping, dining, and retail area interspersed with offices for professionals as well as apartments for young, vibrant tenants who want to live in the middle of—or above—the action.

Live-works have been growing in popularity, and whenever there's a trend, I've noticed the Owen family has their mitts all over it. I've never had any personal dealings with Owen, but I know rich people. They're not that great.

As a former rich person, I speak from experience.

I also know that Gary, the city's former mild-mannered inspector, came into the office with his bottom lip dragging the ground each and every time he had to deal with this site. Gary was a softie, and we all liked him. He was rocking a five-foot-three frame and had a shy way of watching his shoes when he talked. Then he blows up at Daniel? I wouldn't have guessed he'd raised his voice a day in his life before today.

People can surprise you, though, and for me that should come as no surprise.

Gary's despondence, and the possibility that he took a bribe, proves what a bulldog this Owen guy can be.

Bring it on, buddy. I've already been through the wringer.

Daniel's grumping about the mayor isn't totally inaccurate. Rumor has it the Owens grease palms. Mayor Dick Dolans might well be their pet.

I come to a stop the moment I merge onto the highway. So much for taking a shortcut. I-70 is a parking lot, and the heat index on the car's thermometer reads 97° F.

Worse, I'm wearing a synthetic-but-made-to-look-like-real-silk shirt and it's sticking to me like a second skin. Waves of heat waft off the road as if the cars are in the process of being melted down into one big metal glob. The month of June is going out like it has a score to settle.

Again: *relate.*

I crank the A/C down and rest a hand on the steering wheel. I refuse to panic. I'll get to Grand Marin when I get there. I wish I would have dug up some much-needed intel about the site before Daniel rushed me out of there. I know next to nothing about it.

At least I'm wearing my nicest, most slimming pencil skirt and high heels. Not the best getup for tromping around a construction site, but it's a good look when wanting to bust some billionaire balls. I smile to myself, straightening my shoulders.

I'm out for a win for the good guys. A win for justice. I picture myself as Wonder Woman and lift my chin. If she did it in a bustier and panties, I can do it in a pencil skirt and knockoff silk.

Ready or not, Nathaniel Owen, here I come.

ABOUT THE AUTHOR

A former job-hopper, Jessica Lemmon resides in Ohio with her husband and rescue dog. She holds a degree in graphic design currently gathering dust in an impressive frame. When she's not writing super-sexy heroes, she can be found cooking, drawing, drinking coffee (okay, wine), or eating potato chips. She firmly believes God gifts us with talents for a purpose, and with His help, you can create a life you love.

Jessica Lemmon's romance novels have been praised as "purely delicious fun" and "lavish, indulgence-fueled romance" by Publisher's Weekly, as well as "wonderfully entertaining" and "a whole lot of fun!" by RT Book Reviews.

She is the bestselling author of over thirty books that have been translated into a dozen languages and sold in over 30 different countries worldwide, with her debut novel releasing in January of 2013.

Her work has been honored with awards such as a Library Journal starred review, an RT Top Pick!, iBooks Best Book of the Month, and Amazon Best Book of the Month. She has been recommended by USA Today and NPR.com, and has achieved the rank of #1 bestseller on Nook as well as earned a seal of excellence nomination from RT Book Reviews.

Through witty banter and fun, realistic situations and characters you'll want to "sit down and have a drink with," Jessica tackles tough relationship issues and complicated human emotions while delivering a deep, satisfying experience for readers.

Her motto is "read for fun" and she believes we should all do more of what makes us happy.

ALSO BY JESSICA LEMMON

Visit jessicalemmon.com for a complete book list.

Made in the USA
Las Vegas, NV
26 January 2024

84932729R00173